D0583306

NO LONGER PROPERTY OF
SEATTLE PUBLIC LIBRARY

ALSO AVAILABLE BY EMILY J. EDWARDS

THE GIRL FRIDAY MYSTERIES

Viviana Valentine Gets Her Man

VIVIANA VALENTINE GOES UP THE RIVER

VIVIANA VALENTINE GOES UP THE RIVER

A GIRL FRIDAY MYSTERY

Emily J. Edwards

NEW YORK

This is a work of fiction. All of the names, characters, organizations, places and events portrayed in this novel are either products of the author's imagination or are used fictitiously. Any resemblance to real or actual events, locales, or persons, living or dead, is entirely coincidental.

Copyright © 2023 by Emily Steers

All rights reserved.

Published in the United States by Crooked Lane Books, an imprint of The Quick Brown Fox & Company LLC.

Crooked Lane Books and its logo are trademarks of The Quick Brown Fox & Company LLC.

Library of Congress Catalog-in-Publication data available upon request.

ISBN (hardcover): 978-1-63910-268-6
ISBN (ebook): 978-1-63910-269-3

Cover design by Rui Ricardo

Printed in the United States.

www.crookedlanebooks.com

Crooked Lane Books
34 West 27th St., 10th Floor
New York, NY 10001

First Edition: May 2023

10 9 8 7 6 5 4 3 2 1

For David. As always.

DAY 1

Friday, November 17, 1950

The office door shut behind our fashionably dressed secretary, and both Tommy and I exhaled.

Our desks were pushed up against each other, so each time I looked up, I caught the eyes of my boss-turned-partner, Tommy Fortuna. For all his bravado, he tried to look away, but when his eyes stopped ping-ponging around the room, I caught his gaze and couldn't help but notice the tears welling up in his eyes.

"Ladies first," he offered before he couldn't contain himself anymore, and he exploded in high-pitched giggles. He was slapping the knee of his gray wool trousers and wheezing so hard he reminded me of my grandpa. I loved Tommy when he was like this, truth be told. He was happier than ever since this summer's lark, and there was nothing better in the world than Tommy in a good mood.

"You're the war hero!" I whispered for the sake of my secretary's dignity. "You drink it first!"

"The shrapnel in my hip is exactly why you should drink it," Tommy said, his voice booming, not taking into consideration the feelings of the girl only one thin particle-board door away from us. "I've taken enough flak for my country."

"Coward."

I knew I couldn't stall any longer—not unless I wanted the focus of Tommy's teasing to transfer from the coffee maker to me. I lifted the mug to my lips and smelled the hot liquid swirling within. It smelled almost like coffee. I blew on it and sipped.

Tally Blackstone was the only secretary on Earth who could somehow make simple black coffee taste worse than East River water.

"Like . . ." I swallowed the hot liquid hard and felt it travel all the way down my throat; the sensation did nothing to detract from the unpleasantness of the lingering taste, which somehow made my tongue curl up and want to die.

"It has an aroma of pencil shavings to it," Tommy said. "Which I know is a sore subject."

Once my mouth stopped puckering and I was able to use my lips, teeth, and tip of my tongue as intended, I stuck that tongue out at the beaming man across the way. "You're the one who was framed for murder, not me."

We'd managed to acquire our secretary a few weeks ago, after our last big job. Her father, a diamond importer, came to us with a case, and she and I really hit it off. This overlapped, quite accidentally, with an ex-beau of mine coming back into the picture, and through all the upheaval, Tally and I were now as thick as thieves. We'd ended the case with my promotion from Girl Friday to co-investigator, some cramped office quarters, and a new office secretary by way of the debutante, who thought she'd try her hand at being a working stiff, at least for the time being. She'd managed to figure out the typewriter and telephone, but other aspects of the work were taking longer than I'd anticipated. Specifically, the parts that kept me and ol' Tommy boy at a functional level of caffeine.

Tally stuck her head back through the door with a short knock. "How is it?"

"Fine!" I blurted out, and she ducked out again. I gathered my cardigan around me and stared intently at my desk blotter, waiting for the inevitable from Tommy.

I could feel his eyeballs boring into me. "She's not going to get better if you keep lying to her."

"But she's only eighteen!" I whined.

"And you were younger than that when I hired you, ya dummy," Tommy shot back. "And over the course of nearly ten years, how many times did I go out of my way to spare your feelings?"

"That's because you're as coarse as a cheese grater, ol' Tommy Boy," I said, blowing him a kiss. "But you know I love ya."

Tommy smiled. "Tally!" he hollered, and our secretary came back through the door.

"Swill, isn't it?" she said, scooping up the mugs again with her manicured fingers, and depositing them on a small table near the door. "I just poured some for myself. I'll wake up extra early tomorrow to see if I can have Mrs. K walk me through it one more time. Do you think she will, Viv?"

Our landlady, Svitlana Kovolenko, had been extremely skeptical about having a debauched heiress move into one of her empty rooms, especially because that heiress looked like Tally Blackstone, a girl so beautiful she made Bacall look boring. Mrs. K has a teenage son, and she frets over him like a worried hen, and she was absolutely, positively sure she'd have to lock him in their basement apartment to keep him in line. But after a few days of carefully avoiding each other's paths, Tally showed herself to have a teasing, older sister–kid brother relationship with Mrs. K's son Oleks, who was only a year or so younger than she was. Not only did Tally not go for guys as broke as Oleks, but she didn't go for guys at all. While Mrs. K, by and large, kept her nose out of her girls' dirty laundry, she didn't have to know that particular secret just yet, though after nearly a decade of living under her roof, I knew Mrs. K was the kind to accept whatever the world threw her way and, even if she passed judgment, hold her tongue.

"Of course she will," I said. Tommy had expressly forbidden me from making another pot of coffee myself—or taking the time to show Tally all my tips and tricks for making what I considered a more than passable pot of coffee. It was sink or swim for her, and a deliberate way, he said, to make me stop feeling so much like the secretary and more like a detective whose name was now painted on the door.

Tally hopped up on the edge of Tommy's desk, dangling a fashionably-shod foot in the wind. Half a dozen jewel-encrusted rings shone on fingers wrapped around the edge of the desk. Tommy knew he wasn't Tally's type—and she was too young for a man who claimed quite proudly to like a "proper broad"— so he didn't ogle the legs, but there was no way to keep his eyes off the rocks. If they were real, they cost hundreds. If not thousands. But the kicker with Tally was that there was a good chance they were nothing but glass. And much like the names of the girls she smooched, she wasn't going to tell.

"Oh, I meant to tell you, I think someone called with a case last night," she said offhand. I was going to ask when she had planned on telling us, but after a few months of her friendship, I had learned girls like Tally had a strange relationship to time and what was considered pressing information to share. An affair or divorce was at the top headline of morning news, but apparently potential paying work was pretty far beneath the fold.

"Someone called here?" Tommy said. "You were out the door by 4:59."

"No, at home," she added. "It was a family friend."

It wasn't unusual for Tally to tie up Mrs. K's line for hours a night, but even I noticed last evening that her chat session was long and involved a lot less gasping and giggling than her usual catch-ups with friends. But what was a social faux pas in our house didn't read the same way to ol' Tommy boy—right now, there was no way to miss the dollar signs rolling through his eyes. "Family friend" in Tally Blackstone talk meant someone with at least one yacht.

"Okay. When can you get them in here?" Tommy asked.

"Oh, boy. Um, he won't wake up until noon, at the earliest, and it'll take at least an hour for him to drive in from Tarrytown . . ." Tally ticked off the hours on her fingers. "Five or six?"

"It's nine o'clock in the morning, and you're telling me this family friend, who rang you up last night with a case pressing enough to consider summoning a private dick, can't be bothered to get into the city before six PM the next day?" Tommy looked bewildered, but he was clicking his lighter open and shut, undoubtedly counting the pennies that would roll in from doing a job for anyone driving in from upstate.

"He had a *symposium*," Tally huffed. "You can't possibly expect him to . . ." and she shut her trap, remembering that she was now technically someone's employee, and decorum dictated she shouldn't mouth back. From the last few months of having her in my life, I knew that part of Tally's magic came from knowing the rules to every comma, dash, and period— and knowing when to break them. The other part of her *je ne sais quoi* was that she was richer than the state of Wyoming, even with the state of New York seizing most of her daddy's dollars in legal settlements and fines. She was rich on both her mama's and daddy's sides, and I'd seen her throw down wads of bills for even the tiniest bill at the diner. Tommy says she's just desperate to have everyone like her, after the life she had growing up, but I can't see the difference between that and just good, ol'-fashioned generosity. Has the same result in the end.

"Symposium or not, a man doesn't call from the 'burbs if there's not something complex going on," I said. Tommy, like most men, was as jumpy as a man with a rotten tooth when he thought he was being disrespected, but cold, hard cash soothed any savage beast.

"That's true—Buster did sound awful shaken up," Tally said. "And Buster likes things fixed fast. He spares no expense."

"Did he tell you at all what was the matter?" I asked, taking shorthand like always.

"No, he just said that something was wrong and that I was possibly the only person in the whole wide world who would understand," Tally said. "Our whole wide world is pretty big, so it must be strange if I'm the only person in it he could mention it to."

"Well, it'll certainly be a unique situation," Tommy said. "Unique enough to not care if he wastes a stranger's entire day waiting for him to show his mug."

"Should I leave word with his man to come in tonight, or not?" Tally asked. She couldn't tell what the big deal was with Tommy's attitude, but I could see her manners kicking in and telling her to just be polite.

"Yes, please," Tommy said. "Leave *word* with his *man*. Then go hit the deli to get some bagels and drinkable coffee."

Tommy peeled a fiver off a stack of bills in his pocket, and Tally nabbed it before slipping out again, this time to make her calls. For her first few weeks on the job, she doled out her own personal cash for things, until Tommy told her not to, good and proper, but I could tell it still pained her to take greenbacks off someone so *broke*. I had a sneaking suspicion she managed to slip all those bills back into places where Tommy would find them and be delighted by the unexpected windfall.

As she left, Tommy pinched the bridge of his nose. *"'Leave word with his man,'"* he grumbled.

"It's been less than two months," I said. "Maybe we should just have her buy coffee every morning."

"Buy coffee? Every day?" Tommy gaped. "God, what a waste of money."

"The only reason Tally ever entered her kitchen growing up was to get into her private elevator car to get to her daddy's Caddy in the underground garage," I told Tommy. "Give her some time to adapt to us and our strange little world. What's the worst that can happen? The mystery man doesn't show?"

"No, Dollface," Tommy said. "Private Investigator 101: The worst thing that can happen—that can always happen, on every single case—is somebody wakes up dead."

★ ★ ★

It was a long day of cigarette breaks, NBC radio, and waiting. Sometime after the sun was fully hidden behind the neighboring buildings, but before I got up the energy to get off my keister and flick on the overhead light, I heard lively chatter coming from the secretary area of our suite, then a soft knock on the door of our interior office.

"Mr. Fortuna, Miss Valentine," Tally said by way of introduction. She reached into the room and hit the light switch, drenching the office with a dim yellow cast. "This is Buster Beacon. The man I was telling you about."

A man in a fur overcoat and galoshes tramped into the office, and my long-earned and well-honed secretary instinct kicked in.

"Sir, can we take your coat?"

"Tally asked already, and I declined," he said officiously. "I quite like the entire look. And the galoshes . . . well, simply put, I forgot my other shoes, so duck feet it is." He did a small jig to draw attention to his feet. Buster Beacon then strode into the office.

He sat down on one of Tommy's penitent wooden chairs as if it was a velvet lounger. His face was boyish and round, red in the cheeks from either cold or pluck, I couldn't tell which quite yet. His age was blurred by the fact that his clothing was tailored and of good material—the coat itself looked like mink to my eye, and his gloves, clutched in his left hand, were trimmed in a matching pelt. A gold watch glimmered from his cuff; I couldn't get a good look at it, but it was Omega if I had to hazard a guess. His cuffs emerged the requisite half inch from his jacket and were linked by golden disks.

Boys, from my experience, didn't make those kinds of sartorial decisions for themselves.

Tommy stood and shook the man's hand, and I stayed seated, waiting for my cue. I felt a swift shiver of excitement when I realized that this was the first case Tommy and I would approach fully *together*, not just with me playing second fiddle as the girl who took his notes and patched his busted-up mug when he came back from a meeting that went sour. As Tommy had been begging me to realize, my name was on the door, and something told me Buster Beacon would address me like it was too.

"I'm Tommy Fortuna," my boss said, "and this is my partner, Viviana Valentine. Tally told us this morning you might be in need of our services. Would you like to give us some details?"

"Honestly, I'd rather just have the whole thing disappear so I never had to tell anyone else about the goings-on at the house," Mr. Beacon said. "It's embarrassing and ridiculous, but I'm at my wit's end."

"Sorry to hear that," Tommy added.

"But I have to assure you, Mr. Beacon, we've heard some doozies over the years," I said. "When I first started, there was a woman who was sure her son was steppin' out with an unsavory lady friend, but it turned out he was addicted to uppers and couldn't break his pinball addiction."

"That was a great one," Tommy reminisced. "Do you remember the foreign fella—Swiss, I think—who wanted me to tail his Canadian wife?"

"Oh, boy, yeah," I said laughing. I turned to Mr. Beacon. "Turns out the fella—he was Belgian, Tommy, not Swiss—liked to dip parts of his body in chocolate, and when she refused to participate, he took out his frustrations in some unsavory ways. We ended up dropping him as a client, and she got the penthouse."

"And the jewelry," Tommy said.

"I do so love to be in the company of great crackpots and shiftless freaks," Mr. Beacon said.

"Be nice, Buster," Tally scolded from her perch by the doorway. "These are my bosses you're speaking to."

"I am being nice, my dear—you've been to my dinner parties," he retorted over his shoulder. "I was being entirely sincere."

"What's happening, Mr. Beacon?" I asked. "Are things growing legs and walking off? Threats made to your income or person?"

"Hardly anything like that," Mr. Beacon said. He allowed the silence to hang for emphasis. "There are *noises*."

"Noises?" Tommy paled, and his stomach grumbled, reminding him that this meeting was eating into his Friday night suppertime, which, since the summer, he'd been spending at Mrs. K's, cooling off at the end of the week. One kind word about her borscht and she'd been working to impress him ever since, to everyone's delight and full stomachs.

"Woo-woo creaks and ghastly sounds," Mr. Beacon explained back. "And no, I am not insane or losing my marbles or any other such thing. I am queer and avant-garde, sir, but I am not delusional."

"Mr. Beacon, if I turned down every client I thought might be delusional—well, I'd be out on the streets," Tommy said. Buster didn't quite laugh.

"Can't you just check in the other room to see what's making the noise?" I asked.

Tally piped up. "The place is a bit too big for that, Viv."

"I have eight bedroom suites, four parlors for varying purposes, the kitchens and storerooms, the servants' quarters, expansive cellars, several outbuildings, and workplaces in the garrets," Mr. Beacon explained. "The sounds stop before my men can possibly search the entire estate."

"I didn't think there were places like that in the States," I said. "Just back in Europe where they have lords and ladies and counts and countesses."

"There are more than you'd think." Mr. Beacon shrugged.

"Well, off the top of my head," Tommy interjected, "I can't explain away anything that might be giving you the shivers, Mr. Beacon. So I'm assuming you're going to request us to come on up to Tarrytown and have a look-see for ourselves?"

"Took the words right out of my mouth, Mr. Fortuna."

"And when would you like this to happen?" I asked.

"As soon as possible, of course," Mr. Beacon replied. "I may galivant around the city on my own schedule, but the people I hire are not usually given the same liberty." All of the pleasantness was out of Buster's face, and I had no doubt he meant exactly what he said.

I saw Tommy cringe at the display of aggression and superiority, but I was more used to being bossed around by men in nice suits than he was—or at least more used to being bossed around without giving them lip. "Sure thing, Mr. Beacon."

"Now, let's talk remuneration," Tommy said. He gave me the eye, and I slipped out to the front of the office with Tally. Some things were still above my pay grade, and I knew I'd get my marching orders when I needed to.

★ ★ ★

"So, what's he not telling us?" I asked Tally as we traipsed back through the gloomy November evening to Mrs. K's boarding house, our coats and scarves flapping in the wind as the temperature was well above normal for the fact that we were a week out from the Macy's Parade.

"Not much," Tally said. "He said he was at his wits' end because the house is so big. It's been emptier and emptier of staff as the years go on, and he just wants to know what's happening."

"This sounds like a case for private security, not private investigators, though."

"Oh, Buster would never. He abhors violence."

"Security doesn't always mean violence," I said.

Tally scoffed, and I wanted to roll my eyes, but I remembered she had more experience with hired goons than I did. We grew up so far on opposite sides of the tracks, Tally and I, that we were practically from different nations. But after having my house broken into a few times over the summer, I had to admit, I caught myself daydreaming occasionally about having a guard on duty to keep out the riffraff.

"Well, let's take for granted that there's no such thing as ghosts, and the headless horsemen are hibernating," I said to Tally. "Why would anyone be breaking into his mansion?"

"Silver, art, a few nice new television sets," Tally rattled off. "Jewels, the like."

"Is his the only mansion in the area?" I asked. "Does it stick out? Practically have Las Vegas lights screaming, 'Woo-hoo, criminals! Come rob me'?"

"Absolutely not," Tally said. "There's a bit of a row. And just because someone's home is ostentatious, doesn't mean they're *asking* to be robbed, Viviana."

"I wasn't blaming him for his own misfortune," I said. "I'm just saying that burglars are a pretty slow lot. They're not gonna think too long and hard about which house to hit up."

"You had your diamonds nicked from a boarding house in Chelsea, I'll have you recall."

"I'll have you recall they were not diamonds, *missy*," I said, giving her a nudge, and she laughed. "Have the other homeowners in the area experienced similar unexplainable activities?"

"I don't know—Buster didn't say. He's so embarrassed, he probably doesn't want to ask."

"For a tall man who takes to wandering Hell's Kitchen in a mink, he seems to embarrass easily."

"He's been like this for as long as I've known him. A lot of the theatrics are because he's chicken—you know that," Tally said. "The dog with the loudest bark has the weakest bite."

"That's the truth," I said. "How did you come to meet this character anyway?"

"*Ma mère*," Tally explained. "She liked weirdos and oddballs and putting the money from her trust into projects that would drive *mon père* up a damn wall. And Buster was her favorite project. He was my favorite too. I used to beg to go to his house whenever we were in the city. If I could have, I'd have spent my entire childhood there."

"Did your mom and Buster have an aff—" I trailed off as Tally gave me a knowing stare. "Oh, right."

"You really have to get better at reading people, Viv," Tally laughed.

"I can tell who has a gun on them from three blocks away—isn't that enough?" I was howling as we walked up the steps to our boarding house, and Mrs. K flung open the door.

"Who has a gun?" she asked. After our summer of break-ins, Mrs. K was a little touchy and, for the first time in a decade, insisted we always lock the door behind us, even though the culprit was himself locked away at Sing Sing.

"No one! And I could tell if you were packing heat, Mrs. K, so don't try it." I wagged my finger at her in my best impression of a nasty old granny, but clearly Mrs. K didn't think this was a joking matter. She just wiped her hands on her apron and muttered *nedoumkuvatyy* under her breath as she shooed us inside, Tally and I still giggling like schoolgirls. I don't speak Ukrainian, but I figured it wasn't a compliment.

House dinner was a filling chicken pot pie, with Mrs. K's favorite lime Jell-O for dessert, and the other girls were home in time to join us. We waited as long as we could for Tommy, but by seven fifteen, Mrs. K's son, Oleks, was digging in, and we all followed suit. After I'd moved to the third floor with Tally, my windowless room on the second floor, squashed between the rooms of Dottie the teacher and Betty the nurse, had stayed open. Every time I asked Mrs. K if she planned on advertising it, she changed the subject. I'd never asked Tally what she paid for the privilege of living at Mrs. K's, but without that room being rented out, I felt pretty guilty about my landlady losing an extra twenty dollars a week.

"So, how is everything?" I asked the girls as Mrs. Kovalenko dished up the main course. We had the windows in the dining room wide open, and Oleks was fiddling with the radio, trying to find something to listen to. We were six weeks past the Yanks taking the series in four, and Oleks was going through competition withdrawal. He wasn't yet sold on the staying power of those new Knickerbockers, and all he was getting was static and ads for Carnation evaporated milk.

"Preparing for Thanksgiving," Dottie responded. "The usual cardboard Pilgrim hats and hand-turkeys."

"Doesn't that ever get boring?" Tally asked. In the grand scheme of things, Tally was barely older than Dottie's students, but she had very little patience for children.

"It's more about cultivating hand–eye coordination than the turkey itself," Dottie said.

Tally stared at her blankly before continuing on. "Any good gossip on the wards lately, Betty?"

"Nothing," she huffed. She already seemed pretty agitated, and asking about work got her to bristle.

"What's the matter?" I asked. "Normally, you're just brimming with stories when you come home. Sometimes it's hard to keep an appetite when you discuss all the blood."

"Nothing," Betty responded. "I'm just having a rough go of it. But don't worry—I know how to calm myself down. I'm a nurse. Steady hands." She held up her fork, still as death, as evidence of her lack of agitation.

"Well, we're here if you'd like advice or just to discuss your feelings," Dottie assured her. Sometimes when Dottie turned on her teacher voice, it made you feel like you were two inches tall, and sometimes it was exactly what you needed to hear. I hoped this was sitting right with Betty, but by the look on her face, it wasn't what the doctor ordered.

I heard Mrs. K's phone ring from upstairs. "I'll get it."

I put down my napkin and ran up the stairs to the second-floor landing, where Mrs. K's phone sat in a vestibule. "Mrs. Kovalenko's Girls-Only Boarding House," I said into the receiver.

"Viv, good—it's you," Tommy yelled into the receiver.

"It's modern technology, Tom. You don't have to scream," I said back calmly. "What gives? Are you okay? Where are you?"

"Tally's still got a car, right?" he asked, blowing off my questions.

"Yeah, she parks it in a garage near the Garden," I said.

"Good, she's gonna take you to Tarrytown," he hollered.

"When?"

"Tonight."

"Tonight?"

"Yeah, maybe I should keep yelling." Tommy was cross, and I knew it wasn't my fault, but it sure as hell was my problem.

"Where should we pick you up?"

"You're not—I'll be up as soon as I can."

"Last time you blew me off without giving me details, ol' Tommy Boy, your secretary-to-be had sent you on a cross-country train chase," I reminded him.

"My back is still sore," he chuckled. "No, I've got to get some things in order and talk to a contact I have. I promise, I won't follow a girl onto any trains."

The phone line beeped to let me know Tommy's nickel was about to run out. "Well, don't go following girls anywhere, bub. Okay, Tommy. I'll tell Tally and get there as soon as we can. Tonight."

"You're a doll, Viviana Valentine."

The line clicked off, and I headed downstairs to finish dinner and talk to my secretary.

NIGHT 1

Friday, November 17, 1950

"God, it's so dark," I whispered into the freezing car. We'd been on the road for an hour, and even though the day had been balmy, the night was cold, and I felt it settle into my bones. The leather front seat wasn't warming beneath my tush, and the whole ride was brittle and uncomfortable.

"Be quiet," Tally scolded. "I can't see anything with you talking." She was gripping the wheel with her bare hands and leaning so far forward that I thought she was going to bump her head on the windshield. In the city she drove like a bat out of hell, and I thought that she'd at least have a bit more concern in the country, but nothing doing. The heater was blasting, and the hot air, the smell of the motor oil, and Tally's enthusiastic driving were creating a cocktail of nausea in my stomach. Our first night out together, I almost upchucked in this very seat, but Tally didn't seem to recall the sensitivities or limits of my stomach.

We were past Yonkers on the Saw Mill Parkway and deep into the country. There were no streetlights before us at all, and the dense forest at the side of the road was free of leaves—just naked trees with ghastly branches that swayed in the breeze. I fiddled in my bag and pulled out a folded morning newspaper, but with all the country-road potholes, my head started to wobble.

"Just listen to the radio," Tally said, waving her hand at the Cadillac's dashboard. Normally she had the dial tuned to her favorite jazz station and the volume cranked as high as it could go, but this far into the country there wasn't a big audience for bebop.

"I thought you didn't like the noise while you were driving."

"I don't like you *talking* at me while I'm driving."

"Fine. But I didn't want to use the radio, because when I get *out* of the car, I'll have to keep reading," I explained.

"Aren't you excited? Buster throws amazing parties," Tally explained. "The second you pull into the driveway, you'll have to stop reading your stories anyhow."

"I'm not reading *stories*, I'm reading the *news*," I explained. "The president was almost assassinated two weeks ago—don't you care?"

"It's *all* stories," Tally said. "They didn't even get close to him."

"A police officer *died*, Tally—don't you want to know why?"

"Not particularly." Tally gripped the steering wheel harder, and I could tell she was annoyed with me.

"Fine." I shoved my newspaper back into my carryall.

"Did he tell you who was there?" Tally asked. "If it's Devora Bettencourt, you're going to have the time of your life."

"No, I haven't spoken to Buster directly since I left the office," I explained. "This is all Tommy's orders, and sometimes he doesn't fill in all the blanks."

"Well, it should be fun anyhow."

"Let's hope this warm spell stays through the weekend," I said, frowning. "But I don't see how that's possible."

"Well, if it does stay nice, Buster will go boating, that's for sure," Tally explained. "I hope you brought boating clothing."

"I brought clothing, and I can wear any outfit on a boat."

"Okay, suit yourself." Tally was cross as she squinted out the window. "I hope I don't hit a goddamn deer."

"There's a goddamn deer?" I clutched the door of the car and pressed my forehead against the window, trying to spot the beast.

"If there is, you better hope I see it before I hit it," Tally said.

We lulled into a quiet trance as Tally's tires hummed along the pavement. "So, tomorrow we—" I started before Tally cut me off.

"I'm going back tonight." She said it like I was an idiot for assuming she'd be with me on the case at her friend's house.

"You're leaving me by myself?" I'd been to two parties with Tally Blackstone's acquaintances over the summer, and they were exhausting enough. A whole weekend with those types might put me in the hospital.

"I'm seeing a full dress rehearsal of *Guys and Dolls* tomorrow!" Tally whined.

"Buster is your lifelong friend," I said. "Aren't you curious about what's happening to him? It's just a play. This is a man's *life*."

"Nothing on Broadway is *just* a *play*, Viviana," she hissed, and it was clear I'd struck a nerve.

"So you're going to drive through the bleak night, all alone, dodging deer and God knows what else, just so you can see a show tomorrow?"

"And have breakfast with the producer, another old family friend—*yes*, I *am*," Tally explained, lifting up her chin with an air of royal dignity. "Buster will more than understand. I will uphold any relationship with people who are still interested in speaking with me."

"So Tommy and I are chopped liver?" I knew Tally was born into better waters than the secretarial pool, but the only thing stopping me from canning her right this minute was the fact that I didn't want to be left on the side of the road in Dobbs goddamn Ferry. And because I wasn't sure if having my name on the door actually entrusted me with the power of hiring and firing our secretary. I'd have to ask Tommy. When I had a cooler head, for Tally's sake.

Tally didn't say anything but took a hard, sharp exit and careened her Cadillac onto the even quieter streets of Tarry-town, jamming on the gear shift and clearly on the warpath. I closed my eyes—the only way I had found yet to quell my impulse to vomit while I was in a car with Tally behind the wheel. I felt the car travel the country roads—the winding, looping streets, potholes, and swift stops—before coming to a sharp halt not twenty minutes later, accompanied by a long *toot toot* of the Cadillac's infernally loud horn.

"We're here," she said, and I heard the trunk open and close in rapid succession, followed by the door to my right swinging out from beneath my weight. I peeked open my eyes to see Tally hadn't moved from the steering wheel, or even turned the car off.

"Thank you for driving me all this way," I said. "I'll be in touch." A white gloved hand had reached out to pluck me from the car, and a man in a gorgeous wool tuxedo was holding my battered cardboard suitcase in his other paw. "Thank you, sir," I said, and turning to the door, the full grandeur of the house hit me like a pie to the face.

It looked like a fairy-tale castle, but a classy one. No turrets or anything, just a beautiful stone exterior illuminated as if by the grace of nature itself, and with stately, manicured evergreens growing in huge planters out front. To the right, off at the edge of the property, was a large flagpole, properly bare because it was after sundown. I could hear the lap of water coming from somewhere, and several rooms were lit behind what were, I'm sure, expensive velvet and brocade draperies. The effect was enough to knock my breath out, but the tuxedo coughed to break the spell, and I scurried to follow him into the vestibule. As the large front door shut, I heard Tally's tires peel away on the gravel. She was gone.

Buster Beacon met me in his foyer, wearing a garnet dressing gown of luxuriant silk and fur-lined slippers. "Miss Blackstone won't be staying?" he asked.

"Don't look like it," I pouted before I caught myself in front of the paying customer. "No, sir. She has plans in the city tomorrow with a Broadway producer. They simply can't be broken. She sends her remorse."

"I'm sure she does." He winked. "I've known that girl since birth, and she's never shown proper remorse for anything."

I couldn't help but laugh. "Mr. Fortuna will be up as soon as his schedule permits, so unfortunately you've just got me for the time being."

"Nothing unfortunate about that, Miss Valentine. Let's get you warmed up," Mr. Beacon said. "Jeeves will take your valise to your room. Do give him your coat and follow me to the parlor for a drink."

I shuffled out of my overcoat and handed it to the man in the tux, who had my suitcase. "Thank you."

He just nodded, and I turned back to Mr. Beacon.

"Sir, is his name really Jeeves?"

"No, it's Arnold, but Jeeves sounds better, doesn't it?" Beacon responded, but I didn't agree with him. I'm a bigger fan of calling people what they like to be called. "And please, call me Buster. Given name Balthazar, but clearly that just doesn't do."

"No, sir, that's more of a punishment than a name," I said.

"How astute of you to say." He led me through an archway with pocket doors and elaborate floral stained-glass windows. Every surface of the house was ornate, shining, and beautiful. I couldn't pin whether it'd been built yesterday or a hundred years ago.

"Please call me Viv," I said back.

"Oh, but Viviana is so lovely."

"When you say it with your accent it is," I said back. "Hollered out the back door of my mom's house? Not so much."

"I promise I shan't holler, Viviana," Buster replied, stressing the breathy vowels. He led me into a grand central living room, open to the second story, which was filled with comfortable-looking furniture and potted palms. To my right was a five-foot-tall fireplace with a carved wooden mantle; within it, a roaring fire that crackled like Christmas morning. To the left, over a sea of white-upholstered settees, leather club chairs, and spotless end tables, a wall of glass doors overlooked the unlit backyard and the river, now twinkling with starlight and the occasional headlamp of a car making its way across the bridge. At the far side of the room, directly in front of me, there was a marble-topped wet bar, and Buster slid behind it, his dressing gown and smile made all the more spectacular by a backdrop of glistening Baccarat crystal.

"What's your poison?"

"Oh, please, you make that choice," I said, flirting back. "I drink anything."

"Oof, is there any more telling phrase than 'I drink anything'?" Buster responded, turning around to survey the grand display of bottles behind him. He twiddled his fingers in anticipation while he spoke, almost like he wasn't thinking about what he was saying. He wasn't being mean, exactly, but he sure as hell wasn't being nice. "'I drink anything' is the confession of someone who's trying to appear accommodating but, in actuality, hasn't cultivated a preference. You've clearly never had a fine cognac, Miss Viviana, and that shall change tonight."

A lovely amber liquid swirled into a snifter and it was delivered to me with a smile. It looked and smelled like it'd soothe some hurt feelings and raised hackles. "Chin-chin," Buster said as he motioned his own glass in my direction, and we sipped. The cognac felt like a warm hug and lit my lips on fire.

I looked around. "Well, I can tell why you can't just stick your head in the next room to see who's making a racket," I said. "I've never seen any place this big."

"Fascinating, isn't it?" Buster responded. "It's the American dream. Be born into nothing and buy anything that makes you feel even the smallest bit better about yourself. You can see, I feel absolutely marvelous."

If Buster was a friend to Tally and her mother, I knew for a fact that he wasn't "born into nothing," but I figured it was rude to argue about a client's definition of "nothing." Even I thought I had *something* growing up, even if that something didn't include indoor plumbing.

"Do you live here alone?" I asked.

"No, I have some staff, and they all live in quarters," Buster said. "Plus, I am rarely without guests."

"Am I the only person so far this weekend?"

"No, everyone else is changing into their evening clothes; they'll be down momentarily."

"Oh, please don't tell me you have formal dinners," I said, my stomach falling to my ankles. "I didn't pack anything like that. And me and borrowed dresses don't get along."

"No, no, not at all," Buster said. "Things apparently got a bit mucky this afternoon. I, thankfully, was in the city."

I didn't press the strangeness of his statement as several people filed into the parlor, many of the men with still-wet hair and most wearing their coziest evening clothing.

"Everyone! So glad you're refreshed," Buster announced. "This is my friend, Viviana Valentine. She just joined us while you were all indisposed."

Seven adults murmured their greetings, and our host went through the formal introductions.

"First, we have Richard Paloma," Buster offered, "He works in the lab and is, some would say, my roommate." I noted his description of the relationship. I'd have to call on Tally's information regarding that, for sure. Paloma was tall and lean and angular, with a swath of dark hair, dressed in nice pajamas and a lovely red velvet smoking jacket. The effect wasn't as ostentatious as Buster's whole look; Paloma looked more elegant. It suited him, and I found myself wondering what kind of robe Tommy wore around the house when he was alone. If it wasn't some worn-out flannel jobbie with a hole somewhere in the armpit, he probably didn't wear one at all.

"Good evening, Mr. Paloma. I'm Viviana Valentine," I said, shaking his hands. His hands were warm and smooth and lacked a wedding band.

"Oh, we're all first names only here," Mr. Paloma assured me. "Richard is fine."

"Even better."

"Edward Allen, my key investor," Buster said, leading me to an older gentleman, properly dressed in a light sweater and flannel pants, who nodded at me and didn't offer a handshake. "And his wife, Evelyn." She was similarly dressed in casual flannel slacks and a cashmere cardigan knotted across her shoulders, and responded to our introduction by jutting out her thin fingers. They were ice-cold, but her handshake was firm.

"Edward, Evelyn, nice to meet you." The sour pusses on their faces made me realize they were not as casual as Richard Paloma, so I resolved to go back to surnames as quickly as possible. They drifted back toward the edge of the room as Buster continued his introductions. The couple were out of place at their age and, thanks to Evelyn's proper breeding, knew so.

"Stanley Swansea, an old chum from Boston," Buster pointed to a shorter, fair-haired man engrossed in a close conversation with a woman in a dressing gown, about his height and enraptured with his every word. "And he's chatting with Hazel Olmsted. You can say hello once they break apart, if they ever do."

"Have they known each other long?" I asked, noticing Mr. Swansea's hand casually brush against Miss Olmsted's three times in less than a minute.

"About ten hours," Buster laughed. "And finally, a neighbor. Chester Courtland."

Mr. Courtland was the only person properly dressed in a suit—and not a terribly fashionable one at that—and he offered me his hand. "Miss Valentine." He had rough calluses on his thumb and middle finger, the kind you get filling out loads of paperwork by hand—I knew those rough patches myself, no matter how much I tried to get rid of 'em.

"Lovely to meet you, sir," I said. Buster wasted no time shepherding me from the group and back to the privacy of the bar. I turned to him and lowered my voice. "You said 'finally,' Buster, but there's a man by the door?"

"Oh yes. That's Monty."

"And Monty is . . .?"

"Monty Bonito," Buster muttered. "A recent addition thanks to the goings-on. He came highly recommended."

"Ah."

Paloma was the first to break from the familiar group and move to stand closer to our host. "No Tally tonight?"

"No, sir, she had an engagement in the city," I explained.

"Does she ever not?"

"Rarely. I'd be exhausted if I kept her social calendar."

"Surely you're not at home every night?" Buster asked, leaning on the bar. "With a figure like that."

His gaze went down the length of me, and that, along with the comment, would've set off alarm bells if Tally hadn't already clued me in on Buster, so instead I barked out a laugh. "No, sometimes Tommy and I have jobs. Trailing a nogoodnik, peeping on fronts—you know."

"That sounds much more exciting than life up here," Buster said.

"It's mostly standing outside on cold sidewalks, hoping to catch a glimpse through the curtains of someone doing something they shouldn't," I said.

"And this Tommy character," Paloma asked. "He's the one Tally had a lark with, correct?"

"Don't mention that to him. He's still sore about being one-upped by a little girl, or from sitting on a train for six days—I can't tell which," I said.

"Tally's no ordinary little girl," Paloma said with a smile.

"Don't I know it. She moved into my boarding house after the whole fracas, and it's been nonstop since."

"One time," Buster started, "when she was about . . . eight or nine. Before her mother died. They were both up for a long weekend, and Tally decided that everyone should play hide-and-seek. Though she didn't tell a soul we were involved in the game."

"Oh, dear," Richard said. "Is this when . . .?"

"It is," Buster smiled. "I'm not sure if she's told you the full story, but do ask her about her dealings with the Coast Guard when you're in her presence next."

I stifled a laugh with a sip of my cognac. "Noted, sir. I will do just that."

"I do wish she were here," Buster lamented. "Not that I don't trust you, Viviana, but the more people who are putting their minds to our little goings-on, the more sure I'll be that I'm not going crazy."

"Who here has heard them?" I asked.

"I have," Mr. Paloma responded. "Obviously, I live here."

"Monty as well, or at least he's aware of them," Buster explained.

"Anyone else?"

"Myself, Richard, and Jeeves—aside from us, I don't believe so," Buster said, scanning the faces of all the guests and assessing them. "I just simply cannot recall how parties overlapped with the occurrences, but if anyone here has ever heard them, they haven't mentioned it. There certainly haven't been any strange sounds since the guests arrived this morning."

"And Mr. Courtland," I started, "has he experienced anything like this at his estate? Maybe we should ask if—"

"He hasn't heard anything at all." Paloma cut me short. Considering how reluctant Buster was to share the news of his hauntings with me and Tommy, I wondered if he'd asked his well-to-do neighbor for real. We all know what happens when we assume, so I'd have to find a way to surreptitiously ask the neighbor fella myself.

"Looks like we have our work cut out for us," I said, sipping my cognac. It burned like fire but in the best way I've ever felt.

"What do you think of a fine French cognac?" Mr. Paloma asked, inclining his brow toward my glass.

"It's divine."

"It ought to be, it's pre-Revolution," Buster said. I didn't know if he meant ours or theirs, but I guess it didn't matter. "We'll have you passing for an heiress yet." I had to admit the constant barbs were really starting to grate on my nerves. I straightened my skirt to hide my fluster just as Mrs. Allen came over to insert herself into the conversation.

"Good evening . . . Viviana, was it? What a charming name," she said. "Where is it from?"

By her appearance and her manners, I would venture to say Evelyn Allen's family was as steeped in America's history as the tea in goddamn Boston Harbor, so I knew she was asking a pointed question. "Beats me," I said in my thickest hick accent. "Alls I knows is I was born here."

She smiled nicely and retreated back to the wallpaper, taking up a conversation with the mysterious Mr. Courtland, with her husband swooping in to soak up the neighbor's youthful energy. I immediately regretted pushing away a person who might have information about the mystery I was hired to solve, but Buster smiled.

"Have as much fun as you can at their expense," he murmured. "Edward's in too deep to back out."

"Too deep into what?"

"My research," Buster explained cryptically before exploding into a barbaric yawp. "Oy!"

Both the Allens jumped and simultaneously sloshed their drinks on poor Mr. Courtland, who shrieked slightly.

"Sorry, old chum. Arnold will be back in a moment and can tell you where to clean up," Buster said. "But Stanley Swansea, enough is enough. Surely she's going to bed with you—now walk away before she changes her mind. Meet another darling woman, Viviana Valentine!"

Miss Olmsted blushed but didn't argue, and Mr. Swansea jostled up to Buster and fake punched him in the stomach, tottering slightly so that Buster had to catch him before he fell. Such aggressive boyishness didn't become our host, but he let it slide, and settled the blinkered Swansea upright. Hazel, in the meantime, was swooped into conversation with the other trio, though she kept glancing over her shoulder at our little party by the bar.

"Evening, Miss Valentine," Swansea said, smoothing back hair that had become tousled during his fake scrapping. The move highlighted his face—a lock with a slight curl came down over his forehead, showcasing his tanned face, and a high-cheek-boned, almost Slavic handsomeness like that new

Hollywood boy, Kirk Douglas, as far as the eye could see, all of it marred only slightly by the marks a pair of eyeglasses had left on the bridge of his nose. Up close, and eyeing the piece on his wrist, I knew why Olmsted was in for a penny. I couldn't blame the girl.

"Good evening, Mr. Swansea," I said, giving him my hand. He took it gently and gave it a firm squeeze. It was just the right handshake for the situation. Everyone in the whole damn house was measuring up the situation and coming out right. I hated it.

"Stan's fine," he said, taking his hand back and slipping it into his pocket. Nothing he did was awkward or careless, every movement as purposeful as an acrobat's. "What brings you up north for the weekend?"

"Just a splendid invitation from a friend of a friend," I said, covering before Buster could answer. "I've never been to a weekend in the country before."

"Then you shall see everything the country has to offer," Buster declared. "We'll have you scorning the fetid streets of Manhattan before Sunday-night dinner."

"I doubt that's going to happen," I replied. "But do try your damnedest."

"What would interest you most?" Stan asked in a manner that was dripping with innuendo. "Boats? Ponies? Games? Star-gazing? The sky is glittering here—you can practically touch them, like diamonds."

"Ix-nay on the iamonds-day, Stanley," Buster chided. "She's friends with Tally, of course."

"That hasn't turned me off to diamonds, Buster," I zinged right back. "I don't think anything ever could."

"Just as a woman should say." Richard smiled. His voice was husky, and I found myself desiring to know, as soon as possible, if he was just a roommate. Though Stan Swansea knew fully his effect on all women, Richard Paloma was turning it on special, just for me. A heat tingled between us, one that I hadn't felt since the summer.

I suddenly became very aware that I was standing in a room full of men, none of whom I knew or could pick out of a lineup with a foggy brain. I put my drink on the bar and regretted I'd ever been introduced to cognac.

I was bogarting all of the handsome Mr. Swansea's time as he vied with Richard for my attention, so Hazel Olmsted eventually excused herself from the company of Mr. and Mrs. Allen and the neighbor, Mr. Courtland, and joined our party. The chemistry between Richard and me eased substantially as Hazel and Stanley sucked it all up for themselves. Richard moved on to Courtland and the Allens, trying to balance out Buster's obvious inclination toward his younger guests.

"How do you do, Miss Olmsted," I said, shaking her hand. Her touch was warm and kind, her grip relaxing as Stanley's attention went back where it belonged.

"Hazel, please. And quite well, as Buster already shouted to the party," she replied, laying a hand gently on our host's silk-swathed shoulder. "You can't embarrass a woman who goes for what she wants, my dear."

"Then you must have never felt shame in your life," Buster replied.

"Never, I swear it." She broke into a full-bodied, throaty laugh, and I saw Swansea melt into a puddle. He leaned his face in close to hers, and it hovered there, searching for answers and love in her eyes. They were a match made in heaven, bouncing quips off each other like they were auditioning to become the next Powell and Loy.

The pair managed to engross our host, so I tried to mingle. Monty Bonito was circling the room like a stalking cat, and I left him to it. Chester Courtland, the neighbor, was sitting at a window seat and looked ready to snooze. I wondered why he didn't just go home. So I figured I'd ask.

"Evening," I said, sticking out my hand. Courtland's eyes averted from whatever point he was fixed on. "I'm Viviana Valentine, but you can call me Viv. Or whatever you like, I guess— Buster does."

"Hi, I'm Chester." No hand was extended in my direction.

"I heard you're a neighbor," I said. "Must be nice digs."

"Oh, not directly next door," Courtland assured me. "But the general area."

"Oh, good. If you owned a mansion, I'm not sure if I'd have the right manners to chat with you."

"You seem to be able to hold your own," Courtland said, nodding at the bar where it seemed Buster, Stanley, and Richard felt compelled to sing a mathematics-themed fight song, some more enthusiastically than the others.

"E to the u, du/dx!" Buster hollered. He waved his arm in a sort of pirate-like swing, careful not to slosh his beverage.

"E to the x dx!" Stanley followed up. His fist was pounding on the bar as he chanted.

"Cosine, secant, tangent, sine," Buster had cupped his free hand around his mouth, projecting to the entire room.

"Three-point-one-four-one-five-nine!" Stanley was shouting now, red in the face.

"Integral, radical, u dv," Buster sang in a low bass and then playfully hit Richard in the shoulder.

"Slipstick, slide rule, MIT!," Richard finished with a blush. He glanced at me, and even from across the room I managed to see him roll his eyes.

"Do you know what they're talking about?" I asked the man sitting next to me.

"Vaguely," he said. "I remember the vocabulary from high school trigonometry, but God help me if you wanted me to do an actual proof."

I laughed, but God help me if I wanted to know what a proof was—aside from "beyond a reasonable doubt."

"Have you been to the house before?" I asked.

"Once or twice," Courtland admitted. "But it was during the summer—garden parties, that kind of thing. It's pretty swanky inside."

"I'll say—but I have a feeling tomorrow morning I'll see clear as day that it's pretty swanky *outside* too," I said. My eyes were dancing around the room and doing some quick calculations on the expansive silk rug. Cut it up into pieces, and you could use it to carpet all of Mrs. K's, basement to attic. "It's hard to believe that they do experiments in here. I'd be afraid of scorching the rug when something bubbled over."

"I don't think it's exactly that kind of science," Courtland laughed. "But I could very well be mistaken."

"So, I take it you're not a scientist?" I asked.

"Not in the least. Just a lawyer," Courtland said.

"Must be a pretty good lawyer to even live in this zip code," I said.

"There's only one secret to being a good lawyer," Courtland explained. For the first time in our chat, he held my gaze for longer than a moment. His eyes were tired and reddening at the edges. "Get people what they want, and try to make it as painless as possible."

"You make it sound so simple!"

"But I admit, it's the hardest thing in the world," Courtland said.

"What brings you to the party, aside from a regular old invite?" I asked.

"Oh! I have a client who is interested in the goings-on of the laboratory," Courtland said.

"Another investor?" I asked.

"Something like that," Courtland agreed, but declined to go into specifics.

"It must be so thrilling to work for people who are on the forefront of all of this technology," I pushed, but clearly I'd pushed too far.

"Some people think so," Courtland said, shaking his head, along with his glass. "Can I get you anything?" He stood, and made it obvious he was removing himself from my company.

"No, thank you. I'm going to stargaze for a bit, though," I said. "You don't get these in Chelsea."

"No, I doubt you could." Courtland skittered off to the bar, but he left his glass on the edge before slipping out of the door closest to the stairs.

I counted to sixty, slowly, before getting up and sitting by the Allens, who looked like they needed a third party to diffuse a situation.

"Hello, Mr. Allen," I said. "This is quite a late night, isn't it?"

"Oh, I assure you, miss, my mind is sharp around the clock!" he said, his eyes devilish. "Never was one to throw away a productive hour."

"And Buster said that you're funding quite a lot of his current exploits," I said. "That must be very exciting, but nerve-wracking."

"We trust Buster immensely," Mrs. Allen said. "He has quite the mind."

"And a personality to match," I said with a laugh. I knew so little about our host that it was hard to pretend I was an old-time friend.

"Oh my, yes. And he's quite like me in my younger years— vim and vigor like a young stallion," Mr. Allen responded. "Unlike that Stanley."

That Stanley had started swing dancing with Hazel near the bar, with Buster providing hand claps and song for rhythm and music. "I don't know—he looks pretty vigorous," I said.

"Oh, this is much too vigorous for me, though." Mrs. Allen placed her empty Champagne coupe on the small table to her right and stood up. "Edward, I'm heading to bed."

"I will try not to wake you, my dear," he said, tinkling ice cubes at me. "I'd like a bit more of a tipple myself. See what the kids are up to."

"You're old enough to be her grandfather, Edward," Mrs. Allen said, all but sneering. "But enjoy yourself—we're in the country, after all." She gave me a nod and slipped out the door closest to the stairs.

By this point, Buster was cheering, and Stanley and Hazel were glowing with sweat. "What a performance! What a performance! Fred and Ginger, electrified."

"Thank you, Buster," Hazel said, curtseying. "Goodness, I think after that, I need to calm my blood. I'm off to bed."

"Stanley?" Buster raised an eyebrow.

"For propriety's sake, I'll wait at least ten minutes." The boys laughed as Hazel followed Mrs. Allen's footsteps out the door.

"What is propriety?" Buster said. "Ah, Edward, care for a refill?"

"Of course, of course." His eyes still on the doorway where his wife and Hazel had retreated, Mr. Allen slid his glass down the marble bar, and Buster caught it, filling the crystal with a healthy dollop.

"I'm off as well," Richard explained. "Don't want too many cobwebs in my brain tomorrow morning." He gave me a nod and left.

"I think I'll go to bed too," I said.

"Are you sure, Miss Valentine? It seems like you just got here," Stanley said, turning the flirt toward me now that his beloved Hazel was out of earshot.

"Yes, I think I'm sure, I'll see you all in the morning." Buster rang a small bell on the end of the bar, and the butler in the woolen tuxedo silently appeared behind me, ready to show me the way. Chester Courtland had returned to the bar behind Buster and picked up his glass, which our host had refilled without me even noticing. Wealthy people had a way about them, I noticed, like they could always come and go as they pleased while assuring the rest of us that we were at their beck and call.

"This way, miss," he muttered, and I dreamily followed, leaving the assorted men at the bar, three of whom immediately began carousing as if they were still at a raucous party. As I had felt my energy drain through the night, theirs only went up. It wasn't that I was unaccustomed to late nights; it was just that, since summer, most of my late nights had been spent sitting on cold benches outside of bars or in dingy digs with Tommy, scouting marks and learning the ins and outs of being a private investigator. But talking with Tommy for hours on end was as easy as slipping into your favorite pair of shoes.

I wanted to blame my tiredness on my trek from the city, but I hadn't even been the one driving. Maybe it was trying to keep up with the strangers, each and every one of them, I felt, waiting for a verbal misstep to mark me as the one that didn't belong.

"Is Arnold your first name, your last name, or neither?" I asked the square shoulders leading me up the stairs.

In the blackness just between the two of us, I heard a chuckle, and the face peered backward at me. It was a nice face, older than Buster's, but not by any means aged or demeaned. "Well, at this point, I'd rather not say," he smiled.

"Fair enough," I said. "But Arnold or Mr. Arnold, you know why I'm here, right?"

"Yes, miss," he admitted.

"You want to give me the dirt once we're behind closed doors?"

"It would be my honor. But not until then," he said, tapping the side of his nose.

The grand staircase of the home turned upward and deposited us into a mezzanine that wrapped around the second floor of the great central living room. I could hear the chatter and laughs of the gentlemen below and knew that they'd be able to hear every word I spoke to the help.

"The stairs come up in the north wing," Arnold murmured, giving me the overview of the layout. "The southeast, at the front of the house, is the guest suite where the Allens are staying, where they always stay. They prefer morning sun, and let me tell you, it gets blazing hot—I wouldn't wish it on anyone. In the northeast corner are the dual suites for Mr. Swansea and Miss Olmsted. Close, for convenience's sake. And perhaps modesty's."

"So was that all planned?" We were farther down the opposite hallway now, away from the large living room, so I felt comfortable to ask for the gossip.

"Perhaps not planned, but perhaps anticipated," Arnold responded. "This way, to the southwest, are Buster's and Richard's rooms." He left off saying whether that was also for convenience's sake, though I had my doubts, now.

"So, that puts me . . .?"

"Well, Buster had thought you'd want this room closest to the stairs, for overhearing all sorts of comings and goings," Arnold replied, "But I'm sorry, that's a dreadful place to put a young lady. Call me old-fashioned, but I try not to put single women close to the stairs."

"That *is* old-fashioned, especially if there's a lock on the door."

"There isn't," Arnold replied, making a hard right turn to a quiet corridor with three doors. "Buster abhors locked doors. So I put you in the northwest corner. It's a bit shady, but it's safer. The center door in the vestibule is the staircase to my quarters, so I can be with you as soon as you call, if you need any help in the night."

"So one of them is my room and the other . . ." I trailed off.

"Mr. Bonito's." Arnold's voice was terse.

"He's not quite like the rest of them," I said. "Or is he more like me?"

"More like you, is my understanding," Arnold opened the door to my room and motioned me inside. I led the way, and Arnold closed the door behind us.

"He came just after dinnertime this evening," Arnold said, relieved clearly that he could speak more openly. "I have no idea who he is or what his role is intended to be."

This one room at Buster's house was the size of Mrs. K's entire third floor, and then some. The walls were papered in an elaborate red pattern and surrounded an enormous four-poster in the center of the room, made of a gleaming dark wood.

"What the hell is your guy's Old English budget around here?" I asked. "Good god, it's like you've never heard of dust."

"One of Mr. Beacon's bigger peculiarities," Arnold responded. "He says it's because of his equipment."

"Is he a good boss to work for?" My finger trailed over the gleaming surface of a matching desk, picking up not even a speck of filth.

"Surprisingly so," Arnold said with confidence.

I glared at him. "Everyone hates their boss somehow."

"I truly don't, Miss Valentine." Arnold shrugged against his fitted tux.

I gave him a squint before dropping the subject.

"So!" I plopped down into the leather chair beside the desk, letting it swivel with my weight. "Give me the real skinny on the noises."

Arnold leaned against one of the bed posters. "They seem different every time," he admitted. "I think that's one reason we can't track them down."

"Basement, first floor, second floor, attic?" I spied my purse on the desk and unbuckled it, to fish out my pencil and paper.

"All of the above. More! Sometimes you hear things in the boathouse, as well."

"Boathouse? Jesus Christ, I'm only one woman, Arnold."

"Will you be expecting reinforcements?"

"God, I hope so," I said. "Though I did the last case all by my lonesome, so I know I can if I have to."

Arnold looked wary. "Let's hope you don't have to."

He stood up straight and appeared as if he was about to leave.

"Wait! Before you bug out," I said. "What do I have to know about being a guest, so I don't look suspicious?"

"Breakfast is at nine AM, sharp," Arnold said. "Most show dressed for the day. I believe we're to have a warm spell this weekend, so Mr. Beacon will, of course, be primed to show off his new boat."

"New boat?"

"There are three now," Arnold explained. "Though why he bought this most recent one is beyond me. It arrived just two weeks ago—no time left to enjoy it this summer."

They all have at least one yacht, I thought to myself.

"Anything else?" I asked.

"Likely no, Miss Valentine. But if you have any questions, you can dial me on the house phone by spinning zero zero zero. It will ring both in the kitchen and in my quarters."

"Thanks, Arnold. I have a feeling we'll be having many, many chats this weekend."

Arnold responded with a butlerish bow. "I look forward to them, miss." He showed himself to the door and disappeared into the night.

DAY 2

For the past ten years, I've never slept anywhere but in a bed in Mrs. K's boarding house and in the hospital just once. I did not expect anything but a restless sleep at Buster Beacon's house, especially 'cause there wasn't a lock on my door.

It was pitch-black when a thunderous crack of sound woke me up. Sweaty and tangled in crisp linen sheets, I fought against my bindings to get my feet on the floor.

The floor was warm. And it wiggled.

"Watch it!"

"Jesus Christ!" I was back on the bed, standing, holding a pillow, ready to strike.

"It's me, Viv," Tommy said from the shadows. "What was that noise?"

My heart stopped beating in my throat when I heard Tommy's voice. "What I'm here to investigate. We're here. Why are you . . . here? How did you get in?"

"One thing at a time." Tommy, who was still dressed and in his shoes, tossed me a robe to slip over my favorite red-and-white striped pajamas. They were getting a little thin after so many washings, and I was already shivering, either from cold or adrenaline. "Find your slippers. We're going poking around."

I was in my slippers before he even stopped talking.

"Where do you think it came from?" I asked before opening the door.

"Above somewhere, I think."

"Follow me."

I slipped out of my bedroom door, with Tommy at my heels, edging slightly down the hall before opening the door to Arnold's quarters upstairs.

The passageway was simple and clean—none of the showy turns and curves of the public spaces, but orderly. The walls had been painted recently with a new coat of white, and the dark colored carpet on the stairs didn't have a single fray. There was a switch to the right of the door, and Tommy stopped my hand before I flicked on the lights.

"No, not yet."

He went before me in the darkness and crept up the short flight of stairs.

Four bedroom doors stood open to rooms empty of people and furniture, and all the way to our right at the end of a hall, another stood sentry: a big oak door, closed, likely guarding Arnold's personal quarters. To the left was a small kitchenette.

"I guess we have to check on the butler," Tommy said. He pulled a dark leather coin sap out of his pocket and held it in his fist, creeping toward the closed door.

"Don't hurt Arnold."

"If he don't hurt me first," Tommy murmured back.

He turned the handle of the door and found an empty room, with the sheets on the bed turned back in a jumble. There was an attached water closet with a clawfoot tub and curtain, pulled open so we could see that no one was using the facilities.

"Guess it wasn't the butler," I said. "Back downstairs."

"I hate big houses." Tommy pocketed his weapon.

"How come I didn't get one of those?" I asked, and Tommy didn't say a thing. "Do you hear anyone else?"

We were back downstairs in the main house. The door to the guest room next to mine was ajar, and I could hear someone stumble and curse.

"It's fine, Mont," Tommy called in. "Take your time. No hurry or anything."

"You know Monty Bonito?"

"I *sent* Monty Bonito."

"Then sleep on *his* goddamn floor."

Tommy snorted. "We're checking the other bedrooms, Mont. Catch up." He turned to me. "Where *are* the other bedrooms?"

"Follow me. And shush."

We met Arnold—in an ankle-length nightshirt—alongside Buster and Richard, on the mezzanine that connected their wing to ours. The two roommates were in their broadcloth nightclothes, though Paloma had opted for a heavy terrycloth robe instead of his embroidered silk smoking jacket. The lights in the public hallways had been kept on but dimmed for evening, so we were able to assess each shocked face. After a moment of silence, I took charge.

"Buster, you go peek in on the Allens. If they wake up, they'll be less shocked to see your face in the night than any of our mugs," I said. "Monty, go check on the lovebirds."

He looked to Tommy for instructions. Gritting his teeth, ol' Tommy Boy commanded, "Now."

Monty skittered off in his blue-checkered flannels and black slippers.

"The rest of us, downstairs."

Arnold opened the drawer of a credenza and pulled out several flashlights. "Here." He led us down the winding stairs.

At the base, Tommy took a hard left toward the front of the house; Arnold galloped toward the south wing without waiting.

"I'll check the backyard," Richard announced, and tore off toward the rear of the house.

I was left with the internal rooms closest to the stairwell— Buster's several parlors, I assumed, and all the other square footage he'd described in our office not even half a day ago.

The first room I slipped into, without doors, was the library, stately and lightly furnished aside from the floor-to-ceiling shelves filled with books, an ornate table in the center with a book stand and a leather blotter, and a few tall armchairs. The potted plant in the corner was sparse enough that not even a slip of a girl could hide behind it. I traced the perimeter of the room and saw no cupboards or closets. There was literally nowhere to hide.

The next door on the way to the back of the house was a closet, filled with blankets and pillows. All the bedrooms were upstairs, but I supposed that was as good a place as any to store linens.

Toward the back of the house was a kitchen, behind a swinging door. White and black marble tiles created an opulent checkerboard, and I met Arnold in the center of them.

"Did you already check the cabinets?" I asked.

"And the mudroom and laundry room," he said, motioning toward two fairly well-concealed doors in the paneling. "I'm sorry, it's a hard house to search. All the dirty bits are hidden."

"And you really have no idea what the noise was or where it could've come from?"

"None."

Three men found us in the kitchen.

"The Allens are sleeping like angels," Buster reported, pulling a pipe from his pocket, to chew the end. "And I stuck my head into the dining room on the way here—there was nothing."

"Nothing out front," Tommy said. "But maybe I can see tire marks or footprints when it's light out."

"They weren't asleep, but they got alibis," Monty intimated about Stanley and Hazel.

"And Richard?" Buster asked.

"He went to the backyard," I said. "How do we get there from here?"

"The easiest way is through here."

Buster sprung open the door to the mudroom and marched us through a utility door hidden behind a small rhododendron. We were just next to a grand stone patio, naked of furniture and blooming flowers for the winter. There was nothing to block the view clear down to the Hudson, and the boathouse at the base of the bank. No streetlamps or headlights to speak of, but the moon was more than half full, and I couldn't see a soul wandering.

"Monty, with me," Tommy instructed. "Everyone else, stay put."

We watched as the two shadowed figures headed toward the glittering water.

"Do we have to stay put, or should we go back inside?" Buster asked.

"Put." I stomped my slippered foot for emphasis.

He quieted but adjusted his dressing gown to cover more of his chest.

Arnold, Buster, and I stood shuffling and shivering on the flagstones.

"What are you looking at?" Richard appeared at my side and asked a simple question, making me jump about ten feet in the air.

"Tommy and Monty went to the boathouse, looking for you," I said back, trying to keep my voice from squeaking.

"I never went to the boathouse," Richard replied.

"We'll ask where you went once we're back indoors," Buster declared. Now that his roommate was in sight, Buster clearly considered the evening's mysteries concluded, and herded himself, his housemate, and the butler back into the kitchen.

"I guess I'll go get them, then?" I said to no one at all, and walked my pink fuzzy slippers, now soaked with freezing dew, down the lawn to go gather my troops.

★ ★ ★

Tommy called out to me as I approached the small outbuilding.

"Nothing doing, Viv," he said. "At least that I can tell at night."

"Fine, let's just go inside. I wouldn't think we'd figure it out in one crash bang boom anyhow." We fell in step as we marched back to the house. "Okay, you two. Explain."

Tommy started in. "Monty owes me a favor, and he lives in Yonkers, so I called up Buster to let him know he'd be up to lend a helping hand, but to treat him like a guest so no one else would be the wiser."

"They're the wiser, Tom," I said. "No offense, Monty Bonito, but you don't fit in."

"Only at the OTB." He shrugged. "But I'm doing my best."

"How long have you known each other?" I asked. "Monty, I hope you're not insulted, but I never heard your name before."

"The fewer people who know my name, the better, sweetheart," Monty said. "But it's nice to make your acquaintance."

"We go way back," Tommy said. "Late in '42."

"After you got seasoned with the best the Japanese Navy could hurl at ya?" I asked.

"We're both pretty lucky to be alive," Monty said gruffly.

"Were you also at Midway?" I asked.

"No." There was no further explanation.

"No, I was Navy, and Monty was Army," Tommy said. "We met once we got home. Some big meeting for GIs to find out what kind of benefits we wanted from serving."

"They talked about college and houses," Monty said. "We were there because there was free lunch."

"Funny how you all managed to find just the right friends from the war," I said.

"Don't worry," Monty said, "there were plenty of fellas from the war I'm happy to never see again."

"So what the hell were you thinking, sleeping on *my* floor, Mister Tomasso Antonino Fortuna? You scared the bejeezus out of me," I said.

"Arnold let me in when I showed up. He said all the bedrooms were taken, so I just said I'd catnap on your floor."

"All eight bedrooms? There should be one free—me and Monty are two, Buster and Richard are four, Hazel and Stanley are six, and the Allens take the seventh."

"Who'd we miss?" Tommy asked.

Monty piped up. "The neighbor fella. He tied one on tight tonight, and Buster and Mr. Allen led him to the room at the head of the stairs, long after you went to bed and those other two who were makin' goo-goo eyes at each other skittered off to do what they were gonna do."

"Did anyone check on him? His name is Chester Courtland."

"I assumed Buster had?" Tommy added.

"Let's double-check." I motioned for Tommy to follow.

We went back the way we came, behind the bush and into the kitchen, where Arnold had tied an apron over his robe to slap together a midnight snack. Buster and Richard were at the kitchen table, quietly munching away on ham sandwiches, Buster with a glass of water and Richard with a tall glass of milk.

"Mr. Beacon," I started, "did you check on Mr. Courtland?"

"I didn't," Buster responded, not moving from his place at the table. He seemed tired—and looked his age—while working through a blood alcohol level that had before rendered him boyishly charming hours ago but now left his cheeks puffy and sad.

"Okay." I raised an eyebrow at Tommy, and we started back toward the living room.

"Do you want a nibble?" Buster called after us, but we ignored him and kept walking. Monty walked up to the table and picked a sandwich off the platter, flopping into a chair next to Buster.

Once we were outside the swinging doors, the tension in Tommy's shoulders fell. "He don't seem concerned," he said, thumbing back in the direction of our host as we hustled up the stairs.

"About his house, the noise, or the neighbor?"

"All of the above."

At the landing, I hooked a right and Tommy followed. "This must be it." I opened the door and found Chester Courtland an absolute mess.

"Well, he mighta been the thunk," Tommy muttered, bending down to check on the unfortunate soul, who was lying prone on the floor between the entrance door and his personal bathroom.

Chester was only in his shorts, and the smell of him revealed why. He had clearly spent part of his night vomiting, and the result was abysmal. I could hear Tommy start to gag at the scent of the sweaty, filthy man on the floor. Scanning the scene, I spied his suit crumpled in the corner in front of an armchair, and there were no pajamas to be seen—neither Richard nor Buster nor Arnold had even offered him a complimentary pair. Tommy heaved the man to a standing position but as soon as he loosened his grip on the man's chest, Chester fell to the ground with a whimper.

"I can't, I can't . . ." he moaned, barely conscious. He was shivering, and most of his limbs were blue in the dim light—but the lower part of one leg was actively purpling, and swelling to boot.

"I think he's got a broken bone somewhere," Tommy said. "Ankle, leg, or otherwise."

"Drunk himself silly?"

"Or upchucked from the pain," Tommy surmised. "I'll get him into bed somehow; you get Buster to call for a doctor. He needs one, no matter what."

★ ★ ★

I left Tommy to struggle with the mostly naked man and scurried back down to the kitchen. I pulled Arnold aside to the mudroom, to share the details.

"I need you to call a doctor, and a good one," I said. "The neighbor is in dire straits. He's purpling at the feet and covered in vomit. Try not to tell anyone what's happening. Only Buster, if you have to."

Arnold nodded and picked up the receiver of the phone hanging on the wall, and I exited back into the kitchen.

"Courtland seems fine," I fibbed to the kitchen crowd. "And I'm giving Tommy some privacy to clean up in our room before hitting the hay again." I stretched and faked a yawn. Monty gave my legs an eye, and I scowled at him.

"Yes, that's a lovely idea," Paloma said, dusting his hands on a linen napkin. "I think I'll head back toward bed. Come on, Monty. Let's go back upstairs."

He urged the rough-hewn houseguest along in front of him and back toward the stairwell. Monty had no choice but to follow Paloma's lead.

"Arnold is summoning a doctor," I explained to Buster. "Your neighbor doesn't look too hot. But we can handle it from here."

"Are you sure?" Judging by Buster's helpfulness up until this point in the night, I knew his question was for show only.

"This is why you hired us, isn't it? To do the dirty work?"

"I can hire an army to come in, create, and clean up dirty work, Miss Valentine," Buster said. "And still, I often find myself with filthy hands." He sighed as he plucked his napkin off his lap, nodded at me, and left the kitchen.

Arnold returned to the kitchen. "A generalist from Columbia-Presbyterian will be here shortly," he explained.

"How's he gonna get here so fast?"

"He lives in White Plains, about a ten-minute drive."

"That explains it."

In the meantime, Arnold began washing the dishes.

"What aren't you telling me?" I asked, plucking half a ham on rye off the board before putting it back down, remembering I'd already brushed my teeth and that the flavor combination of Pepsodent and rye bread didn't sound all that appetizing.

"Nothing pertinent, Miss Valentine," Arnold said.

"Call me Viv."

"Yes, Miss Valentine."

I rolled my eyes. God forbid anyone call a girl what she wanted to be called.

"So, what's in the basement of this lousy place? Anything I have to worry about?"

"Wine, mostly; some antiques gathering dust; the furnace—the usual."

"Any way in from the outside?"

"There's a coal chute, but I don't have the strength to open the door; it's been rusted for ages."

"And we've been up to the attic . . ." I mused to myself.

"What part?"

"Your part. The part you told me about. There's more parts?"

"Four parts," Arnold explained, wiping a long chef's knife on a pristine towel, the blade of it glinting in the low, yellow light flicked on above the sink. "Each corner of the house essentially has its own above-stairs quarters; there's nothing above the living room and gallery. I'm in the southwest, as I explained. The southeastern wing is bereft of anyone and is locked despite the master's general distaste for the mechanisms. The garrets above Buster and Richard's quarters are for their professional use."

"Tally mentioned he was in the city the other night for a symposium."

"Yes, I believe he was."

"What kind of symposium?"

Arnold dodged and looked at the clock on the oven. "The doctor should be here soon, and I don't want him ringing the bell and waking the house. I'm to wait by the door. Will you be so kind and put the sandwiches in the icebox?" Arnold untied his apron and left me alone in the kitchen.

The help is always there to clean up the messes. I considered pilfering a sandwich or two for snacks when Tommy and I reconvened after our meeting with the sawbones, but thought better of it. Courtland was pretty well encrusted with vomit, and that was enough to make even Tommy lose his appetite.

★　★　★

I snuck up to the guest bedroom at the head of the stairs and entered just as the doctor was putting away his stethoscope in his little black bag. He stopped speaking as he saw me.

"Don't mind her," Tommy explained. "She's with me."

"Yes, sir. Well, this man almost certainly has a sprained ankle and a fractured fibula, for which we can do absolutely nothing more than wrap it and tell him not to walk on it," he continued. "He's breathing, albeit not entirely normally, and his blood pressure is fine, though by the—well—smell of his vomit, he was not intoxicated."

"So what's got him messed up, Doc?" Tommy asked.

"I can't tell exactly without lab tests, but it would not surprise me in the least if, as they say, someone slipped him some kind of mickey."

"He's drugged?" Arnold asked.

"Drugged enough to stumble for a bit and sleep like the dead, but not enough that he won't feel the pain of his leg when he wakes up," the doctor said. "I'd give you painkillers, but as I don't know what's in his system, I wouldn't want to do more harm than good."

"So when he wakes up, he's gonna be a real mess," Tommy said.

"That's the professional assessment, yes."

"How long 'til we can give him something for the broken bone?" I asked.

"At least twelve hours, if not twenty-four," the doctor said, glancing over his glasses at me. "I can come back tomorrow night for reevaluation and with the results of laboratory tests."

"Please do," Tommy said, shaking his hand. Arnold took the doctor's kit and led him from the room, no doubt discussing the cost of the midnight house call. And how to keep the record of the doctor's visit between parties who needed to know.

"So, what do we do?"

"Arnold promised to stay with this jamoke while he slept it off," Tommy said. "But while we're alone, we go through his stuff."

Tommy was already pulling open the nightstand, which revealed itself to be empty.

"Start with his pants, Tom," I said. "He didn't even have jammies—he wasn't intending to spend the weekend like the rest of us. He probably meant to hoof it home, but something got the better of him."

I plucked the trousers off the floor and cringed at the cheapness of the fabric.

"There's no way in Hades this man owns a neighboring mansion," I said, turning the pants around so I could find a pocket. There was something heavy weighing down the lefthand side. "Look at the shine on these knees."

I pulled out a creased black leather billfold and tossed it to Tommy, who flicked it open.

"Not on a government salary, he doesn't," Tommy said.

"You find a business card?"

"No," Tommy said. "A badge." A shiny piece of brass was attached to the right side of the billfold.

"Cop?"

"FBI."

"Holy shit, Tom."

"You're telling me." He slid the billfold into his own pocket.

"Oh, I got a no—" We both heard the doorknob turning, so I clammed right up.

"It's just me," Arnold whispered into the dark, bumping a small plastic bucket against the doorframe. "I'll clean up and stay with him. You can go rest now. Thank you for everything."

"No problem," Tommy said. I slipped the small leather pad into my robe pocket. "We'll wake up early and help set up breakfast, won't we, Viv?"

"Of course," I agreed. "Tommy can attest I make a mean pot of coffee."

We slipped out the door and shot down the hall to our room, shutting the door behind us and wedging a chair beneath the knob for security.

As soon as Tommy turned around, I jumped at him, throwing my arms around his neck. "Oh, thank God you're here." I buried my face in the crook of his neck.

"I wasn't going to run off—or get run off—like last time," Tommy said, hugging me back.

I didn't feel like letting him go, but the evidence we just discovered was pulling my mind away from Tommy. I fell off his neck but stayed close. "He's a Fed?" I asked. "Let me see."

"Come over here by the light." Tommy pulled away and sat down on the side of the bed, flicking on the bedside lamp. I perched next to him as we both snooped through the man's documents.

"At least he didn't lie about his name—that we can tell," I said, pointing to the driver's license. "And he's got a whole hundred dollars in small bills tucked in."

"What's that gonna do in a place like this?" Tommy asked. "Was he going to tip the butler? You said you had to know something before Arnold came in."

"I started to say that I got a notebook—haven't flipped through it yet," I admitted, handing it over. "If there's anything else . . . Well, maybe Arnold won't snoop."

"He's a butler—that's his job."

"How do you know? How many butlers have you ever met?"

"Oh, quit it, would you?" Tommy said, tossing me the notebook. "Here, you can read chicken scratch better than I can with these ol' eyes."

I flipped open the pad and immediately recoiled. "No one's reading this," I said. "It's doused in alcohol and maybe some vomit. Stinks like the devil, and the ink ran like the devil too."

Tommy looked a bit crestfallen but got up, collected the notebook, and went into the bathroom. He emerged without the evidence.

"What'd ya do?"

"Wedged both behind the toilet tank." He pulled out his tucked shirt and took off his belt. "I'll get into my pajamas in the bathroom once you're asleep, Viv, but toss me a pillow. That floor is hard."

"I am not tossing you a pillow, you idiot," I said. "Just get in the goddamn bed. My virtue will not be tarnished."

I walked to the far side of the bed, leaving Tommy the side closer to the door.

"And you better change. You smell like upchuck."

I tossed my robe on the desk and got under the covers while Tommy disappeared into the bathroom to clean up. He reemerged in his flannel pants and smelling of Colgate. Tommy clicked off the lamp and sidled in beside me. Lying flat on his back, with his hands behind his head, he studied the ceiling.

"Turning into a case, isn't it?" he asked in the dark.

"Seems like it."

"Thanks for giving me a soft place to land."

"Happy to do it, ol' Tommy boy."

Within no time, he was sawing logs. But with the additional presence in my bed, I had to flop around like a dead fish before I found a comfortable way to lie; I rolled on my side, facing Tommy, and fell asleep to the sound of his deep breathing.

I awoke to the sound of a strange buzz in my room. The sheets tangled around my legs, and I stumbled from the bed. "What? What? What is that?"

Tommy exited from the bathroom in just his blue-striped shorts, half of his face shaved. "What did you hear? What's going on?"

"A really odd buzz."

He laughed at me. "It's called a Norelco, Viv." He disappeared back into the bathroom, and I heard a small click, followed by the buzz. It was Tommy's electric razor.

"Oh." I turned to go sit back down on the bed and wait for Tommy to finish his ablutions. The clock on the nightstand said it was just after six.

"Did you get enough sleep?" Tommy asked, coming out of our shared bathroom, pulling an undershirt over his head. He didn't seem to notice or care that he wasn't decent; it was like any old day at work.

"Enough—that's all that matters," I said. "We have to be down soon to help Arnold with breakfast."

"You hurry up and get dressed," Tommy said, stepping into a pair of cotton slacks. "I'll sneak into the G-man's room to take another pass for information, and then I'll join you downstairs."

"Sounds good."

By the time I was done with my morning preparations and fully dressed in my favorite, blue-striped sailor dress—the fabric, I noticed, laughing to myself, nearly matched Tommy's underpants—Tommy was gone, and I laced up my saddle shoes, to head down to the kitchen.

Arnold was busy cracking a pallet of eggs into a large mixing bowl.

"Good morning, Miss Valentine," he said over the sound of hissing butter. "The coffee station is over there, if you'd do us the honors."

There was a nook in the kitchen with an electric percolator, outlet, and hand-cranked coffee grinder. I filled the latter with beans and set to churning. As soon as the coffee was brewing, I watched a master butler at work.

"What else can I do?" I asked.

"Not much, sadly, I really have gotten used to doing this for so many people on so little sleep," Arnold admitted. "But it's nice to have company."

"How was your night?" I plucked a piece of toast out of a silver rack and munched it.

"There was some more"—he paused as he saw me eating—"stomach unpleasantness, but just before I came down, the man was finally awake enough. I explained all I knew, and he asked for a phone. Simple as that."

"Too simple."

"You don't say." Arnold smiled as he poured his gleaming, steaming scrambled eggs into a silver chafing dish. "Ah! The help is in transporting this to the dining room, if you please, Miss Valentine."

"No problem, boss." I bumped the swinging kitchen door with my hip, deposited the dish on the sideboard, among all the other matching dishes, and returned to find Tommy in the kitchen. He looked almost like he belonged here, in boating shoes and a loose-knit cotton sweater I'd never seen before.

"So, who knows about us?" he asked pointedly. Arnold took the opportunity to answer.

"Myself, of course, and Mr. Beacon, Mr. Paloma, and Mr. Bonito," he explained. "That leaves Mr. Courtland, Mr. and Mrs. Allen, Mr. Swansea, and Miss Olmsted none the wiser."

"Swansea and Olmsted were the ones, uh . . . otherwise engaged last night?"

"Correct."

"And the Allens?"

"Real pills," I said, cutting Arnold off. "Money folk. Awful. Rude and proper and properly terrible to be around."

I swore I heard Arnold chuckle to himself, but Tommy was clearly debating something in his head before sighing and pulling a small box from his pocket.

"Put this on," he said, tossing it to me. "It's our cover."

I plucked the small, cream-colored cube from the air and found a small latch, opening it while rolling my eyes.

Inside was a ring with a honkin' stone.

"What the hell is this?" I asked.

"About two carats of diamond," Tommy responded.

"Did you get it from Tally?"

"Or don't put it on, Viv, and get all sorts of runaround from the Allens," he said. "Up to you."

I slipped the ring onto my finger and put the box in my pocket. "You're the boss."

"We're partners, Viv." His ears looked pink in the sunlight. "What else can we do, Arnie?"

Arnold smoldered at the nickname. "Pour Miss Valentine's coffee into the silver pot, please, and then go sit at the table as if you're early for breakfast, please."

We did as we were told.

Nothing had changed since I had deposited the eggs, except that Buster was now seated at the head of the dining table, buried in the *Times*.

"Guten Morgen," he said chipperly.

"Morning," Tommy responded, placing the coffee service on the table in front of our host.

"My apologies—I thought you were Arnold," Buster said, folding the paper and slipping it beneath his plate. "How fared ye, after my departure?"

"Courtland got too much in his drinks," I explained. "Poor Arnold was up to his elbows in it last night."

"We ended up calling in a doctor," Tommy explained. "Courtland wasn't responsive, and we figured it better to be safe than sorry. On top of that, his ankle is damaged, so you might have a houseguest for longer than you expected. Not sure how much the visit set you back, though."

"Not a worry at all." Buster waved away the thought of money. "No ideas on our little mystery?"

"None yet, sadly," I said. "Where's Mr. Paloma?"

"Delayed, but en route, I assure you," Buster said. "You two hit it off last night."

Tommy gave me the eye.

"We all had a sip of something, and you know how charming I can be," I smiled. I reached for the coffeepot.

"Didn't hit it off well enough, apparently," said Buster, eyeing my hand. "Are congratulations in order?"

"It's a cover," I said, switching the pot to my right hand and slipping my left beneath the table. "If Tommy's going to be staying in my room, we might as well be slightly decent about it. You already have Swansea and Olmsted making a show. I don't want your investors to think you're running a brothel."

"Swansea and Olmsted are indeed making a show," a throaty voice agreed from the doorway. Hazel stood looking smug and relaxed, and Stan's arm was looped around her waist. "Where shall we sit?"

"Anywhere you'd like," Buster said. "But you know breakfast is self-serve."

Hazel deposited Stan at the table and went to make their plates. Tommy gave him the eye, but Stan didn't seem to notice or care.

"How did you sleep, Stanley?" Buster goaded.

"Deliciously," he responded, winking.

"Glorious."

Richard Paloma was the next to enter, harried and out of sorts. He bent to whisper in Buster's ear, then disappeared again.

"Ah, Richard will join us later," Buster said, getting up to pluck a bagel from the sideboard.

"What's on schedule for today, Buster?" Hazel slid a plate of food in front of Stan, and he looked doubly happy. She sat and unfurled her linen in her lap, delicately taking bites of her eggs and sausages.

"Oh, goodness. Well, I'd like to take the sailboat out, but I need a head count, and the Allens aren't with us yet," he said. "We'll have to fully figure out how to entertain the campers when everyone is present and accounted for."

"Except Richard," Tommy pointed out.

"Yes, except Richard."

"Aren't you going to introduce us?" Hazel's eyes glittered at Tommy, and I felt myself tense up and get defensive.

"Of course—forgive me," Buster said. "I forgot that several of you had, uh, retired before Mr. Fortuna could join us. Ah, on time as ever, Allens!"

Edward and Evelyn sat as close to Buster and as far from Hazel as they could muster. Monty rushed in after them, with a piece of toilet paper stuck to a shaving cut on his chin. He plunked down next to Hazel and Stan, and ever so tactfully gave Stan a punch in the shoulder.

"Everyone, we do have one more guest for you this weekend," Buster announced. "This is Thomas Fortuna, Viviana's . . ."

"Well—now fiancé!" I pulled my hand from beneath the table and made sure the diamond caught a beam of light.

Hazel gasped. "My goodness!" She said, "Congratulations."

"What a rock!" Monty was not being subtle. "Where'd you manage to pick that up, Tom?"

"And you are . . .?" Tommy feigned ignorance of Monty's identity and stood up to shake hands with him over the table, looking all the more like Randolph Scott as he straightened up and out and put on airs.

"Oh, right. Sorry. Montague Bonito, friend o' Buster's here. Yeah, we go way back, all the way. Everyone calls me Monty."

"Nice to meet you, Mr. Bonito," Tommy said.

"Have you set a date?" Evelyn Allen asked.

"No, Mrs. Allen," I replied. "It only happened last night."

"The first night Viviana was ever out of Manhattan and so far away," Tommy said, throwing his arm around me. "I just couldn't stand it. I came up from the city and simply had to pop the question."

"And you happened to have that already?" Hazel asked.

"Had it since the day she turned twenty-one," Tommy said, taking his arm back. "So, who wants to go boating?"

Monty's was the first hand in the air.

"The entire reason I came," Mr. Allen mused. "Must get in one last sail before winter truly moves in. I'm amazed it's held off this long. Have you put up the others?" he asked Buster.

"No, not yet, I'm playing with fate," Buster replied. "Evelyn?"

Mrs. Allen didn't look pleased. "No thank you, of course," she declined. She turned to Tommy to explain. "I never go."

"Neither does Viv," Tommy replied, crushing my hopes of getting on the boat. I had been envisioning one of those giant tall-mast ships, like on the Old Spice bottles, and climbing around the rigging like a little monkey. "Terrible seasickness, this one. She can't even make it to Staten Island."

"Awful affliction, isn't it." Mrs. Allen got up and fetched more eggs.

"Obviously, I'll take the helm, and hopefully Richard's little issue will clear, and he'll be able to join us," Buster said. "How about the other lovebirds?"

Hazel looked a bit disgruntled to have her romantic lead taken away by Tommy's little ring stunt. "Oh, that's up to Stan," she said, and deferred to him.

"I'm not much of a sailor, as you know," he said, "but provided I don't have to work the ropes, I'll join."

"Splendid," Buster replied. "No, I think Mr. Fortuna and Mr. Allen will provide the support needed. Okay with you, chaps?"

"Fine by me," Tom responded, and Mr. Allen glowed with importance.

Within an hour, the partiers had sailed away on one of the most glorious ships I'd ever seen—not quite a mast ship, but nothing to shake a stick at—with Tommy acting like a tourist and taking photos of the estate and fellow revelers with his prized Polaroid Land camera. Mrs. Allen and I rested on the back slate patio, transformed from a barren autumn bog to a warm summer's retreat. Arnold had gotten busy in the short amount of time between making breakfast and seeing off Buster with a basket of sandwiches—the cushions had been returned to the chairs, pollen and dead leaves dusted from the table, and even a raggedy begonia had been found and plunked into an empty planter for some color. A small, portable radio sat on a table between the loungers.

The yard in front of me was still an endless sea of green—two days of heat perked the blades right up, and it was uncanny to have such a summer vista in front of us when Thanksgiving was just around the bend. Not even the grass in Central Park was this lush, with all the fields tramped down by kids and dogs and picknickers whenever the days got sunny. Normally, at this time of year, I'm up to my knees in mud and maybe snow, but now I just heard the clack of branches and the swish of waves in a balmy breeze. The lawn was divided into a top field, right next to the slate patio, and a few small steps led to a slope that went all the way down to the banks of the river. From here, it was like I was sitting on the grounds of a European palace—before the bombs peppered lawns with craters like the surface of the moon.

I sat in a lounge chair, a respectful distance from Mrs. Allen but close enough for conversation, flipping through a fashion magazine entirely in French. I didn't speak a word of it, but mentally marked pages for Tally's next spending spree. She tried to buy me presents and treats, but I refused. Not only did it feel morally wrong to carry a handbag worth more than I made in a year, but there was no convincing my secretary that cutpurses were attracted to the scent of new leather like wasps to rotten apples. Mrs. Allen sat at a wrought iron patio table with her travel desk, a lovely, hinged case of black leather filled with correspondence.

Arnold came outside, bearing a tray of iced tea with fresh lemon slices.

"Arnold," Mrs. Allen began without even looking up, "does Buster happen to have any airmail stamps? I seem to be out again."

"I believe so, ma'am," Alan responded. "Miss Valentine, do you need anything?"

"No, thank you, Arnold."

He disappeared with a shuffle on the slate.

"Goodness. Do you always maintain your husband's correspondence, Mrs. Allen?"

She looked as if I'd poured a bowl of split-pea soup on her head. "This is my own work, Miss Valentine. We are not all in service to our spouses. Or our intendeds."

My blood boiled as I felt the rock on my hand grow heavier. So. It was gonna be like that.

I opted to say nothing. Arnold returned to the patio with an array of postage stamps, all of which Mrs. Allen squirreled away in her case; then she closed it, latched it, and walked inside.

I looked up at Arnold to find him staring. I tried to think of a witty retort, but I was left blank. "What a bitch."

"You have no idea." Peeking around to make sure no guests were in the line of sight, Arnold took Mrs. Allen's untucked chair on the patio and her untouched tea.

"Would you care for some information?"

"Yes, please." I joined him at the table, notebook already in hand.

★ ★ ★

"Let's start with those who I think will be the easy ones . . ." I said, thumbing to a fresh page. "Hazel is a very good place to start."

"Hazel is unique," Arnold agreed. "This is not her first time to the house, though it's not Swansea's either. But they managed never to overlap before."

"Where is she from?"

"Connecticut," he replied. "A deeply established family. Related to the greensman of the same name, though I don't think directly."

I had no idea whom he meant, but scribbled, *Greensman??* in the notes.

"Line of work?"

"Work!" Arnold nearly guffawed.

"It's okay, I know those girls. They don't always bother me." Though, at the moment, my favorite diamond debutante was on my shit list for leaving me at this party without backup. "Is she on the hunt?" I asked.

"I'm sorry?"

"Husband hunting. Does Hazel want or need to get married?"

"No, I don't believe so," Arnold added. "Or at least her fortune is ample without a marriage and family benefit."

"Surely you have something that's juicier than that?"

"Honest to goodness, she's a very rich girl who enjoys her leisure. She's visited a handful of times."

"Does she always find a paramour when she visits?"

"Never." Arnold was resolute in that, at least.

"Now, what about Swansea? He and Buster and Richard all went to college together?"

"That's correct," Arnold confirmed. "The Massachusetts Institute of Technology for their undergraduate degrees; they whiled away the inter-War years all together. Buster and Rich-ard stayed on at MIT for their postgraduate study, but Mr. Swan-sea left for the California Institute of Technology to continue his work."

"From MIT to CIT?" I asked.

"They call it Caltech," Arnold corrected. "Don't ask me why they changed the naming conventions."

"And what is his work? It's different from whatever Richard and Buster do?"

"Very."

"Care to elaborate?"

"I hesitate, miss, as it's both complicated and secret."

"Complicated and secret are usually two very good reasons why people get hurt," I pointed out. "Maybe the neighbor fella is up to something."

Arnold was quiet, though he didn't seem compelled to con-sider the thought long.

"I ought to check on dinner, Miss," he said, and scuttled back inside. There was nothing to do except turn on the radio, sit back, enjoy the sun, and catch up on *Roy Rogers*, which was the only thing on that wasn't the news. And after finding Ches-ter Courtland, I needed a break from reality.

★ ★ ★

Despite the warmer weather, it was still late fall, so the sun began to set shortly after four, illuminating the sailboat as it came back to the dock. I trudged down the lawn to meet the vessel and found myself admiring it, to boot. Over the summer, I'd man-aged to step foot on my first yacht and found myself liking the experience. Buster's toy was a stunning, low-slung boat, white on the bottom, with wooden decking all along the front and sides. There was a hole in the middle, for people to go below deck, and a huge mast in the center and another sail just tied to the front and side. At the pointy end was the name—*Captain Ryder*—in a beautiful gold script.

A small group was clunking along the dock, backlit by a roaring sky. Buster was at the front, towering over his companion who, judging by the slow gait, was Mr. Allen. Shortly behind them was the equally small Monty Bonito, clearly trying to eavesdrop, though neither Buster nor Mr. Allen seemed to care. Third were the necking and handsy Hazel and Stan, her arms around his waist. Behind, lagging as he stood and looked out at the water, like Gatsby himself, was Tommy.

Slipping past the other boaters, I went to him, stepping through the picturesque lawn that, upon closer inspection, was mostly crabgrass and dandelions holding on for dear life.

"How was your day, Dollface?"

"Spent the day trying to garden a little."

"Digging up some dirt?" His hands were in his pockets, and he shifted forward on his toes, like a little boy anticipating something.

"Arnold has seen his fair share but hasn't shared anything wildly useful. He skittered off before I could ask questions about most of the guests." I sighed. "I don't know if that's a butler thing or an impeding-an-investigation thing, but only time will tell. I did a head count, so it looks like no one had to take a swim."

"No, no. But my camera did." He shrugged at my gasp. "Bound to happen sooner or later. Swansea lurched when we hit a wake, and into the drink she went. I managed a few photos, we'll check them out later. But all in all, it was old Mr. Allen playing young, Stan and Hazel being Stanley and Hazley, and Monty and I trying to fit in."

"Did you get the couple's backstory?" I asked. "The canoodling has to be hiding something."

"Not necessarily," Tommy refuted. "Let's go get dressed for dinner."

"But . . . I didn't bring a dinner dress."

"It's lasagna, Viv. And I just need to wash the sea spray off my face and tend to a few cuts and bruises. By the way, Buster's quite impressed with you," Tommy added. "He wants to make sure you do your best work here. And so do I."

He slipped his arm around my shoulder, and we dodged gopher holes in the lawn on the way back to the house.

NIGHT 2

Saturday, November 18, 1950

The Allens sat in their customary spots next to Buster, leaving the rest of the people on the guest list to congregate at the opposite end of the dinner table, with Monty and Richard creating the bridge between what were now clearly two parties instead of one. Edward was in deep conversation with Buster about timetables and deliverables, with Evelyn silently cataloguing every word, and I strained to pick up any spare hints of what they were discussing, but the loud chatter from the younger guests made that all but impossible.

"Oh, it was *such* a shame that you couldn't join us," Stanley said, placing his hand deliberately on my shoulder. Tommy put on a glower, but I could tell he was trying to hold back a laugh at Stanley's obvious machinations. "It was a gorgeous day. Won't be another like it for at least six months."

"It really wouldn't have been that nice for me," I lied. "Better for me to have my shoes on solid ground than a wobbly boat."

"It isn't a *boat*," Mr. Allen chided from the end of the table. "It's a *ship*."

"I'll have to remember that, Mr. Allen—thank you."

"Nothing beats the sea spray and sunshine," Stanley continued. "Makes you feel alive. Invigorated." He made a little growl and Hazel laughed.

"I tried to capture the essence for you in photographs, Viv," Tommy said.

"I am sorry about that, old friend," Stanley said. "I'll cut you a check for the replacement."

"Kind of you," Tommy said, accepting graciously.

"Evelyn, how did you pass your day?" Hazel asked politely.

"Reading." The older woman didn't even look up from her pasta as she answered the question respectfully tossed her way. I watched as she sank the side of her fork into the noodles, and the layers didn't cave. I'd have to ask Arnold his secret after we cleaned up.

"Did you find something new in the library?" Buster asked. "You know I haven't added volumes to it in half a decade. Perhaps some new stories wandered in on their own little feet."

"Not books, Mr. Beacon, only correspondence."

"Ah, of course," Buster acknowledged. "Mrs. Allen no longer goes in for bestsellers and talked-about tomes. It takes a very special book to get her to pick it up, even."

"Fiction is so . . ." She paused to find the right word, then continued, "unbelievable."

"Until you find the right story, and then it is the full and honest truth," Buster replied with a soft smile, and I swore to God, up and down, I could see a faint blush on Mrs. Allen's cheeks, but I knew better than that. "However, the news of the globe cannot wait! No rest for the wicked; the world never stops turning—sunrise, sunset, and so on."

Richard spoke up. "It's true. I had intended on staying in the laboratory all day today, but Buster, you have that amazing ability to talk me out of work. You always have."

"Isn't that the truth?" Stanley followed up. "It's amazing to me that you have all of *this*, without half the work that Richard and I put in." If I wasn't mistaken, there was a hint of a snarl in his question, and I was second-guessing myself until I felt Tommy poke me under the table to make a note of Stanley's resentment.

"How many times would we come back from putting in hours, and he was still in bed at dinnertime?" Richard asked with a laugh.

"Do you recall the time," Stanley started, "when we were coming back at two in the morning, having spent all night working out that differential equation—"

"And he was coming back to the rooms with that Labrador retriever?" Paloma interrupted, and laughed.

"Where did you get a dog?" I asked him.

"To the best of my recollection, I won him in a bet," Buster said smugly.

"What was the bet?" Mr. Allen asked.

"Smucky Jones was sure that he could recite more digits of pi than I could," Buster Beacon said, straightening up and squaring his shoulders. He was daring us to let him show off, and obviously, we were going to take the bait. Richard and Stanley settled back into their chairs, knowing what was coming, and I caught Richard rolling his eyes.

"And I take it you won?" Tommy asked, finally making the spark.

"Three, point, one, four, one, five, nine, two, six, five, three, five, eight, nine, seven, nine, three . . ." Buster began, before stumbling. "Well, I knew more in my twenties."

"Did you ever think that maybe Smucky Jones did not want the dog?" Tommy asked.

Richard laughed.

"What did you name the pooch?" I asked.

"Foetidus," Buster said, and Stanley laughed. "He had a bit of a flatulence issue."

"And . . . what happened to the dog?" Hazel asked, and I had a feeling I didn't want to know the answer.

"Ran away at his earliest convenience," Buster said.

"Buster was not great at remembering to feed him," Stanley said.

"That's terrible." Hazel was staring at both her friend and her lover, and I gathered that the latter relationship was becoming more and more temporary unless Stanley was really earning his place in her bedroom.

"Some people are nurturers," Buster said with no remorse. "Regrettably, I am truly not one of them. He was a lovely animal. I'm sure someone scooped him out of the gutter like a Victorian urchin."

"Speaking of caring, has anyone checked on poor Mr. Courtland?" Hazel asked.

"I believe Arnold has been nursing him today," Buster replied. He lifted his right hand to jingle a small, crystal bell on the table, and Arnold emerged from the kitchen. "How is our patient at the moment? Inquiring minds wish to know."

"Well as he can be, sir," Arnold responded. "The doctor will be back this evening with some test results and a further course of treatment."

Hazel piped up. "Thank you, Arnold. I was worried."

"Yes, Arnold, do keep us apprised," Mr. Allen said, and his wife rolled her eyes.

The butler received a nod from his boss to affirm there was no other reason for his attendance, and returned from whence he came.

"Imagine being so unlucky," Richard said. "To break your ankle just because you're *borracho*."

"He must've really tied one on," Tommy continued. "He wasn't yet awake even when Viv and I checked on him this morning."

"Isn't that kind of you," Mrs. Allen said. "Spending your first weekend as an engaged couple tending to the sick and infirmed. Even if it was a man's own actions that led to his infirmary." Her caveat about Chester Courtland's actions was delivered with venom.

"Ah yes, well," I stammered, patting Tommy's hand affectionately. "Such a large part of our relationship is built on, uh, service." Tommy offered a nod and a considerate, churchy smile.

"Back in our day," Mr. Allen piped up, "we just spent our courtships petting in the back of the movie theater."

A hush fell over the dining room before Buster began to guffaw.

"With that visual," he said, dabbing at his eyes with his linen napkin, "shall we retire to the parlor for drinks?"

The double-story room was icy at the edges, and Arnold was poking to life some kindling and logs in the massive stone hearth, the mantel of which was about at the same height as Tommy's eyebrows. "It appears, sir, as though our warm spell is over."

"Oh, drat," Buster replied. "I was hoping to get the boat out again tomorrow."

"The radio says we'll see snow again tonight," Arnold replied. "I wouldn't recommend another trip out."

"I'm not as young as I used to be," Tommy added. "Not sure if the old bones could take another day of grappling with ropes and sails."

"So be it," Buster replied. "Call the winterizer—I can't bear to do it myself. The two sailboats, and we should do the speedboat as well. Who would like a snifter?" The guests congregated at the bar, with Monty, Tommy, and myself frozen out at the fringes.

Arnold nodded at his boss, then made eye contact with Tommy. A poke and a point informed Monty to stay put and stay sober, and Tommy and I skirted upstairs behind the butler.

"The physician arrived as you were finishing dinner. I already showed him up."

"Any news?"

"Courtland hasn't spoken, but he's conscious in fits and starts," Arnold said with concern. "Whatever he ingested was not just alcohol. Any more than that, the doctor hasn't said. But I dare say he has news."

Arnold noiselessly turned the knob and led us into the cursed bedroom at the head of the stairs. It smelled of sick and body odor, though the window was cracked to let in some fresh air. I stood by it and welcomed the scent of snow on the wind, sharp and clear, to break through the heat and the stench.

There was a bottle of fluid hanging from a twisted piece of wire from the headboard, with a long tube that ended in a needle in the sleeping man's arm. The doctor was putting away his stethoscope and nodded at a pile of clothing on the floor. "He was burning up," he said. "He probably has an infection, either the leg or the injection site."

"Can you give him something for the pain?" Tommy asked. "Look at him." I wanted to look, and I knew it was the right thing to do, but my eyes still stayed glued to the point on the floor where my toes met the wood grain. Now was not a time for crying, and I felt in my guts that one glance would open up the waterworks.

Something rang in my head, and I had a question too. "And what do you mean 'injection site'?"

Clenching every muscle in my body and willing myself to stay stone-faced, I finally looked up and considered the G-man lying in bed, underneath a pile of quilts. Chester Courtland's face was blanched—nearly the same color as the starched pillowcase—and his mouth was twisted into a brutal grimace, but there was no motion at all behind his eyelids. His hair was matted to his forehead, and his arms lay motionless at his sides. None of the quilts moved, and I couldn't help but wonder if the weight of the blankets was making it even harder for him to breathe. And no matter how poorly his leg felt, I knew in my guts that his pallor was caused by something else. He looked like a saint they painted up on church walls, pale and tortured and full of either righteousness or regret.

"I can't do a damn thing, really," the doctor responded. "At least not about what's going to kill him."

"Kill him?" I squeaked.

"Per the laboratory at the hospital, he's received a dose of a poison called curare, miss," the doctor responded. "I had them run every test I could think of, no matter how strange. As I recall from school, curare is a hunting poison developed long ago in Central America. Injectable, like a smallpox vaccination. Most effective—kills through paralysis. Starts with the extremities and works its way toward vital organs. In small prey, it kills quick. And I suppose it kills prey that is six foot two, two hundred pounds, and is a healthy American male around forty years old, almost as fast."

"This is a murder?" Arnold asked. "You're positive?"

"There are far easier ways to take one's own life," the doctor responded. "And in all my years in medicine, I've run across very few people who take their own lives at dinner parties in a neighbor's house. Now I have only one pressing question: Do you want to call the police or should I?"

"I'll call the police," Tommy said, taking out his wallet and pulling out a small, white card—his private investigator's license. "Both Viviana and I are private detectives, sir. We're here to investigate suspicious activity, and now, it seems, a killing."

The doctor slid his glasses down his nose to inspect the card. "The girl too?"

"The girl too." I stepped forward to show him my own license, nearly identical to Tommy's.

"I don't envy you," the doctor said, slipping his glasses back up his nose and finishing his packing.

"*I* don't envy me." Tommy was as sober as a judge.

The wind picked up, and the open window flexed in its frame. "I ought to be going, before this gets worse," the doctor said. "I've set up an atropine drip, the best I can, which may counteract the effects. He either dies or he lives—he may pull through if there's a miracle. I'm sorry I couldn't bring you better news."

"And if we need you, can we reach you at the hospital?" I called after him, just as the sky opened. A hard, pounding rain mixed with pellets of hail began bouncing off the sill.

"The better question is if, after this storm moves through, I will be able to reach *you*, miss."

The words of the physician hung in the air and were underscored by the rapid and alarming change in the weather. While just this morning it had been warm enough to go yachting in summer clothes, the skies had flipped, and in addition to frozen rain, lightning streaked across the sky.

"What the hell is this?" Tommy asked as a pile of ice accumulated beneath the cracked window.

"It wasn't going to stay nice and sunny for that long in November, Tom." I slammed the window shut and grabbed a dirty undershirt from the floor to mop up the moisture as best I could. "The newsman on the radio said a big storm was going to move through, and soon. Now, since we're alone, and Arnold will probably be busy lighting fires and battening down hatches for a few minutes, let's take the time to root through this guy's stuff some more."

Just his underclothes were lumped up on the floor, and they were completely nondescript; not even his name was written in his shorts. Tom was already in the closet, searching the jacket pockets for more clues.

"Nothing," he said. "Or at least, nothing left."

"Check his body, for me, will ya?" I said. "There will be a bruise around where he was stuck with the needle."

"It must have been a drive-by poking," Tommy said. "You didn't see anything?"

"Pretty sure I woulda mentioned it if I had seen someone lurking in the living room with a giant syringe," I snapped. "Check his ass, Tommy boy. If I was going to poison someone, that's where I'd stab him with a needle."

"You're an interesting woman, Viviana Valentine." Carefully, Tommy scootched down the waistband of Chester Courtland's recently procured pajama bottoms and found a dime-sized bruise on a pale cheek. "Coulda been the physician, though."

"Coulda been, but I'm not betting on it," I said. "He only told us about the arm."

Tommy wiggled the pajamas back into place as Arnold arrived. "Did you find the injection site?" the butler asked.

"It was a sloppy job, but it was done," I confirmed. "He would've felt it. Do you remember him behaving strangely in any way last night? I was distracted and went to bed before Courtland did. I didn't even know he was staying the night." I didn't make eye contact with Tommy.

"Nothing of note," Arnold said. "But I was out of the room quite a bit."

"It's okay, Viv. We thought we were here for ghosts, not murders," Tommy said. "But now that we know—no funny business anymore."

Arnold surveyed the room. "You ought to go back down. You're here to weekend, remember?"

"I always forget that 'weekend' is a verb up around these parts," I said. "Come on, ol' Tommy boy, there's nothing else we can do here, and our cover is being blown."

Tommy and I left the room, and I spotted Hazel standing in the shadows, waiting in the chilly hallway for us to emerge.

"I'll join you downstairs in a minute, honey," I told Tommy, squeezing his arm and nodding toward Hazel.

"Okay, Dollface." Tommy went down the stairs and left me with the nervous woman.

"Is he okay? Two doctor visits in a day," Hazel said.

"Here, follow me to our room," I said, pulling Hazel to the wing that housed Monty's and my room. I opened up the door and felt immediate relief because of the heat trapped in the over-sized bedroom and the scent of Tommy's cologne in the air. "He's not looking great, Miss Olmstead."

"Please, really, do call me Hazel," she urged again. "This is so awful, I feel guilty about being downstairs and enjoying myself. Maybe he can hear us."

I wasn't quite sure about the effects of poison on Courtland's ability to hear, but I patted Hazel's shoulder, regardless. "It's fine, I'm sure." In my heart, I thought it was pretty tacky too, to keep carrying on with a man as ill as Courtland in the house, and if I didn't know it to be a crime that had put Courtland up in dire straits, I would've insisted Buster make the revelers go home. But someone on the premises had dosed the G-man with something that might send him to an early grave, and right here in front of me, I had a dame concerned for his prognosis. Maybe *too* concerned.

"The doctor is a little worried that Mr. Courtland took something before we found him," I explained. "It may be mixing with the alcohol he drank, or maybe mixing with something the doctor gave him for pain, and it's making him feel real bad."

"Goodness gracious," Hazel said, sitting on the leather chair next to the desk in our room. "Can that happen? I admit, I'm not much of a party girl myself. If you can believe it. I've heard of people doing all sorts of sordid things at parties . . ." She trailed off.

"Buster—you've been to his weekends before. Is he normally doling out nose candy?"

"I'm sorry?"

"Cocaine. Snow. A white powder that most people inhale through their nose," I explained, tapping mine. "It makes 'em real giddy and happy, sometimes frisky."

"Wow, goodness no, I don't think so," Hazel said. "I've never been here for anything but rest and relaxation. God's honest."

"So, opium maybe?"

"You know a lot about these things, Miss Valentine," Hazel said suspiciously.

"Forgive me," I said, thinking as fast as I could for a way to explain. "But Tommy and I do a lot of outreach to people in hospitals for all sorts of reasons."

"How lovely of you," Hazel said, softening. "But no, Buster gets his jollies from boats and a nice Scotch and little else. That I'm aware of."

"Perhaps Mr. Courtland brought this in himself," I said. "I've heard of it before."

"How awful, to be in the throes of that," Hazel said. "Well, please do let me know if I can help in any way. I'm not a dab hand at first aid or nursing, but I can run and fetch. I know where everything is in the whole house—I know the whole place, top to bottom."

"You're too kind, Hazel. But let's get back down to our host," I said, corralling her out of the room. I noticed my shorthand pad was out on the nightstand, and I hoped she hadn't snuck a peek. "Mr. Courtland probably just needs rest, and there's nothing we can do."

★ ★ ★

We slipped into the party room unnoticed, with no one anticipating a report on the man upstairs. Edward Allen and Buster were having an animated conversation near the bar, and Richard could get no word in edgewise, though he clearly had something to say about the subject at hand. Tommy was hovering at the edge of their conversation, while Monty Bonito sat just down the stretch of marble, alone, staring at a beer. Evelyn and Stanley were nowhere to be seen.

"I'm going to go find Stan," Hazel said to me. "But thank you for the information." She headed back up the stairs to her section of the house, and I hoped she found the solace she needed in the arms of the other scientist fella.

I moved to the bar, between Monty and Buster.

"Wanna get a girl a drink, Mont?"

"Sure." He rounded to the back of the bar without causing any pause in the scenes around us.

"What's your specialty, by the way?" I asked. He picked up a siphon and added a nice spritz of soda water to a concoction before him and slid it across the bar to me.

"General sneaking, pilfering, and filching," he said with a smile.

"Sneak or filch anything good before we got here?"

"No filching—not on a job like this," he assured me. "But sneak, sure. The upstairs—the way upstairs. Got some funny junk up there."

"Costume jewelry? Ugly portraits? Wives?"

"*Wives* is not likely."

"That's not a commentary on Buster, Monty, it's a book."

"I ain't read it."

"Anyway," I said, taking a sip of my drink. There was no alcohol burn to speak of, but it was sweet and complex. "How'd you learn to mix a drink this good, Monty Bonito?"

"Ah, girlie girl, some of us had an interesting Prohibition," he smiled. "And Atlantic City ain't that far away."

"Well, if you ever want to give up sneaking and filching, someone would pay you a pretty penny to be a barman."

"But then I'd have to say 'yes, sir' and 'no, sir' and 'yes, ma'am' and 'no, ma'am,'" Monty Bonito explained. "In my current line of work, I don't have to say all that much."

"It does pay to be rather quiet when one is a sneak or a filcher," I agreed. "Can you tell me what you saw when you had your poke around upstairs in the lab?"

"Lots of boxes, like radios but with tiny movie screens. Dials everywhere. Big ol' electric things, tubes like they got on the top of phone poles. All sorts of funny stuff, but I guess they're scientists."

"Of what kind, no one's told me."

"Would you know what they meant if they did?" Monty had a point, there, I had to give him that. He came back to the customer side of the bar and plopped back down on his seat, waiting for orders.

We swiveled on our bar stools to observe the rest of the party. Tommy was on the far loveseat, now alone, and it was just us three nogoodniks in the room, with Richard, Buster, and Edward yakking away without a care that we'd overhear.

The conversation got hushed, and Buster reached up to put a hand on Mr. Allen's shoulder. "If anything happens to me—" But the sentence didn't finish. There was a crack, a whoosh, and the living room fell to near darkness, now only lit by the fire in the enormous hearth.

The snowstorm had moved in. The electricity was out.

"So much for a summery weekend," Buster mused in the darkness. A candelabra floated to the bar and was set down by its bearer, undoubtedly Arnold in the gloom.

"I'll go bring illumination to the others," he said.

"I'm sure you will, oh sage and gracious butler," Buster responded. "Oh—Arnold. Did you manage to reach Courtland's man before the storm moved in? That he'd be staying with us for the time being?"

"No, sir, it slipped my mind."

Another voice, Richard's, spoke in the dark. "I did, Arnold. Not to worry."

"Thank you, sir." Arnold moved through the darkness like a cat. "I'll try to bring candles to Mrs. Allen and . . . the others."

"I don't think they mind," Monty scoffed.

"Will the lights come back on?" Tommy asked.

"I sure hope so," Buster agreed. "At the very least, Edward, you have to understand how our work may be delayed even further if this usual winter picadillo continues to plague us."

"You're a set of geniuses and you can't figure out how to keep the electric on?" Edward Allen's voice was angry but, more importantly, drunk.

"Power grids are not under our control." Buster's voice had a crystalline edge to it.

The butler was back, this time with more modern illumination in the form of a military-grade flashlight.

"Arnold, do take the car and check on the bridge," Buster commanded. "Drive safely." Arnold handed him the flashlight and walked away in the pitch dark.

"The doctor jinxed us," Tommy said.

"You think we're stuck?" I asked.

Monty was growing more and more agitated. "I got work in the city, Tommy. You said this was a day or two, tops."

"I was, apparently wrong, Monty. I'll pay you more."

"I'll double it," Buster added.

"You don't even know what I'm doing here, you bozo," Monty spat at the host.

"Your name is Montague Bonito, and you've been arrested at least two dozen times for petty crimes that"—Buster paused for emphasis—"when one knows who you truly work for, are not petty in the least. You're an advance man, Mr. Bonito. Layouts, maps, entrances, exits, resources, keys, and reconnaissance. I do not let anyone stay in my home without knowing them inside and out."

Monty swung around to Tommy, ready to hurl a punch. "You ratted on me?"

"Calm yourself, Mr. Bonito. Mr. Fortuna did not 'rat.' I'm a man of resources."

"Watch yourself, Buster," Paloma soothed, but not enough to change the tone of the room.

Mr. Allen was agitated. "Why is anyone paying your houseguests, Buster?"

"None of these people are guests, Mr. Allen, though they are here for nothing that is of your concern."

"Of course it's of my concern, Balthazar." He was near shouting. "I'm paying for this whole goddamn operation!"

"And what operation is that, Mr. Beacon?" Tommy finally asked. Buster was cornered, and he knew it. The three sneaks and the money man needed details, and there was no one around who didn't deserve the truth. Though there was a small chance that someone who wasn't me, Tommy, or Monty was the one who stuck the fella they thought was a neighbor. But why, I couldn't yet guess.

"Oh, for God's own sake, do calm down, all of you." Buster's fake face of calm was bothering me, waxy and alert in the candlelight. "I'm getting a brandy and will meet you by the fire."

He shooed us—honest to God, *shooed* us, like children—to the couches by the hearth. And we all went, because we had no other choice.

"Well, then," Buster descended onto the couch next to me and across from Tommy and Mr. Allen. Monty was standing near the fire, silhouetted in the darkness, and Richard's leather-soled footsteps retreated into the house. "Mr. Bonito, please do share with your compatriots what you saw when you went sneaking around upon your arrival."

"I didn't sneak," he said. "Sneaking implies that the owner of the house doesn't know what you're up to. You knew."

"Fair enough—what you found during your reconnaissance."

"Upstairs on one wing," he said, pointing with his whole arm, "is the butler's stuff. Standard issue, but I think you could afford some more insulation for the fella who does everything but wipe your a—"

"We get it, Monty," Tommy said.

"Then two other wings are locked. I don't like locked doors, especially ones that are locked with two Yale dead bolts."

"I thought your purpose was to get past those locked doors," Buster said in the dark.

"I promise you I can. I just didn't have enough peace and quiet to get it done. Sue me," Monty said.

"Then they shall be opened for you at our earliest convenience, sir," Buster assured him with condescension. "With keys. For your inspection and approval."

"Then up above your rooms," Monty continued, "there's a lab."

"We know," I said. "I'm assuming Mr. Allen does as well."

"I paid for the lot of it," the old man replied. By his slurring, I wasn't sure if he'd make it to the end of the story without falling asleep. "I won the bidding war, and don't you forget it."

"And what was happening in the lab, Monty?" Buster's voice was pointed and cruel.

"You know as well as I do that I have no idea. I was just tellin' Viv, it was a lot of stuff run on electric."

"We work with military technology," Buster explained. "Well, to advance existing military technology, with the aim of selling it back to the government, for their benefit and our profit."

"You're looking to *profit* from war?" Tommy said. He shifted on his cushion away from our host, crossing his arms over his chest, where I knew very well he had some silvery scars from shrapnel he got at sea.

"Who isn't?" Mr. Allen slurred.

"Anyone with a goddamn conscience," Tommy muttered. "So, try me, Mr. Beacon. What kind of technology are you working with?"

"Communications, mostly," Buster explained. "If all goes according to plan, we have the dreams of making your sacrifice obsolete."

"My sacrifice?" Tommy got hurt bad in the war, and even though he joked that all the metal in his hip helped him always find true north, he never griped about the aches and pains. For all I was worth, I don't think Tommy saw it so much as a sacrifice but a duty. At least eight years later, he did.

"Imagine if one could operate boats, guns, planes from farther away," Buster said. "Remove men and their ever-so-frail bodies from the theater of danger."

"'Ever so frail,' my ass," Monty said.

"You spent the war in a classroom," Tommy barked at Buster.

"I spent the war in a *laboratory* so that maybe in the future you wouldn't have to go to war at all, Mr. Fortuna." The red was rising in Buster's face.

Monty scoffed, audibly angry and audibly inebriated.

"Do you want to tell the room where you spent your war, Mr. Bonito? You weren't one of the lucky boys in dance halls in Montmartre," Buster reminded him. "Do not put on the bravado and imply you would like to go *back*."

To that, Monty was silent.

"And where does Mr. Moneybags fit in?" Tommy asked.

"In case you could not tell, I am not the United States government," Buster responded. "I needed some help acquiring their technology."

"Is this house even yours?" I asked.

"Yes, Miss Valentine. The house, by the grace of my forefathers, is mine."

The front door slammed and we all jumped. "*Guten Abend*, Arnold," Buster called into the darkness. "How's the bridge?"

"Out," Arnold called back.

"Ah," Buster said. "Alas, friends, that means we're snowed in."

"Do we go up and tell everyone?" I asked Tommy.

"No need," Buster cut in. "At the very least, everyone was expecting to spend tomorrow here at the house, and perhaps the city will fix the issue by the expected departure time."

"But you do have a very, very ill man upstairs," Tommy advised him, eying Mr. Allen as the old man descended into a fitful, drunken snooze. If he fell into a deep sleep, we could speak openly, but if he drifted in and out of wakefulness, we'd have to watch our tongues.

"That very well may be," Buster said, agitated. He was used to calling the shots, not being held up against a firing squad of questions. "But although I am a physicist and engineer, I am not a structural engineer and am as useless at rebuilding a bridge as you are."

"I don't know about that," Monty sneered. "Tommy and I got some rough hands for rough work."

Buster was lit, his rage fueled by a steady supply of fancy French spirits.

"Be that as it may," Buster said, getting up to get another drink, "I have hired you to ascertain information for me, and you've yet to deliver anything useful."

"You hired me to investigate a noise, one I haven't heard yet," Tommy said. "And neither has Viv. Or Monty. And you've done nothing but show off and give us the runaround for a day. We'll leave as soon as we're able and given a full refund."

"You will do nothing of the sort," Buster said. "I need your expertise."

"And we gotta find out who put that man up there in bed," Monty said. "I don't like leaving a fella."

"You're right," Tommy said. "Well, Mr. Beacon, you're stuck with us 'til the bitter end."

"Why don't you show us *what* your expertise is in, Mr. Beacon?" I asked sweetly. "That way we can make sure any noises we do hear aren't just regular, run-of-the-mill science stuff."

This only did the damage of ruffling Buster's feathers more. "We do not do any *'run-of-the-mill'* science in my laboratory, Viviana."

"Ah, well," I said, exhausted from coddling just so many grown adults' feelings for one day. "How about this: just show us your fucking lab." Tommy snorted and got up. The shift of movement on the couch caused Mr. Allen to slump off to his side. He was out like a light.

"Monty, care to guard our fella?"

"Not a problem." Monty sidled back to the dark bar. "So long as I can watch him from here."

"Not a problem," Tommy assured him. "If he takes off, I am confident you can catch him, even if you're piss drunk. Now, Buster. Where are the flashlights?"

DAY 3

Sunday, November 19, 1950

The mantle and Grandfather clocks all sounded at the same time—a succession of dings and bongs told us it was midnight, and respectable company would be asleep, or, at the very least, in bed.

"Just tell me your Frankenstein lab is heated, Buster," Tommy shivered, rubbing his arms through his summer sweater.

"Warmest room in the house, I assure you," our client slurred. "By nature of the tubes and screens, of course, but Edward also funded significant renovations to that part of the house."

"None of this is gonna make my hair fall out and my jaw fall off, right?" I asked.

"Nothing in here is radioactive, Viviana." Tommy's question about working heaters was met with less condescension than my question about radiation, I noticed. Buster clearly assumed that anyone who hadn't gone to MIT, or college at all, was a yutz. Tommy had four credits at City College before his stint in the service, and I supposed Buster could tell.

"Hey, listen, bucko," I said, trying to lighten the mood, "despite this rock on my hand, I'm still waiting on that Prince Charming. Can't lose my good looks just yet."

The joke was met with silence.

"Is Richard asleep or working?" I asked.

"Likely trying to record everything he could from whatever experiment he was running before the power went out," Buster said, leading up the stairs to his laboratory. "We simply cannot do that much work without electricity."

"Who's with you?" An accusatory boom came from the dark cavern at the top of the stairs.

"Thomas and Viviana," Buster replied.

"Not Allen?" Richard Paloma stood at the top of the flight, barely illuminated by a flickering candle. The lack of electricity hadn't halted the work of the steam radiators, and the hair on my head stood up and tingled.

"Lord, no. He sniffled a second snifter and fell asleep on poor Montague," Buster replied.

"Do you just keep him drunk so he doesn't ask questions?" Tommy asked.

"I keep him drunk because he's a miserable old man when sober," Buster replied. "Not asking questions is just an added benefit."

"Okay, boys, stop bluffing and finally tell us what you do," I said.

"Oh, God, how do we make this simple?" Buster asked, plucking at paperwork on his desk.

"Should have thought of that before you hired two nincompoops, eh?" Tommy was bristling. By the twitching of his fingers, I could tell he wished he still had his camera, though the likelihood of Buster letting him take pictures of his top-secret laboratory was next to nil.

"It *is* simple, Buster—stop being a jackass." Richard Paloma's voice was smooth and suave. "Viviana, what do you know about radio waves?"

"They're those little bolts that come out of the RKO tower at the start of the pictures," I said.

"Oh, God, this country is doomed," Buster slurred behind me.

"One more word out of you, Balthazar," Richard threatened. "She's not wrong, and you know it."

"I understand that is a simplification," I assured him. "I'm not educated, but I'm not stupid."

"Radio waves," Richard continued, "are the manifestations of energy created by electricity and magnets. They can be tall or short, and far apart or close together." I could tell he was moving his hands to demonstrate, even though the room was extremely dark. His voice was kind and patient, and if I'd ever had a teacher as smooth as Richard Paloma, maybe I wouldn't've dropped out of school.

But I mighta been kicked out.

"Because of radio waves," he continued, "we can broadcast the electrical impulses of something like a sound—like using a radio communicator in the war or flicking on your wireless in your living room. With a different apparatus, called a cathode-ray tube, we can broadcast television with radio waves, turning what many people think of as sound into moving images. Lovely things, those tubes, though they make so much static electricity."

"Movies at home sounds pretty great," I admitted. "No one to try to slip their hand up your skirt in a dark movie theater."

"That happens?" Richard asked, aghast.

"Do you not have a sister?" I returned. With the silence that came back, I assumed he did not.

"But our radio experiments are more about, say, making sure that when you broadcast, you don't broadcast to the whole world, but rather to the person you intended on broadcasting to."

"So, maybe no more codes, like in the war?"

"Things will always be encoded," Richard said. "But maybe they can be automatically decoded. But the ultimate goal is, if I wanted to share a special message with just one person—without the whole world hearing it—I would be able to."

"But isn't that why we have direct-dial phones now? Everyone says they're getting fewer and fewer connections at the telephone exchange thanks to them."

"Yes, that's very true. That's not what we do, but it does require electricity to carry the information. I could share with you my phone number, and you could reach me any time you want so long as you were in a place where your electrical impulses were free to travel down the phone wires."

"Ah yes," I flirted. "My free impulses."

"Now just imagine, Miss Valentine, if you weren't tied down." There was a cough from the dark of the attic to remind us we were chaperoned. "By wires."

"How do you mean?"

"We think that we will be able to control radio waves to make secret voice communications between telephones not linked by wires."

"Goodness."

"Goodness, indeed."

"Imagine what you'd be able to say," I murmured, "if no one was listening in."

"My, yes. Wouldn't that be nice."

"Your guest rooms have a little radio on the nightstand," I said. "Would I be able to pick up on any of your transmissions up here, using that?"

"Oh, not likely," Richard said. "And even if you did, all we broadcast out of the house is beeps and noises."

"So you don't worry about any of your houseguests ever listening in?"

"No one has any interest in all of our little noises," Buster said from the darkness.

"It's true," Richard added swiftly. "It'd take a concerted effort by a very educated mind to figure out what we were doing up here, all hours of the day and night."

"Brilliant," I added. "Nothing worse than the butler listening in."

"We're doing our best, Miss Valentine," Richard Paloma assured me. "The most secure form of communication should no longer be the postal service. We're in the twentieth century now."

"And Arnold mentioned that what Stanley works on is similar but different," I said.

"Arnold should not be mentioning those sorts of things." Buster's voice was a slurred whisper.

"Arnold wants to help. So," I said, reaching out into the dark and placing my hand on Richard's bicep, "explain to me how the work is similar but different."

"Well," Paloma started, "the radio waves Buster and I work with are big, big waves. Like when a big, lumbering ship bobs in the water. They are what we call 'low frequency' and 'low energy.' Stanley works with microwaves. Teeny, tiny waves that are high frequency and high energy. 'Toddler-splashing-in-a-bathtub' waves."

"I think I understand."

"So while our research is mostly about secure communications, Stanley's microwaves could be used to control the behavior of electrical components at a distance."

"You lost me," I said.

"Think of it this way—when you want to change the radio station from CBS to NBC, how do you do it?"

"Well, sir, I reach out my little hand, and I turn the knob."

"And what if you're listening from across the room?"

"Well, I saunter my way to the wireless, reach out my little hand and turn the knob."

"Aha! There we go. What if you were so tired from catching dirty scoundrels during your day, your slippers were nowhere to be found, and there was no one there to save you from that desolate trek from your warm bed to the radio. What if you didn't have to walk to the wireless to change the station?"

"I don't think the American military cares about turning the station from CBS to NBC, Mr. Paloma," I said. Richard Paloma was imagining me in my bed. I was imagining Richard Paloma in my bed. If that ever happened, I wouldn't give a fig what was on the wireless.

"I assure you they do not, but that's a simple way of explaining what we all do up here, all hours of the day and night," Richard assured me. "Stanley is hoping to be able to use electromagnetic waves in his research, to manipulate electronic devices at long range."

"And how would that keep me from getting blown the hell up?" Tommy's voice came from across the garret.

"Presumably, in time, one of the devices one would be able to manipulate with radio waves would be a ship, a submarine, an airplane," Richard explained. "Piloted planes without a pilot."

"You'll need a pretty big tower for that," I said. "It's a long way between here and Leningrad, buddy."

"Ah yes. One of my many limitations." At my mention of scientific failure, Richard Paloma's fire was extinguished. Touchy boy.

"So you two," Tommy piped up, "must know all about sound."

"A fair amount, though the practical applications of sound waves are different from electronic waves and magnetic waves," Buster said.

"I may not have ever taken a physics class, but I know it's all energy," Tommy said.

"It is."

"And you really can't pinpoint what the noises you hear are?" I asked.

"They're electrical," Buster assured us. "Not language nor the sound of a real object—say, a violin, or the banging of a pot and pan—being broadcast."

"They don't oscillate," Richard continued.

"Which means . . .?" I asked.

"They don't repeat. It's not, for example, a continuous pattern," he explained. "It's not the same sound over and over again. One of the ways we test our radio receivers is by sending out a very consistent pattern, so we can tell when it breaks up or doesn't get through."

"Is it Morse code?"

"Not quite that rhythmic," Buster explained. "Morse has that clipping urgency to it, and the dots are all one length and the dashes are all one length. And what we hear is not a pattern. It's a *sound*."

"Well, if it's electrical, we won't be hearing it tonight," Tommy said. "And I'm wiped. I'm going to tell Monty to cover Edward with a blanket and go to bed." His heavy step let me know he was truly leaving.

"And I am afraid I'm closer to Mr. Allen's state than I thought," Buster said, announcing the obvious to the room. "Goodnight, dear ones." His slippers tapped down the stairs after Tommy. I was alone with Richard in the candlelight.

"Thank you for explaining everything," I said. My skin was tingling again, but I knew it wasn't the cathode tubes.

"Of course, Miss Valentine. You're a fast one." With that, I felt a hand on my arm, and I moved that hand, swiftly, to my hip.

"Normally, I slap a man who accuses me of being fast, Mr. Paloma," I assured him, as he stepped into me.

"Is this going to get me in trouble?" he asked, moving his face closer to mine. There was very little I wanted more than for Richard Paloma to kiss me—easy-like and probably meaningless, but fun while it lasts—but with memories of my summer flashing in my eyes, I knew I had to stop this before it started.

"No, but it won't end well for me," I said, stepping back. "I'm on an investigation."

"Which I assure you, I want to help and not hinder," Richard said back. "This can wait."

"For now." I smoothed down the skirt of my dress, even though it had been only threatened with a rumpling.

"Is there anything you wish to ask me while we're alone?"

"I overheard Buster say, 'If anything happens to me,' just before we came upstairs," I said. "What *would* happen to the lab if Buster wasn't here to look after it?"

"Well," Paloma demurred, "I can certainly run the science."

"It looks like you're running the science even when he *is* here," I pointed out. "But what about the mansion? Does he have family?"

"I don't believe he has any close family. I suspect it would stay with whoever is running the laboratory," Paloma said. "Which is rather generous."

"So," I was slow to point out, "*you*. *You* might get it."

"Myself, Stanley, about six other men between Washington, MIT, and Caltech," Paloma said. "Not to mention a few international connections Buster has."

"That's an awful lot of competition," I said.

"I'm used to battling competition," Paloma said. "And winning."

I took a large step in the dark toward the stairs. "I'll see you at breakfast, Mr. Paloma."

"Indeed, Miss Valentine. Sleep well."

"You too."

I went downstairs to find my bed, with Tommy already in it and looking at his photographs from the boat trip. He had Coke-bottle glasses I'd never seen before perched at the end of his nose and a flashlight cradled between his jaw and shoulder.

"What do you notice from these?" He looked up at me and through the lenses, which made his blue eyes the size of marbles. He spread the photographs out on his lap.

"A fun day that I didn't have, because I was sitting on a stoop with the sourest puss in the Northeast?" I said, peering at the photos. "And that Stanley Swansea can't stop necking with Hazel."

"What is Buster putting in the water here?" Tommy asked. "Good grief."

"Nothing happened, Tom."

"Hey, if that's how you want to pump him."

"Jesus!"

"For *information*, Viviana—Christ."

"Sorry, ol' Tommy boy, I'm just not used to flirting to get what I want."

"Like hell you're not, Dollface." He smiled at me. "But I mean it—I'm wiped. I'm going to bed."

"Leave that torch on for me while I get changed."

"Can do."

I slipped into the bathroom to put on my pajamas and brush my teeth. I went back out into the darkened room, flicked off the flashlight by Tommy's side of the bed, and promptly dropped it on the floor. "Damn. I can't see a thing. I'm gonna kill myself in here."

"Just climb over, then."

I put my knee on the side of the bed and ambled over Tommy's legs.

"I don't like the country," I said, shuffling underneath the covers and sticking my frozen toes into Tommy's legs to get some heat, leading to a quick yelp from my partner. "Too dark. Too cold. Too scary."

"Don't worry," Tommy muttered into his pillow. "I promise I'll get you home as soon as I can."

★ ★ ★

The sun was just starting to peek through the velvet draperies when I heard the sound of the house coming back to life.

"Power's on," Tommy said for no one's benefit, into the back of my neck. In the heatless night, we'd managed to huddle together beneath the comforter, he at my back with his arm over me, his hand beneath the curve of my waist.

"Thank God," I said, slowly pulling away. The room was freezing, and my subconscious did not want to pull away from Tommy's warm body. "Ah, whoops, my hair's caught in your stubble."

"Anyone ever tell you you snore like a freight train, Doll-face?" He was laughing into my hair and poked me playfully in the rump.

"Ya know what? *No.* No one's ever been so rude, now that you mention it," I said, finally wiggling away and flicking on the lights. "Here, hand me those photos, I couldn't see a thing last night with your dime-store flashlight."

"Dime store!" Tommy scoffed while handing me the photos. "I stole that good and proper from Uncle Sam during the war."

I switched on the bedside lamp and curled up next to Tommy underneath the blankets, spreading the Polaroids across the duvet. "Mr. Allen looks happier than a pig in mud," I said. "He stayed out of his drinks while on board?"

"Thankfully, Arnold only packed lemonade," Tommy said, stretching. Four different things in his back popped and he moved to examine a scar on his left bicep, a bullet that would have killed him proper if it'd been three inches closer to its mark. "Though that doesn't mean he didn't sneak something in on his person."

"You know, something is off here," I said, flopping and turning three photographs in front of Tommy like I was waiting for the river. "Look at Stanley."

"Like I said, constantly necking with this Hazel broad," Tommy said.

"Yeah, like you said—always got his face . . ." I led.

"In the crook of Hazel's neck."

I touched the tip of my nose to tell Tommy he got the answer. "Now you gotta tell me: she's a pretty woman, but is she *that* hot of a tamale?"

"I wouldn't kick her out of bed for eating crackers," Tommy said modestly.

"All I'm saying is, I don't like this. He don't like her perfume *that* much."

"I don't like it either," Tommy said. "But listen—"

Whatever Tommy was going to say was cut off by the sound of a low, piercing moan.

"Let's go." Tommy and I were out the door of our room, both in bare feet without a robe or sweater in the freezing house.

"I'll get the south wing, you get the north," I said.

"If you run across anyone else," Tommy said, jogging toward Stanley and Hazel's suite and shouting across the mezzanine, "deputize them."

The sound was clearly from a machine, but one I couldn't place. It was soft and almost melodic, but with the tendency to become shrill without any notice. It sounded muffled, like it was coming through walls, and made me feel like I was in a spooky movie.

I first popped my head into the bedroom by the stairs and saw it empty of anyone but Chester Courtland's grim face. I closed the door and ran down into the main portion of the house.

"Arnold!" The butler was zooming from the area of the kitchen as fast as his legs could carry him. "Basement!" He doubled back to show me a hidden door in a panel of wainscotting just inside the kitchen and led me downstairs.

As we hit the dusty cellar, it stopped.

"God, we are never going to find it, are we?" I was out of breath and freezing, my bare feet standing in a wafting pile of filth.

"You will, you will," Arnold assured me. "But you do see why you were called in?"

"It's so unsettling," I said as I trailed him back up the stairs. "And you've never once been able to find it?"

"Never once," he assured me. "I can't even figure out what it is."

We emerged from the basement as Tommy came down the stairs, still in his pajamas and undershirt.

"Where'd you check?" he asked me.

"Basement. It only got quieter once we were down there, before it stopped."

"No outside entrance?" Tommy asked Arnold. "You're positive?"

"As I said," Arnold assured him, "there are storm doors, locked from the inside, and a coal chute that has been rusted for some time."

"Not that I don't believe you, but we'll check it again later." Tommy shoved his hands in his pockets.

"You?"

"Tried the lab, but nothing was on. Tried Buster's room—empty. Tried Richard's room, but he was in the shower."

"Well, it's at least something," I admitted. "Tommy, let's go discuss. What time even is it?"

"About a quarter to eight," Arnold responded. "I need to get on breakfast." The butler scuttled off back to the kitchen.

"Something infuriating is happening with him," Tommy said.

"I know what you mean. I know a butler's job is hard, but he always has something better to do than give information," I said.

"Buster is the same," Tommy said as the man in question rounded the banister on the stairs and came into view.

"Handsome? Debonair? The life of the party?"

"Cagey and combative, actually," Tommy said. "Come on, Viv, we have a man to check on and a mystery to solve."

I held my head high and followed my partner back up the stairs to our room.

"The sooner this is over, the better," Tommy said, sitting on the side of the bed. "And I don't know what those guys are getting at, but there was something familiar about the noise, wasn't there?"

"Yes, but I can't place it," I said, picking out my clothes for the day. Everything had been hung up in the wardrobe for me, and even the blouse I'd worn yesterday had been laundered and pressed. Arnold was a ghost, coming and going from every room. It gave me the willies.

"Did you bring boots?" Tommy asked.

"I have these." My scuffed white leather ankle boots were lined with a graying flannel. "I wore them up. I don't think Mrs. K would've let me out of the house if I'd just been wearing my loafers."

"She's a good housemother," Tommy said. "We're going for a walk after breakfast."

"Wanna find the building the FBI is using to stake the place out?"

Tommy got up from the bed and put his hands on either side of my head, kissing my forehead. "How are we always thinking the same thing?" He scurried past me into the bathroom, to hog all the hot water.

★ ★ ★

After we got dressed, we checked in on Chester Courtland, but as Tommy opened the door in front of me, he flipped around to stop me at the doorway. "Listen, it's just . . ." he said, holding my shoulders.

"It's not easy watching a man die, Tommy," I said. "But I've done it before."

I knew by the look on his face I'd caught him by surprise, but he let me follow him to the bedside of our dying Fed. His skin was gray and waxy, and his chest barely moved.

"I'm going to stay here, okay?" Tommy didn't look back at me as I slid an upholstered chair to the bedside. He sat without thinking and folded his hands in his lap.

"Do you want me to bring you anything?" I whispered, and his head shook, but just barely.

★ ★ ★

I was trembling as I entered the breakfast room, and Buster greeted me with no understanding of the tragedy occurring just upstairs. "Miss Viviana!" He toasted me with a porcelain cup of coffee. "Goodness, you look frigid. Arnold, fetch her Richard's cashmere cardigan when you get a moment—she needs it."

Richard himself didn't blink at the suggestion of the butler raiding his wardrobe, but he did join me at the buffet table to take my plate out of my shaking hands. "Go and sit," he murmured. "It's okay."

There was an empty chair next to Richard's at the table, and I slid into it, avoiding eye contact with the rest of the morning party. Evelyn was strung as tight as a piano wire next to her flushed husband, whose eyes were bloodshot and evading his wife's glare. She stabbed at her bacon and eggs, clearly hoping her husband would feel the jabs. Hazel and Stanley were quiet at the far end of the table. Monty was silently plowing through a plate of sausage and scrambleds, though he stopped to direct a short nod at me when I sat and grabbed the closest coffeepot.

Richard slid a plate of lightly buttered toast in front of me, along with a cup of tea. "Viviana—would you like to take a walk with me after breakfast?" The conversation in the rest of the room was so muted, it was clear that everyone heard.

"That sounds wonderful, thank you. I need some fresh air." Cutlery scraped and china tinkled. "I love seeing everything blanketed in fresh snow."

"How does that new song go? 'It's a marshmallow world in the winter, when the snow comes to cover the ground'?" Buster was eyeing us. "'Take a walk with your favorite girl'"?

Paloma shot him daggers.

"I believe she's already someone else's favorite girl, Buster." Evelyn Allen's voice was as icy as the windowpanes rattling behind me. "Sadly for poor Richard, all the women this weekend are otherwise engaged."

"I'm his partner, not his property, Mrs. Allen," I said. "Besides, Tommy is at the bedside of Mr. Courtland this morning, and I don't believe he's inclined to leave."

"Oh, how's his leg?" Stan Swansea piped in.

"Not well, I'm afraid." I tried to scan the whole table for reactions, but there were just too many faces to read, everyone caught in the act of shoveling down French toast. Arnold arrived with the sweater at that moment, and all eyes turned to watch me put it on. It was scented like bay rum.

"That's a shame," Hazel purred. "And I couldn't imagine leaving the house in such atrocious weather. You're a braver girl than I, Viviana."

"Besides, we'll be able to take a glance at the bridge," Richard cut in. "I know I adore all of your company, but surely you all have Thanksgiving plans and will want to leave sooner rather than later."

"Ah yes," Edward Allen slurred. "The Boston contingent calls, no matter how hesitant we may be to join up." The way Evelyn glared at her husband let us all know the Boston contingent was her side of the family.

"Not visiting your family, Mr. Allen?" I asked.

"No, no. Not going to Washington." He went back to prodding his plate.

"Oh, I'm sure Buster wouldn't mind us staying and creating a great, big, happy family," Stanley interjected. I noticed that Richard, who also lived in the house, wasn't considered in the preferences.

"Of course I wouldn't," Buster replied. "But if the roads don't open, it will be quite the nontraditional meal. I doubt Arnold has a turkey yet."

"What are circumstances like this for but making new traditions?" Hazel asked. She was staring at Stanley with big, moony eyes, and it was clear to me the girl who wasn't on the hunt thought she'd bagged a stag. Her mind was made up, and it was time to finally get her M-R-S.

"Isn't that so, Hazel?" Buster was peering over the edge of his china teacup and gave me a wink. Buster also read Hazel's tone like a book. "Well, I'll tell you one tradition that I can't quite shake, and that would be heading to the office to while away the more fruitful hours of my brain. Richard, I'll read your reports from last night, of course."

"I saved as much data as I could," Richard responded, placing his napkin on the table. "Viviana, would you like to meet me at the front door in about fifteen minutes? That will give us time to put on our warmest layers."

"Of course," I said. "May I keep the cardigan on?"

"You may keep it altogether," Richard said on his way out of the dining room.

I rushed upstairs to put on my coat, hat, and muffler, and hoped that my pockets would be enough to keep my fingers warm. I also grabbed my notebook, just in case Richard needed to get anything detailed off his chest. On my way back down to the foyer, I stopped in to check on Tommy.

"Not long now, Viv," he said when he felt my hand on his shoulder. "Who are you going out with?"

"Paloma."

"Business or pleasure?"

"Business, at least on my end."

"Good."

Chester Courtland's eyelids flickered, and the rasping sound in his throat lost its rhythm.

"I'll tell Arnold on my way out."

"Thanks, Viv. Tell Paloma too."

"Are you sure?"

"Pretty sure."

★   ★   ★

The snowstorm had left over a foot of snow, carpeting the entirety of Buster's Tarrytown neighborhood, and the banks of the Hudson itself were encrusted with ice. But the air was still and the sun shone brightly, glinting off the pure white banks and directly into my eyes.

"I ought to have brought sunglasses," I said, squinting into the distance.

"The most dreadful sunburn I've ever gotten was because of the snow," Richard said kindly. "Buster dragged me to St. Moritz once, and after a week, I thought all the skin on my face was going to peel off."

"I'm sorry, I have no idea where that is."

"Don't apologize. No one decent *should* know where St. Moritz is."

"Does that make you indecent?"

"Quite," Richard said. "Aspen? Gstaad? Megève? I've seen them all and have nothing but guilt over it all."

"Why don't you tell me what's eating you, already?" I snapped. My boss was trapped in a palace at the moment, watching a man die, and I was in no mood to coddle a stranger's feelings. In my pocket, I nervously twisted the diamond ring Tommy had given me around my finger.

"I sent for him, you know." Richard stood on the road between mansions and looked out to the river like he was waiting for a ship to come sailing in.

"Who?"

"Chester Courtland. The agent in the spare bedroom."

"Does Buster know?"

"No."

"It's Buster's house."

"It's no one's house," Richard said. "It's true Buster inherited it from family and is a man accustomed to certain conditions. He couldn't afford it himself in a million years—his trust isn't what it used to be. But he's one of the only people in the world qualified to do what the government wants him to do. He is in the position to make demands. So the house is kept for him."

"On my dime?"

"Paid for by the government, yes."

"Must be nice to be so special."

"Yes, well," Richard agreed. "One issue with being so special is that when your unique and specific research begins to show up elsewhere, you are the obvious culprit."

"Buster's a spy?"

"I wouldn't think so," Paloma said, "but there's no other explanation."

"I mean, it could be you."

"It could be, but I swear on my life it isn't. And it would be my life on the line if I had chosen to leak the information."

"What about Mr. Allen?" I asked. "If he's an investor . . ."

"That man can't even understand how a battery works," Paloma said, as if that was sufficient explanation for his inability to transmit information to enemies of the state. "I don't *want* it to be Buster, I don't want to look back on our entire history of friend-ship and have it be tainted by this. But, there's no other option."

"Well that explains the G-man, then."

"That explains the G-man." We strolled down the subur-ban street, toward the washed out bridge. Behind every tower-ing iron fence was the same scene, as wholesome as a Normal Rockwell if Norman Rockwell painted the goddamn Vander-bilts. Each and every spectacular home was blanketed completely in white, and a man with knee-high rubber boots and a thick overcoat was shoveling his way down a meandering drive toward frozen gates. Without a doubt, the owners of every mansion were hiding behind battened hatches, as evidenced by smoke trickling out of at least one chimney per roof. The occasional shriek of a playing child pierced the stillness, but most people were behind closed doors. Unless their bosses had told them to go shovel. We walked through the street itself, and there wasn't a car to see.

"Buster says he knows everything about everybody who comes in his house," I pointed out.

"Not to be uncouth, but the FBI has some experience laying a false trail even most PIs can't sniff out," Paloma shrugged.

"Tommy's not most PIs"

"What about you?" he asked.

I let the question slide because I wasn't in the mood to banter or have my bona fides questioned. "Are they continuing surveil-lance?" I asked.

"Yes, of course, but they're starting to be concerned for my safety. And your safety, should anyone figure out what you and Tommy are doing."

"When the noises came through this morning, where were you?"

"In the shower. Your fiancé burst in on me."

"We're not actually engaged."

"I know. I just like to tease you." The feeling of tension between us changed, from flirtatious to dangerous.

"Do you know the extent of Mr. Courtland's injuries?" I asked.

"I know about the broken leg, but that doesn't explain how quiet he is. Even if he is on a painkiller drip."

"He's not on morphine, Richard." The man next to me slowed, and he grabbed my elbow, I suppose to stop me from continuing, but Tommy had instructed me to blab. "Chester Courtland has been poisoned."

"It wasn't in the food or the canapes," Richard said. "I ate everything Courtland did that day."

"He didn't eat it, he—"

"Was it the cocktail? Did Buster slip something in his drink?"

"No, but he—"

"Is he going to die? Are you doing anything? The doctor gave him something?"

"Yes, something called atropine, but for all the good it's doing him, it's like he got nothing at all. He was jabbed—injected, that is—with a poison. It's going to kill him. It's something called curare."

"Soviet."

The one-word response struck me dead in my tracks. "How do you know?"

"Well, when you call up the FBI to ask them to spy on your oldest friend, they give you a handbook, so to speak. Things to look out for."

"And one of the things was a specific poison?"

"I paid more attention to the deadly aspects than the boring things like phone calls and letters," Richard said.

"Most people would," I admitted. "Do you have a way of getting in contact with the Bureau again?"

"They have a safe house on the other side of the river," Paloma said. "A small bungalow in Nyack."

"And what are they doing there?"

"They've placed bugs in the entire laboratory," Richard said. "They don't understand a word of what we're saying, but it makes them feel better."

"And you said there was no one listening in," I pointed out. "Are there any communications devices—aside from the bugs—in that lab of yours? Telephone, ham radio?"

"No telephone, and I'm sure it would take no effort at all for Buster to manufacture a rudimentary radio transmitter with what we have on hand, but they haven't said anything to me about overhearing messages."

"Could he be speaking or sending in code?"

"If he is, it's a devious one. I've been sent transcripts of what he says when I'm not there in the post—unmarked envelopes, very hush-hush. Aside from complaining about me or Arnold, it's all just statements about the work, observations—mutterings like anyone does when they're alone. No one's mentioned anything to me about encoded messages."

"Well, that's a toughie then. You need to inform them about Courtland, lickety-split."

"I know, but I don't see that happening." Richard was starting to despair. The man might have been as sharp as an arrow, but he wasn't used to being blown off his course. "I generally go in person, to avoid anyone in the house. Say I have to run an errand, take my car, just drive. But the bridge . . ."

"Well, then Tommy and I need to be extra focused on our investigation, which will take some time."

"Then let's get to the bridge, talk to the workmen, see how much time we've got before the police show up at the house," Paloma said. "Or, I guess, how much time you and Tommy will get to figure out who did this."

As we walked north through the neighborhood and farther away from the protection of houses, the wind off the river grew stronger. And on the wind was the sound of men yelling and tools clanging. A low, concrete bridge spanning a frozen body of water was noticeably missing a footing, and part of the masonry had smashed through the thin ice that encrusted the whole scene.

"I'll go ask for an ETA," Paloma said. "Be right back."

Richard shuffled through the snow to a man wearing a Navy peacoat and knitted skull cap and who looked angry at the clouds, the sky, the trees, and the water. His dungarees were sodden to his knees. After a few moments of violent hand gestures, the man eventually laughed, and Richard Paloma came back with an answer.

"Well, at first it was the expected: *'It's finished when it's finished.'* But I may have mentioned that my wife's family"—he gave me an eye at the mention of spousal relations—"were stuck here, and I wanted them good and gone. So he said by Thanksgiving was his best guess."

"Nothing binds men together faster than anger toward their wives, real or not," I muttered. "But that gives us the rest of today, then three more days, to try to figure out who's a secret Soviet infiltrator. Any guesses?"

"Like I said, it gives me no pleasure to assume it's Buster, but the sheer specificity of the information the government has intercepted leads them to believe it is surely him."

"Well, that's the pits, isn't it."

"For me, it is," Richard said. "And not just the personal loss, of course. The competition in our line of work is very stiff, and I've received no confirmation from Buster that I'd be the one to carry on our life's work."

"But what about Mr. Allen?"

"That blustery old fool," Paloma said as the mansion came into view. "He was fit to be tied when Courtland said he was representing 'interested parties,' but Buster soothed that. He'll take any gadget the government doesn't want, thinking it'll make him a fortune, and Buster's promised him the moon."

"And the government doesn't have an issue with him being in the house while you do your work?"

"They have files on everyone who enters the premises and haven't denied his entry yet."

"Including me?" I squeaked.

"Of course." Richard Paloma shrugged as we bounded up the front steps and opened the door. "They have files on everyone."

★ ★ ★

Arnold was in the foyer looking grim.

"Courtland?" I asked, and he nodded.

"Go to Tommy," Richard said. "You have a lot to tell him."

I ran up the stairs as fast as I could and burst into our bedroom. Tommy was sitting with his hands in his lap, and Monty Bonito was perched on the desk, clearly not sure what to say.

"Oh, God, I'm so sorry." I ran to Tommy and threw my arms around his neck while he leaned his head into the crook beneath my chin.

"I've seen men get their arms blown off, you know," he said. "Shot, too, and I'm not proud to say that I've been the one to shoot 'em. But that. That was horrible."

"You can tell me if you want to."

"I don't. But whoever did it . . ."

"Don't worry, we'll get them, we have to."

Monty, relieved of duty by my presence, spoke up. "You all heard the racket this morning, right?"

"Of course," I said. "Arnold and I checked the basement. Nothing there but some dust and dead mice. Tommy found Buster and Richard and cleared them."

"It was strange though, right?" Monty pushed. "Did yous guys ever see that movie, *Rocketship* something or other that came out in the spring?"

"No, but I'm not really one for space movies," I said.

"Well, no matter what, it had that same feeling as Mars. Made me feel all spooky."

"You know, come to think of it," I said, "when I first heard it, I thought of horror movies."

"So it's man-made?" Tommy said. I didn't drag Tommy to the movies anymore after he fell asleep during *Key Largo* and started to snore.

"No other way to make it, I don't think. I've got an idea— let me make a phone call."

Monty scooted off the desk, and I picked up the receiver and spun the zero. "Operator, please connect me to Svitlana Kovalenko's Girls-Only Boarding House in Manhattan. It's in Chelsea."

"That's long distance, sweetie," the voice on the line reminded me.

"I don't care what the charges are—please connect me, thank you," I said, and that got a giggle out of Tommy. "Wait 'til I tell you who's really paying for it, though, buddy."

The girl rang through to Mrs. K's, and on the third bell, I heard someone pick up.

"Hewwo?" It was Betty, and she was crying.

"Betts! It's Viv. What's the matter?"

"I was canned," she said through her tears. She blew her nose hard and didn't apologize, but the honking cleared up her voice a little. "They let me go at the hospital."

"What finks!" I said. I put my hand over the phone to tell Tommy. "Betty got fired."

"That's no good," he agreed. "I wonder why?"

"I don't know—she seemed really down about work on Friday," I whispered before putting the receiver back to my mouth. "But at least you don't have to walk to work in the snow for a while?" Tommy's accused me of being a turn-a-frown-upside-down people pleaser before, and I winced to realize that's exactly what I was doing to poor Betty.

All I got back was a sniffle.

"And right before the holidays too, honey," I said, filling the silence. "Did they tell you why?"

"No, but I think I know. I don't want to talk about it. Are you two alright?" Betty harbored a crush on Tommy, and we all knew it.

"Well, for now. But I need you to corner Tally for me, if you can."

"Sure. She's out right now . . .'

"Huh, while her bosses are working!" I said, and that got a laugh out of my friend. "But I need her to ask all her artist friends—how do the movies make the noises heard in a movie called *Rocketship* something that came out earlier this year?"

"That's not a lot to go on, Viv," Betty said.

"That's why we pay her the big bucks," I added.

"Viv, you barely pay her at all."

"Well, that's why she has the big bucks then," I said. "Tell her to call us at Buster's when she has the answer."

"Stay safe, Viv, I can't wait to hear how you saved the day."

"Thanks, Betts. We'll figure out a new job for you when I get back." I hung up the phone and gave a look to Tommy. "If anyone can just call up Hollywood and ask, it's our secretary."

"Too right," Tommy agreed. "Did Betty say why she was let go? She seemed to really like her job."

"She wasn't specific. All she said was that she didn't want to talk about."

"Let's hope it's just because her feelings are still smarting," Tommy said. "But if it isn't . . ."

"I know what you mean. Betty was a good nurse, and she liked the work. I don't know how to help."

"Well, nothing else to do right this second. Let's go check on dinner."

NIGHT 3

"Terrible news to report," Buster said as Arnold placed a large standing rib-eye roast in front of him on the table and retreated back to the kitchen. The meat smelled divine, nestled into a forest of fresh rosemary. The spread on the table looked like a major holiday itself—a large tureen of potatoes, two different kinds of vegetables, rolls, a chutney . . . Arnold kept himself busy during the day, and I wondered how he had time to do anything else.

Although Buster was about to make an announcement, my stomach gurgled. There was a gleaming silver fork and honed knife just to the left of our host's elbow, and he picked them up, rubbing them against each other with a metallic scream.

"Unfortunately, our patient passed away this morning." Buster's tone was his normal, boyish voice with a slight tremble of laughter. I'd heard of people getting giddy in bad situations before, but I thought a man that was used to performance would be able to put on and maintain a sad face.

"Chester?" Hazel said, her voice catching in her throat, and tears threatening in her eyes. "Oh, that's so awful. Even though the doctor came twice?"

"It *is* awful, my dear. I am sorry it happened at all."

"All from a broken leg?" Edward asked. "That's impossible."

"I suppose the doctor will do an autopsy," Buster said, and stood to carve the roast. Almost every party around the table winced as the blade sank into the dead animal flesh, liquid oozing at each slice. Plates in a stack next to him each received a cut and were passed down the table in turn.

"I *have* heard of it happening," Evelyn said pointedly as she accepted her plate. Her husband seemed to accept her word as fact, and he began piling green beans on his own plate. She turned to the crowd to explain. "People dying from broken bones, that is. I was a nurse on the front in World War I."

"Oh, that's impressive," Richard said. "Whereabouts?"

"Vosges, Moselle, Siberia," she said, not slowing down. Mrs. Allen was on a tear. "But certainly, most of my casualties were from bullets or bombs, but you *can* die from an embolism."

"What's that?" Monty asked before we could stop him. After years of living with Betty, I knew the stomach-turning powers of hospital shop talk at the dinner table. I was used to it, but there was no way that most of the collegiate set was prepared for gruesome details.

"The fat dislodges from your bone marrow—oh, you can see some here, peeking out the end of this cow rib, yes, looks just the same as ours really, surprising number of similarities between cow carcasses and humans, I suppose—and causes quite a surprise death," Evelyn explained, poking at the bones of her section of roast with the tip of her serrated knife. "It causes the patient to suffocate, and there's nothing that can be done about it. So uncomfortable. Would you pass the mashed, please?"

We all gaped at her as she scooped potatoes onto her plate and moved on to slice her meat.

"I know I'm not a doctor, but thanks to that, uh, *colorful* description, it all sounds unlikely," Stanley said, taking the bowl of potatoes from Evelyn. "I've broken plenty of bones in my years, and I'm still here. I'll bet someone offed him."

Tommy forced a look of shock, and Edward gasped. "Son, that is nothing to joke about," the older man said, gripping the handle of his steak knife.

"No one would have any reason whatsoever," Hazel agreed. "That's *atrocious*."

"It's not atrocious," Stanley countered. "It's human nature."

"To murder a stranger?" Hazel asked. Her face registered confusion, like she was mortified and horrified at the same time.

"He may not be a stranger to someone here," Evelyn agreed. "Buster, you said he was a neighbor?"

"I did, Evelyn," Buster said, softly. "That's what Richard said."

All eyes shot to Paloma. "I've met him while out for walks," Richard countered. "He lives nearby. Often is out with his springer spaniel."

"I hope someone is there to take care of the dog," Monty said, adding fuel to the fire.

"Quite," Paloma agreed. "I wouldn't say Mr. Courtland and I were friends per se, but I was interested in getting to know him. It's only polite to be kind to your neighbors."

"But in murder mysteries, politeness is what does people in," Stanley said. "No one wants to be the one to incriminate himself by bitching and moaning about the guy who wakes up in the billiard room with a knife in his back. Stiff upper lip, act like you're distraught over the death of a stranger, and so on and so forth."

"I have nothing to bitch and moan about," Buster said. "Goodness, you've seen how I live—how could I complain? Do you, Richard? Air your grievances." Buster's jokes were honed now, and there was no way to miss the challenge in our host's tone.

"Well, I do wish you'd stop leaving your outdoor shoes in front of the fireplace," Richard said with a forced laugh. "But not enough to kill you over your thoughtlessness. But since Arnold is the one that puts them away, perhaps he has a motive." A polite tittering of laughs reminded us that this line of conversation began because there was now a dead man, wrapped in bed linens, awaiting a coroner.

"Well, all this being said, I'm sorry to dampen the weekend," Buster said. "We've informed the authorities, but unfortunately, because of the bridge being out, they won't be able to get here for some time."

"That's dreadful," Hazel whispered. "Just dreadful."

"Does the man have *any* family?" Edward Allen was tearing up as he sipped his wine. "Goodness, I would hate to find out that my son had passed and was left at some stranger's house. A father's nightmare."

"None," Richard said. "He doesn't have any family at all."

"A small blessing, then," Edward said. I had no idea if this was true of our G-man, but I had to agree with Mr. Allen that I hoped he was actually all alone and that there wasn't even a springer spaniel to miss him.

"Was he well liked in the neighborhood?" Mrs. Allen asked. "Oftentimes, domestic squabbles can accelerate beyond our wildest dreams."

"I believe he was, Evelyn," Paloma said. "He kept a neat yard, trimmed his trees, shoveled the sidewalks."

"You mean *hired* someone to do that," Mrs. Allen said with a laugh. "I don't fathom anyone in this area trims their own trees."

"When you're right, you're right, Evelyn," Buster said, patting her on the hand. She pulled away and grabbed her dinner roll, ripping off a piece and slathering it with butter. All the news of embolisms and murder didn't stop her stomach for one second. I guess it was a shared trait of nurses—Betty had a tendency to chow down on Mrs. K's dinner while telling us about guts and glory.

"Did the bridge show any sign of being fixed, Viviana?" Monty asked.

"Well, they're in the process." I explained our walk through the snow and the reluctance of the project foreman to put too fine a point on the date of completion. "Depending on your transportation plans, we may be having Thanksgiving together after all."

"I'm sure your mother will be upset," Evelyn said pointedly at me, glancing down at the diamond ring still on my finger.

"She's dead," I fibbed. My mother was really alive and well but didn't give a damn if I showed up for a big family meal or not, and I hadn't seen her for a holiday since I was sixteen and moved to Manhattan. We each sent a Christmas card and a note for birthdays, but other than that, we weren't terribly sentimental. I try not to tell outright lies—I gathered it would make a case more convoluted, trying to remember 'em all and who you told them to—but this one about my mother was pretty harmless, unless she found out.

Mrs. Allen said nothing.

"I find it exciting," Stanley continued, taking a large swig of red wine out of his crystal goblet. "I'm going to be having a holiday with a murderer."

"Stanley, do stop," Buster chastised. But the tone of his voice egged on his fellow scientist. Buster and Stanley were caught in their own macabre comedy routine.

"No, but think of it. We're snowed in, and no one can leave. Dollars to doughnuts, someone here managed to kill a man without anyone noticing," Stanley said. "It's a devilish challenge. My money is on Mr. Allen."

Mr. Allen was caught so off guard he choked on his beans. Once he regained his air, he was growling. "I would do *nothing* of the sort!"

"Oh, calm down, Edward," Buster soothed. "Stanley is just being off-color. Do stop it Stanley, or I'll throw you in the river."

"Oh, so *you're* the murderer," Stanley added, and Buster sniffed. "I'm kidding, I'm kidding. I'll stop. What's for dessert?"

"I'm so sorry, if you'll excuse me," I said, getting up from my place. "I'm afraid that walk in the snow really took it out of me."

Tommy gave me a small nod, and I slipped up the stairs.

While the rest of the guests were distracted by baked Alaska and the itch between their shoulder blades caused by watching their spurious fellow houseguests, it was time to do some snooping.

★　★　★

Without even pausing at my room, I marched into the Allens' bedroom and began pawing through their belongings. I didn't like Stanley's accusation against Mr. Allen, but I really needed some dirt on why there were here at the mansion. Edward Allen was investing, but was he seeing anything in return?

The desk was covered with pages and pages of technical drawings, which made no sense to me at all. Virtually every page included Buster's name and few other words beyond "hertz" and a whole slew of numbers. A cryptic blue script filled the margins, demanding to know cost and variables. Without a doubt, Mr. Allen's business mind was humming along at a higher frequency than Buster was giving him credit for. There were two nearly identical travel writing desks, each on their own luggage stand. I recognized one was Mrs. Allen's, and the other was surely for her husband. I fiddled with the toggles but both were locked, and I lightly cursed that I had left my hair down that morning—I hadn't even a spare hairpin to jimmy them open. On a stand near the window was a pitch pipe, handwritten sheet music, blank lined paper, and a pen. One or both of the Allens was in a choir and trying their dab hand at writing their own tunes. I wondered if they rehearsed loud enough for Stanley and Hazel to hear at night.

"So, what'd you find?" A familiar, smooth voice rang from the doorway behind me. "A bloody hammer? A confession letter? A great big bottle of pills with "Poison" written on it in red letters?"

"Nothin' much like that, Stan," I said, turning back around. "You know, instead of lurking behind me, why don't we break the ice and have you bring me to your part of the lab."

"Well, sweet cheeks, how do I know you won't run off with all my secrets?" he said. "If you do, I'll have to take you out."

"You don't know," I zipped right back. "And I run real fast, let me tell you."

"Fine. Come upstairs." Trailing a finger down the walls, he led me away from the Allens' room, back down the mezzanine and toward the wing where he and Hazel had been cozied up. Both of their doors were closed—my guess was to hide rumpled sheets. A nondescript door between their rooms, similar to the one between mine and Monty's, led upstairs. Stanley took a single key out of his left pocket and unbolted the doors.

"I'm surprised Buster lets you lock the door," I pointed out. "There are no locks on the bedrooms."

"Buster has a key," Stanly said. "It was the only way he'd let me secure the lab."

"Does anyone else have a key?"

"Maybe Arnold," Stanley said, squinching up his face for a think. "It's always clean up here, but maybe Buster unlocks it for him."

"You don't leave your lab clean?" I asked.

"I do my best thinking with a cigarette and a bottle of something very nice. Or very cheap, depending on the problem at hand."

"Buster has a thing about dust. I imagine he'd be furious if you left full ashtrays all over the place."

"Then it must be Arnold that cleans," Stanley figured, "because it isn't me. Or Buster—I can promise you that."

The garret was tidy and bare, with far fewer tubes and electric gizmos than Richard and Buster's well-funded lab. "It's only here to fiddle with when I'm visiting," he said, pointing at a workbench covered with wire and tools. "I don't do my main research here."

"Where do you work, normally?"

"Princeton."

"Someone else footing the bill, then? Just like Buster."

"Yup, just a regular university stiff," Stanley said. "But I could only wish to have a benefactor like Buster has."

"You ever try to lure Mr. Allen away?" I asked.

"Mr. Allen, and before him, Mr. Conaway, who didn't seem to think he got quite what he'd paid for," Stanley admitted. "I turned my attention to this Mr. Courtland as well, but, . . . he's not on anyone's side anymore."

He plucked a small wooden box off his desk and tossed it to me. Over a hole in the center were three metal tines, like a fork, of varying lengths. "Pluck each one from left to right. Just with your thumb, like you're flipping a coin."

I did as he said and three tinny notes reverberated through the attic. At the last *plink*, a television in the corner, ten feet from either of us, turned on and began to scream static.

"What gives?" I put the box down on the nearest table.

"What part? The kalimba or the remote control?"

"Either. Is that what you call this thing?" I said, picking up the small wooden box again. "A kalimba?"

"You got the pronunciation right on the first try, good job," Stanley said, like I was a toddler. "I told Montague it was a thumb pianny."

"Jesus, between you and Buster you must be amazed we three can recite the alphabet," I said.

"Forgive me, that's just part of the culture of higher education," Stanley said.

"I won't forgive you until you stop doing it," I said. "But why don't we continue?"

"It's an African instrument," Stanley said, "based on a traditional percussion instrument in Southern Rhodesia. I used it here because I just like the sound, and it's consistent. But you can use anything that makes a frequency."

"To do what?"

"To make the television go on," he said. "Or a radio or a toaster if you can hook one up to the circuits that listen."

"I don't like to tell you that I have no idea what you're talking about," I said, "but I'm afraid I have no idea what you're talking about."

"It's fine—it's all very new," Stanley said, walking over to pick up the thumb piano. "Have either Richard or Buster explained the difference between what they do and what I do?"

"Yes, vaguely. They said they work with big, slow waves, and you work with high, fast ones."

"Essentially. Normally, in my laboratory at the University, I work with microwaves, which are electromagnetic energy that, yes, can be summed up as 'high' and 'fast.' Here, I sometimes like to putter around with ultrasound—different kinds of energy, but those waves also go high and fast."

"And you turned on that television using sound?"

"Correct. There are circuits in the television that can sense the sounds you just made on the kalimba and then, essentially, tell the television to turn on. Or change the channel, if you make the sounds in a different order."

"So if your cat accidentally walks on the kalimba and plucks the tines, it can change the channel you're on?"

"Why must you always look for the negative, Miss Valentine?" Stanley scoffed. "Richard said you did the same to him. Always looking for the fault, the flaw, the weakness."

"Guess I'm too much of a dunce not to," I retorted. "Did Hazel know enough to just ooh and aah?"

"Of course she did," Stanley replied. "She was raised *correctly*."

"You have funny feelings about how a lady should act," I said. "Now show me how you use your little pianny to turn off the TV."

Stanly tapped the three keys in reverse, and the television turned off. "Satisfied?"

"By you?" I asked, giving Stanley a small curtsey. "Hardly." I left him to fume in his little attic alone.

★ ★ ★

I padded down the lushly carpeted hallway, making my way back to my bedroom. Too many people in the house gave me the creeps; all these science boys seemed to think they were God's gift to the future of mankind, but none of 'em seemed to know how to make normal human conversation. Everything was a little too clinical, a little too cold.

"I don't know," I said to myself, twisting the knob to open the door, "I like a man who knows how to take a joke." As the door cracked open to show me my room, I spotted a looming figure in silhouette and hit the floor. One look at the mink-lined slippers and I got up, dusting myself off.

"Whatcha doin' in here, Buster?" I asked, as the tall man sheepishly placed my train case of makeup back down on the desk that sat next to the window.

"Good evening, Miss Viviana," he said, once again stressing all those goofy vowels. I realized he had a funny way of winning people over, always trying to charm the pants off them, even if he didn't care for what was underneath. "You've caught me red-handed."

"Yeah, but red-handed doing what? I don't think you're here to borrow my Pan-Stik," I said, walking forward and snapping down the lid to my case.

"Oh, nothing specific, nothing specific," Buster said, picking up a hairbrush and feeling the weight of it. "I just like to know things."

"So in addition to being a scientist, you're a goddamn snoop."

"Curiosity," Buster said. "It's natural. Inevitable. When one has as many people through one's house as I have, everyone always makes the same conversation, the same comments about the food, the view, the boats, the politics—no matter who's in office. What really makes people interesting is what they *don't* show you."

"So, tell me about myself," I said, hopping up onto the desk.

"Well, I like that little stack of newspapers in your night-stand drawer," Buster said. "You're trying to improve yourself by reading the news."

"Curiosity," I said. "It's natural. Inevitable."

"Yes, well. Hazel has a case at least three times this size and never travels without it. You, I think, have been wearing that particular shade on your lips for more than a few seasons."

"I like what I like."

"And the perfume is always the same too, I imagine." For a gent who lived among gents, he had a lot of opinions about how a lady should keep herself.

"My housemate Betty steals it at least once a week," I explained. "I don't want to catch her off guard."

"How considerate. Yours and Tommy's bathroom toiletries are all mixed together, I noticed," he added with a wink.

"Tommy's a slob who's never put something back in the same place twice in his life," I pointed out. "I should know. I'm the one who's always finding things for him."

"Ah yes, but it does suggest an intimacy," Buster countered. "Perhaps subconscious? I should tell my analyst about you two. He'd have a field day."

"I've literally sewn Tommy back together, Buster," I pointed out. "You don't get much more intimate than that."

"But what I couldn't find—"

"Was notes on the case?" I interjected. "Evidence collected? A smoking gun?"

"Yes, well, of course. I'd assumed you kept records."

"I do," I said, purposefully looking at the desk, which I gathered Buster would take apart, looking for my steno pad, the next time I was out of the room for more than half a minute. He didn't have to know that my notebook was taped to the back of the headboard, at the suggestion of Monty Bonito. "But you're the client here, Buster. All you have to do is ask."

"Asking questions someone already knows the answers to, Miss Viviana," he said, brushing past me on the way to my bedroom door, "is just so deadly boring." He left and shut the heavy wooden door with a flourish, leaving me alone to flip him the bird and wait for Tommy to show his face. I got into PJs and snuggled myself into the coverlet, flicked on the bedside radio, and was drifting off to Jack Benny when I heard the door open once again.

Tommy returned, wordlessly, from helping Arnold and Monty bring Courtland's wrapped body to the freezing cold boathouse. He got into his pajamas and climbed into bed, the luxuriant sheets and feather down comforter lulling him into sleep after his long day. There was never a good time to tell him about Buster's snooping, so I chalked it up to harmless behavior—for now—and let him sleep. I was fitful and not nearly as pacified by the nice digs, and as soon as Tommy's breathing was low and rhythmic, I slipped out from bed, put on my slippers and robe, and went down to the parlor.

Richard was behind the bar. I could smell his bay rum.

"I was hoping you'd come down," he said. The fire coals were glowing, and there were spotlights beneath the pharmacy of bottles behind him. Everyone else had gone to bed. "Pick your poison. Oh, God. It just slipped out—I'm sorry." He cringed and turned his back to me as he waited out his embarrassment with his face to the bottles.

"Whatever is the most expensive," I said, not missing a beat. "I don't care what it is—just make sure it costs a fortune."

"I have just the thing." Paloma reached underneath the bar and pulled out a dusty bottle with an engraved label, dinged with time. "How about some Scotch?"

"Don't mind if I do," I said, and I watched him fill up a crystal rocks glass, and I took it from him gingerly, using both hands.

"How on earth did you end up working with Tommy?" he asked as I sipped. The booze was strong, but smoother than I thought it would be, with a heavy dose of smoke.

"I was walking through Hell's Kitchen, in dire need of employment, and I saw him through a window," I said. "Walked into his office, fixed a problem, and I've been there ever since."

"Why that window?" Richard asked.

"God's honest?"

"Please, if you don't mind." He took a smug sip of his own Scotch.

"The yellow gold, bracelet-strap, Rolex Datejust around his wrist."

Richard bit his fist to keep from howling with laughter, so as to not wake the whole house. "You're kidding."

"Not in the least. I'm a watch thief by expertise, but any kind of pick-pocketing suited me just fine until I landed at Tommy's."

"That is amazing. You noticed he was wearing a Rolex from the sidewalk?"

"And down a floor, don't you know."

"Incredible skills of observation, Miss Valentine. I don't suppose you could tell me what kind of timepiece I'm wearing right now?"

He looked so sure of himself, so thrilled at his trap that I couldn't help myself. I pulled his watch from my robe pocket. "It appears to be a cheap little Timex jobbie," I said, flicking it by its band to get a look at the back and front. "You can afford better, can't you? Or just steal one of Buster's?"

Richard Paloma felt his wrist, in a panic I knew all too well. He found his left arm naked beneath his sleeve. "*Díos*, how did you do that?"

"I won't tell you how, but I'll tell you when—when you passed me this little tipple. Easy as one, two, three, especially because you never thought me capable."

"I will never make the mistake of thinking you incapable ever again."

"It benefits men to view women that way," I said with an arched brow. "I'm sure Hazel and Mrs. Allen—heck, even your mother—all have stories that'd make your skin itch."

"And it took how long before Tommy realized you were more capable than he was?"

"Hey, now. I know you mean well, but Tommy's one of my closest friends," I said, feeling unexpected tears spring to my eyes. "He's the most capable man I've ever met."

"But you know that I'm right." Richard Paloma took a smooth stance behind the bar, his hip leaning against the leather padded rail. His eyes gleamed at me over the rim of his crystal glass, and he took a sip of his own cocktail.

"We've been in this business together for a long, long time," I went on explaining. "I was sixteen, seventeen when I started, and Tommy just in his early twenties. We were a sight, scrapping together, making the whole thing work."

"Six*teen*?" Richard scoffed. "A baby!"

"Maybe in some tax brackets," I rolled my eyes at him. "But not in the one I'm from. Most girls I knew were already married with babes of their own."

"Start young in the country."

"That's why I went to the city!" I said. "Found myself a nice, clean boarding house, a real steady job. Boss out carousing with a new dame every night, I was there like clockwork to clean him up in the morning. Good respectable work."

"That's respectable?" Richard looked like he'd licked a toad.

"Do you think this is winning me over?" I asked. "We may not be running experiments in our dirty little office, but the work we do is important. And difficult."

"One of the reasons Buster keeps me around," Richard said, leaning over onto the marble of the bar, "is because I can run through entire experiments in my head before we even test them. Observe, research, hypothesize, experiment, analyze, conclude. The scientific method. And I could tell the moment I saw you that you were an experimental anomaly. A uniquely special woman."

"How kind. A freak of nature." I put my glass down on the bar. "I'm no different from any other dame you've had at this house."

"No one could run a scam on you," Richard said, not yet turning off the charm, not yet realizing I was no longer receptive to the signals he was putting out. "You're a brilliant girl who could do so much more."

"If you knew anything about where I came from, Mr. Richard 'private-university, skiing-in–St. Moritz' Paloma, you would know *this* was pretty goddamn good."

"Isn't the American dream always to strive for more and better?" Richard asked. He still thought this was playful banter and didn't see that all the words he said were fightin' words.

"It depends on what you want more of and what's not quality to begin with," I flung right back. "I needed more freedom and quality friendships. So I moved from the middle of nowhere to the big city and found Tommy."

"And Tommy's turned you into a sneak thief," Richard retorted. "When you could be quite the interesting young lady."

"Don't you kid yourself—I've always been interesting."

"I have no doubt about that."

"Tommy didn't turn me into a sneak thief—I was one before I met him. Started out snitching when I was just a kid," I pointed out. "Being with Tommy has *kept* me from being a thief. Finding Tommy is the best thing that's ever happened to me in my life."

Richard seemed to ponder this while intently staring at the bubbles in his glass. "You're here under false pretenses, though— you must admit that," he said, changing tack. "Some people get very angry when they find out they've been deceived."

"If I thought anyone would tell me the truth if I told them who I really am, I'd be telling everyone my address and blood type," I pointed out. "But Stanley is right on one thing—no one likes airing their dirty laundry to someone who's ready to submit evidence to a court."

"Well, I'll be happy to tell you anything at all." The low lighting of the evening highlighted Paloma's sharp cheekbones and, to my surprise, a dimple.

"Really?" I lowered my voice and gazed at Richard through my eyelashes. "You'll answer *ab*-solutely anything at all?"

"For you, Viviana Valentine, of course."

"The first night, when Chester Courtland made the noise," I started, wrenching my gaze up to stare directly into his eyes. "You said you would check outside, but you never made it to the boathouse in all the time the rest of us were searching the main house. Where did you go, and what were you doing? What were you afraid was happening?"

"Good grief, Viviana, is everyone a suspect?"

"There's a dead Federal agent in a house filled with state secrets," I said, deliberately controlling my voice so I wouldn't shriek, which is what I wanted to do at this absolute buffoon. "Of course everyone is a suspect."

"I know that, and I'm the one who summoned him here. I'm responsible for his death."

"Watch your words, Mr. Paloma," I warned. "Think about what you're saying right now. Someone may be listening."

"Indirectly, I mean. Imagine how I feel about what is happening here."

"You said you would answer my question, Richard." I downed the rest of my expensive whiskey like a shot of Old Crow. "But you're doing everything but. Thanks for the hooch. It's wasted on a girl like me—I don't like to drink with liars."

I tossed his watch in the empty glass and turned on my heel to go back to my room.

DAY 4

There is nothing like death to motivate my boss.
Tommy was up before the sun—and well before breakfast, making a game plan for the day. Which meant *I* was up before the sun and well before breakfast, to receive those plans.

"Slow *down*, Tommy—my hand is cramping up." I shook out my wrist and accidentally flung my Ticonderoga No. 2 across the room. I still couldn't give them up, even after the summer. Rather than paw around under the radiator, I mentally declared my note-taking time over. "I thought I got us a secretary for this."

"Speaking of, has she called back yet?"

"No, but I'll ring Betty after breakfast," I yelled, slipping into my dress for the day. "I'll try the office first, though, just in case Tally had the good sense to show up to work."

"You better," Tommy said.

"*'You better,'*" I muttered. I know he had taken the brunt of Chester Courtland's condition off my plate, but what else he was bringing to the table right now was beyond me. Was he the one sneaking around in the Allens' room or getting patronized by the likes of Stanley Swansea? I didn't think so.

"But, Dollface, what I think I also need from you today is for you to cultivate some girl time," he said as loud as he dared over his Norelco, even though the only other dames in the house were so far away from us they might've well have been in the Bronx. "We still don't know how Hazel and Mrs. Allen factor into all of this."

"Handling Mrs. Allen is going to take some kid gloves," I said, standing next to the window and peering into my compact to paint on my lip, the same shade of pink as the day before. I wondered if Buster would mention it. "I think she thinks I'm some kind of simpering China doll."

"You've never simpered a day in your life," Tommy said. He emerged from the bathroom, slapping on some Charter House, with a fluffy, white, brand-new towel over his shoulder, thanks to the live-in butler. "Believe me, sometimes I think life would be easier if you simpered just once."

"Do you really need aftershave with an electric?" I asked.

"Nah, but I like the way it stinks," he said, shrugging. "Sue me."

"I like the way you stink without it, too, ol' Tommy Boy," I said. "I'm heading down to chat with Arnold. Now, there's a nut that needs crackin'." I kissed him on his freshly shaved cheek as I walked out the door, leaving a telltale smooch.

"He's on my list, Dollface," Tommy said, leaning over to smack me on the rump on my way out. I couldn't help but laugh. "On my list."

★ ★ ★

Arnold was in the kitchen, humming to himself while flipping some bacon. The entire room was warm and smelled like home. Maybe not Mrs. K's and definitely not my mama's, but someone's home, and I liked it.

"Need me to make the coffee?" I asked, and the tall, broad-shouldered man hopped and quit humming in an instant.

"*Need* is not the word, but I won't turn down help," he replied. "And you are correct, you have a way with it. Half the time, I admit, even mine is too bitter."

"You can keep humming if you want to," I said. "I don't mind. You have a lovely voice. What was it?"

"It's called 'Spring Wind Floods Water.'"

"Awkward name, isn't it?"

"Sounds a bit better in Hungarian." In a rich baritone, the butler began to sing.

Tavaszi szél vizet áraszt
Virágom, virágom
Minden madár társat választ
Virágom, virágom

The last two words repeated until he just began humming again.

"What does it mean?"

"Oh, the usual folk music themes—spring and water, beautiful flowers, choosing a companion. Every child learns it before they get yea high." Arnold reached down to his knee to demonstrate just how low "yea high" was.

"When did you leave Hungary, Arnold?" The percolator was going full tilt, and I went to grab a teaspoon from the crock on the counter, slipping along beside the butler, but I ended up putting a heel right into the instep of his right foot. "Oh, I'm sorry, excuse me."

He was wincing but butlerish in response. "Quite all right. I left in the confusion of the Aster," he said. "*Leaving.* It's still all a blur, I was such a young man."

"Did you serve in the war?" Arnold's face looked more tired with each passing day, but even without the stress of the past week's parties and sitting vigil at the bedside of a slowly dying man, Arnold was visibly older than Tommy by quite a few years. Maybe he'd missed the first big war and the latest one.

"No, no. I never stayed in one place long enough. Spent some time in Prague, some time in Bonn, some time in Bern, some in Belgrade, before coming here. I didn't see any direct fighting."

"Small blessing," I said.

"Indeed." He plucked the crispy bacon out of the pan and set it in a chafing dish. "The silver pot, miss. As usual, if you can." He bumped the passageway door to the dining room with his hip and limped in with the meat.

"So if you're from Hungary, why does Buster talk to you in German?" I asked the stove, but neither O'Keefe nor Merritt had an answer. I managed not to drip coffee on the silver tray and brought it into the dining room, seating myself at the right hand of Buster Beacon. I poured myself the first cup, adding two sugars and a dash of cream for kicks. I took my time, and I could sense Buster getting agitated, but he didn't say *boo*; after all I was the one who had made the coffee.

Though a man had died in the house little more than twelve hours ago, the remaining houseguests were showing only the smallest bits of sobriety and reverence. Hazel and Stan were less handsy—taking pains to sit kitty-corner at the table—and there was no noticeable change in the Allens whatsoever. Monty was a bit jittery and kept his eyes peeled on anyone who crossed behind his chair, which was a shame, as he was sitting with his back closest to the food. He looked like he was suffering from St. Vitus's dance, and he was starting to raise my hackles with all of his twitching, but I couldn't blame him—if someone managed to stick Chester Courtland during the party, there was no telling what they could do at breakfast.

Arnold was leaving the room with a tray of food and a napkin, presumably bringing it to Richard, who thought it best to stay away from communal spaces after he'd insulted Tommy to my face last night. Or maybe he'd just had too much Scotch and couldn't make it past his own bedroom door. Silently I hoped he wouldn't take a spill, another injury that similar to Chester Courtland's would upset the tourists.

The rest of breakfast passed silently, with all the partygoers offering small stories or tidbits gleaned from their radio listening the night before.

"Did you hear? Ike is now head of NATO," Monty said to no one in particular.

"Good for him," Buster muttered.

"Think he's gonna run for president?" Monty asked.

"I hope not," Mr. Allen mumbled, putting an end to it.

It was a stilted, awkward party, with no place to run off to. Arnold cleared the dining room of cold and dirty plates. Monty sat around, occasionally jawing with the womenfolk and Mr. Allen, waiting for something—Tommy, in all likelihood, to come and tell Monty what to do at some point in the morning. Buster remained glued to his paper, sipping an endless cup of coffee.

"Hazel," I started, "Arnold has asked me to help him prepare for a Thanksgiving snowed in, but I have to admit—I've never thrown a dinner party in my life. My expertise is limited to making coffee and buying donuts. Do you think you could lend a hand?"

"Goodness, of course," Hazel said, flattered. "I'm an old hat at organizing a sit-down. You know, there's much more to it than just telling the cook what to cook. And I suppose at this point we'll be relegated to whatever is in the larder and icebox." She was yammering, and I gave her credit for trying to fill the silent air.

"Oh, and I have to say, I haven't cooked anything in years," I said, this time not lying. "Breakfast and dinner is included in my lodging, and Tommy and I have a standing lunch date daily. I have no idea what ingredients can become what. I'm sure Arnold will lend a hand with that."

"Shall we meet just before lunch?" Hazel was giving me a polite smile, not daring to open her lips and reveal her pearly whites, like a puppy who's been kicked one too many times.

"As good a time as any, thank you so much."

"And it's excellent practice for wedding luncheons," she said.

"My goodness, I think you're right," I said, flopping my hand in appreciation, all while showing off that damn rock Tommy had saddled me with. "I will appreciate your expertise."

"Mrs. Allen—would you care to join us? We want to make sure we can accommodate as many families' traditions as we can, don't we?" Hazel was tittering nervously, but Mrs. Allen's New England social superior had offered her an invitation not to be turned down.

Mrs. Allen grimaced, like we were offering her a seat on the express train to hell rather than standing-room only. "That's so kind of you, Miss Olmsted. I would love to be included."

"Wonderful!" Hazel's eyes were watering, and her voice was brittle. "Goodness, we have our work cut out for us this week, to try to make the most of the holiday. I'm going to go have a poke through the pantry to get started." With that, the blue blood got up and disappeared toward the kitchen. Mr. and Mrs. Allen didn't flinch.

Tommy entered the room with a fresh plate of food from the kitchen and sat down next to me, giving me a quick peck on the cheek. He was dressed in a flannel shirt and dungarees.

"I suppose I should head down to the bridge myself today and bother the foreman," he said. "Monty, do you want to come with me?"

"Of course," replied our resident sneak. "Anything to help."

"Hazel and I were just discussing planning an impromptu and creative Thanksgiving, honey," I said. "Mrs. Allen agreed to help us with the menu planning."

"How wonderful," Tommy replied. "That will certainly help with planning a wedding luncheon when the time comes."

"Almost as if you were eavesdropping at the door," I muttered to him, and he pinched me on the side of the thigh under the table.

"Have you gotten closer to finding a date?" Mrs. Allen asked. It was this discussion of our phantom wedding that got Buster to fold down his paper and stare at me, barely suppressing his amusement as I improvised my responses.

"Oh goodness, no. I suppose that depends on the church, doesn't it, Tommy?" I asked.

"Of which parish are you a member?" Mrs. Allen questioned. Tommy blanched. The last time Tommy had seen the inside of a church was at his own christening.

"Church of the Most Precious Blood," I replied. I hadn't seen a pew in a decade or more, either, but I pulled a name out of a hat—even though it was in Little Italy, it was next to my favorite Chinese food place. "Certainly you can't imagine that Tomasso Antonino Fortuna and Viviana Viola Valentino, changed to Valentine at Ellis Island not too long ago, would go to St. *Patrick's*." I didn't add that the cost of a St. Pat's wedding would be more than Tommy and I could afford in a million years, even if we were actually engaged.

"No, no, of course not," Mrs. Allen responded.

"Where are you from?" Mr. Allen asked.

"Manhattan," Tommy responded. The edge to his voice could have cut Mr. Allen's throat.

"No, where are you *really* from?" Mr. Allen asked again. These were fighting words, and I could feel Monty straighten up to see how Tommy handled it. Buster leaned forward and rested his chin in his hand.

"I'm actually from Pennsylvania," I added, trying to diffuse the tension. "Believe it or not."

"Oh, you know what I mean," Mr. Allen continued. This man was a stone-cold idiot, and I braced myself for Tommy's response.

"If you're asking what part of Italy our families immigrated from," Tommy explained, in a more measured voice than I was expecting, "please know that my traditions are from the island of Sicily and Viviana's family traditions are from the Campania region, near Naples itself. Thus our dedication to the church of San Gennaro."

"I'm familiar with San Gennaro," Mrs. Allen said. "All those feast days just turn the North End into a bloody mess."

"I can't imagine you spend much time outside of the safe confines of your own WASP's nest, Mrs. Allen," Tommy said. Monty giggled but I don't think Mrs. Allen got the dig.

"We travel quite extensively," Mr. Allen said. "We've been all over the world—Italy, France, Australia. Just last month we were in Finland. Bet you couldn't put that on a map."

"You got me there." Tommy dolloped some ketchup on his scrambled eggs and shoveled them into his face, chewing loudly with his mouth open for all the world to see. "Hey, Monty Bonito, where was you born?"

"Pilgrim State Hospital, Tommy, and proud of it," Monty said, curling his lips into a smile and fondling a silver butter knife. "And then taken in as a ward of the state, given my mother's particular condition. Other than that, I gots no idea where I come from."

"If you want to know our dirty laundry, Mrs. Allen, just ask. Let's go, Monty, see if we can't put our hands to good use."

Monty wrapped Tommy's leftover biscuit in a stark white napkin and pushed away from the table.

Mrs. Allen looked startled and addressed no one in particular. "Are we sure those boys haven't met before?"

★   ★   ★

With the men gone and the Allens silenced, if not humbled or chastened in any way, I finished my breakfast in pleasant quiet until Arnold came back into the dining room with a message for Buster.

"Sir," he began, and Buster looked up, "that was the boat winterizer. He said that since the bridge is out, he simply must fill his appointment schedule with other clients who are more accessible on a first-come basis."

"I suppose that's reasonable," Buster demurred. "Though I would tip him favorably if he got on a raft and forded the river to attend to my every demand. Will he be able to come at all before the next snowfall? I'd hate to see what damage the weather may bring to the new boat."

"I'm sorry, sir, he couldn't say, as we do not have any time estimations on the bridge."

"Very well, then. Perhaps Richard can help me later in the week, but in the meantime, please tarp over the new boat and move the speedboat to the cover of the boathouse."

"Yes sir." With a slight bow of his head, Arnold disappeared into the kitchen and presumably out the back utility door.

"What can happen to the boats if they're not winterized?" I asked. I had no idea what the process could entail, but I had to ask.

"The hoses may burst, the engine may crack, and worst of all, every last inch of teak on that deck might splinter and be destroyed, m'dear," Buster explained.

"Sounds expensive."

"'Tis." Buster went back to his *Wall Street Journal*.

With breakfast chatter now all but dead, I flitted upstairs. First things first was to check the contents of Arnold's now-empty pockets. It wasn't much really—a small ring of keys with no identifying marks. I'd have to leave them on the floor of the kitchen, probably underneath the stove, for him to find later and think that he'd dropped. Next step was to call on my secretary. In our bedroom, I picked up the heavy, Bakelite phone on our desk and plunged the receiver. The operator picked up immediately.

"Operator, could you please connect me to the office of Tomasso Fortuna, private investigator? It's in Hell's Kitchen."

"Of course, honey, but that will be long distance," the voice on the other line purred back. "Hope everything's okay."

"It's fine," I assured her. "I work there too. And the client's paying."

"Ooh, that's saucy." The anonymous voice on the other end of the wire seemed excited to listen in as she connected with operators down the line.

"Sorry to disappoint you, but you'll just hear me yelling at our secretary," I said as I waited. But after flicking the ring for what felt like ages, no one picked up.

"Ah, well, I'll try again later," I said to the operator.

"We're always here." She rung off and I hung up the phone.

"Oh!" I suddenly realized the only other place Tally could be, and I picked up the receiver, only to hear a man's voice over the line.

"That river might be running dry," Stanley Swansea said, only to be acknowledged by a grunt. "Things are getting a little too hot for me to handle." I immediately held my breath, hoping no one would hear that there was an eavesdropper on the call.

"I thought you liked it!" A thick voice came through with a throaty laugh.

"That's usually the appeal." Stanley laughed. "But no, no, we have to wait for the next one."

"If you say so," the voice acknowledged. "You're the one doing the work."

"All of it, actually." Stan's bravado was unbecoming, and I was starting to pick up so much double entendre, my arms were full. Stan was calling up some lug outside the house to brag about bedding Hazel.

"You lucky dog." The phone clicked off, and I was met with silence once again. I let out my breath, took another deep one, depressed the plunger, and got the operator.

"Operator. How may I direct your call?" The voice asked.

"Svitlana Kovalenko's Girls-Only Boarding House in Chelsea, please," I asked.

"That's long distance, hon," the operator warned.

"It's okay," I shrugged. Even if Buster ended up with a three-hundred-dollar phone bill, I was going to be paying for some of it. Eventually I heard Mrs. K's distinctive ring.

"Mrs. Kovalenko's Girls-Only Boarding House," Betty crooned into the receiver.

"Betts! How are ya?"

"Hi, Viv, I'm okay." She sniffled. "Thanks for helping me take my mind off things."

"What do you mean?"

"Well, I can't find Tally—she's been here, but only when I'm out or I'm asleep, I think," Betty said. "So I hope you don't mind, but I got the information you needed from Tally, about that movie and the sounds in it."

"Oh, Betty, that's not fair to you," I said. "I'll get Tommy to pay you for your time."

"That would be swell, but it was nicer to have something to do," Betty said. "Sitting around in my room and filing my nails gets real boring."

"Wait just a minute—do you have connections in Hollywood I don't know about?" I teased. "How did you find everything out?"

"Lordy no, I wish! I just called the library."

"You called the library? Do *they* have connections in Hollywood I don't know about?"

"They have an informational line. They know everything! It's like having a room full of Dotties."

"Betty, you're brilliant!"

"We sometimes got bored on night shift," Betty said. "For a little while we'd call 'em up and try to stump them. Never happened once. They know everything—I swear to it. Anyways, the movie you were asking about was called *Rocketship X-M*."

"Never heard of it!"

"Neither had I! But there's a small theater on Forty-Second still showing it. I called, and they said it would be there through Christmas. We should take it in when you get home," Betty said. "But they said there was a new instrument being used in the background. Everyone's talking about it."

"It's not every day that a new instrument appears on the market," I said. I picked up my pencil and scribbled in my shorthand. "Tell me about it."

"It's named after the fella who invented it, a Russki named Leon. Termin was his last name—Tango-Echo-Romeo-Mike-India-November. The thingie's been around for a while—they did concerts with it, the whole nine yards! But it was first used for the silver screen in a Hitchcock flick in '45."

"Well, how about that," I said. "And you said the fella was Red?"

"He was! Moved to the States in '27," Betty said. "He did a scamper back there in the late '30s."

"I don't suppose the library knew why?"

"Best they could say was 'politics,' but that could mean anything this day and age," Betty said glumly.

"Betty, you really are a girl's best friend," I said. "And tell Tally to call me if she ever shows her face, would you?"

"Will do, Viv. Say hi to Tommy for me." I could practically hear her wink over the phone.

"Oh, do I have a story for you, Betts," I said, holding up my hand to catch the glint of the diamond in the morning sunlight once again. "Talk soon!"

"Bye, Viv!" She hung up.

"Well, that's something to chew on," I said to no one. "And I guess it's already time for lunch."

★ ★ ★

Hazel was in the empty dining room, staring at an array of forks the way I've seen Mrs. K stare at tea leaves. "Buster, Richard, and Stanley are in their labs," she explained, picking up some cutlery and putting it back down. "And the *proper* menfolk are still out at the bridge."

"Where does that put Mr. Allen?" I asked, coming into the room, and she gave me a friendly hug.

"Two guesses and the first one don't count!" Hazel said. "I don't think I could live with a lush, between you and me."

"Me neither, though Tommy has been known to hit the bottle at the end of the day."

"He is a dreamboat, your man," Hazel said. "I bet *he* knows how to change a tire."

"I don't think he's owned a car in his life," I said, laughing, "but he probably could." I'd had a flirtation over the summer with a beat cop who'd gone on to motor pool, and I hoped he was doing okay. From here on out, though, I'd stick with men who took the subway.

"What's it like to know your future is secure?" Hazel fell into a chair, and our pretense of discussing menus was on ice.

"We're far from secure, Hazel," I said. "If Tommy's business goes belly up, we won't have a pot to piss in."

"You have a two-carat Tiffany solitaire on your left hand, Viviana," Hazel said. "That's enough security for me. And most girls."

The stone twinkled in the weak light of a winter day. "It sure is something, isn't it?"

"Oh yes, young love," came the voice of Mrs. Allen from the doorway. "Edward and I didn't get married until we were older."

"I had no idea," I told her. "You two have the comfort with each other that looks like it took years."

"Well, we always got on," she said modestly. "But I would never have dreamed of being married before I was thirty."

"Yes, well," I said as Hazel flinched. "It is a very intimate decision for all of us. Despite what the movies say, I don't know a single girl who'd marry a man without asking all sorts of questions first."

"Speaking of questions," Hazel interrupted, desperate to change the subject, "what sorts of things should we serve for Thanksgiving if the fates allow us to spend it here?"

We marched into Arnold's spotless kitchen to tear apart the pantry.

"Viviana, what are your traditional dishes?" Hazel asked, pencil at the ready above a note card filched from Buster's stationery in the library.

"Well, I rarely make it home for the holiday," I said truthfully. "So Tommy comes over to my boarding house to have dinner with me, my landlady, her son, and whoever else is there. And my landlady is from Lviv, so our dishes can be a bit nontraditional, though she really does like doing the whole bird-and-stuffing routine."

"Goodness, how colorful," Hazel said, without cruelty.

"Well, we opt for the American tradition," Mrs. Allen said haughtily. "Edward's family goes back to Mayflower times."

"How nice." Hazel was pointed and almost dismissive. "So, nothing adventurous."

"I wouldn't quite put it like that," Mrs. Allen replied. The quarters of the walk-in pantry were cramped and no place for a catfight, but the two were circling.

"Oh, I would love a classic Thanksgiving if we can make one," I assured Hazel. "I don't think I've ever had one, start to finish."

"We have a pair of roasting chickens in the icebox," we heard a voice pipe in from behind us. It was Arnold, ready to lend some backup. "Not turkeys, but they will present nicely at table."

"Well, that's certainly a start," Hazel said. "Thank you. Corn, mashed potatoes, stuffing . . . ?"

"Frozen corn only, I'm afraid, but I can make that quite delicious, and mashed potatoes would be simple," Arnold agreed. "Plenty in that basket that was by your right toe, Mrs. Allen." I tried to scoot past the older woman to take a performative look at the spuds, but she didn't budge.

"I can help make the bread for stuffing if we have nothing on hand," I told Arnold. "I have some practice." I'd made a loaf, once, with my grandmother, who didn't speak a lick of English, but it wasn't technically a lie.

"That would be generous of you, Miss Valentine."

"I do not suppose you have fresh cranberries?" Mrs. Allen inquired.

"No, ma'am, but I have some jarred sour cherries in the spare larder in the basement," Arnold responded. "Perhaps I can make a spiced relish of some sort with that."

"That will have to do." Arnold nodded and, sensing the coldness, left the room, apparently immediately needing those jarred cherries.

"Mrs. Allen, you mentioned the other day you were in the First World War," I led, being sweeter 'n a lollipop. "And you didn't marry Mr. Allen 'til . . . later. What did you do in the meantime?"

"Much like you, Miss Valentine, I had a career."

"Was it nursing the entire time?" Hazel asked.

"God no, nor was I a teacher. I generally abhor what society considers 'women's work.'" Hazel was getting pummeled like she was in the ring with Joe Louis, but it opened me up to winning Mrs. Allen's favor. *Duck and weave, Hazel,* I thought to myself, and took my shots.

"I know that I do work for my intended," I said, wagging that rock again. Tommy was right that it opened doors with the Allens that Hazel's lack of jewelry certainly slammed shut. "But I find my work utterly fulfilling."

"And what is it that you do?" Hazel asked.

"Corporate research," I responded, stealing a line Tommy had used once in the face of an inquisitive husband who'd come barging into our office, looking for an errant wife. I knew for a fact that, at the time, the wife was buttoning her blouse back up behind Tommy's closed office door, but he was cool as a cucumber in deflecting the anger of the galoot. "Accounting, split-offs, and sometimes we'll go into background checks for select clientele." It wasn't entirely a fib. Tommy's cases were usually about theft or divorce. And we always tried to dig up as much dirt on people as possible.

"And that leaves you satisfied?" Mrs. Allen asked.

"Very. But I am so curious about other working women."

"Yes, well. After nursing and field surgery, the world of medicine was open for me, but while in the service, I was theorizing how I could look inside a person without X-rays," she said. "I went on to pursue engineering."

"Goodness! You have a college degree?" I asked.

"More than one." Mrs. Allen's feathers were dutifully fluffed.

"Goodness gracious," I said.

"You're young yet," Mrs. Allen said. "You could get a degree before you have children, if you do actually want any."

"Oh, I doubt that. I didn't graduate high school."

"You didn't?" Hazel asked. "But you're so smart!"

"Intelligence and schooling are not even remotely the same thing," Mrs. Allen said. Hazel's eyes were watering. Mrs. Allen was sinking barbs in her like Hazel was Julius Caesar.

"Oh, it's much the same thing," I replied. "I wasn't smart enough to know how many doors stayed locked without one having even a high school diploma."

"But Tommy opened some for you?" Hazel asked.

"More than he knows." That bout of sincerity set off the waterworks, and Hazel removed herself from the kitchen.

"Well, I don't think Miss Olmsted got what she expected out of this weekend," I said. "Poor girl."

"She's better than that Swansea fellow," Mrs. Allen said, her tone just this side of gracious. "He just wants her money."

"What makes you say that?" I asked.

"It isn't her looks," Mrs. Allen said.

"Hazel is gorgeous!" I gasped.

"She's holding together for her age," Mrs. Allen said. "And my husband seems to think she's quite the stunner. But Stan's almost as blind as a bat."

"Well, that would explain why he's always so close to her and why he moves as deliberately as he does. Was he born with poor eyesight?"

"Ha! Hardly. It's the microwaves, dear. The energy cooks his eyeballs from the inside out."

"You're pulling my leg."

"I am absolutely not. Do not go in his laboratory when he's working, Miss Valentine. That can be very dangerous science."

"Good God. But when Richard was showing me the other lab, he said it wasn't dangerous."

"Low-frequency radio waves won't hurt a fly, but microwaves are different."

"And his hobby? The sound stuff?"

"Oh, is he working in ultrasound too?" Mrs. Allen asked.

"If that's what it's called, I think so. He showed something off last night."

"I didn't know he was dabbling in that. Goodness, these boys are so diverse, aren't they? How clever."

"Incredibly." I smiled and tried to make her feel like I was an independent woman and not just some strong man's future little wife. But Mrs. Allen seemed agitated. "Is Mr. Allen's investment extended to Stan?"

"Lord no. But if he catches wind of the other work, he will want to take a look at it—anything aside from microwaves. I should speak to Stanley." She glanced at her Cartier wristwatch and toward the door. "I should check with Arnold about the post. I am expecting an important letter, but with the bridge out, perhaps it won't arrive. I suppose he has Thanksgiving under control and doesn't truly need our help?"

"No, I doubt he did after all."

Mrs. Allen left the kitchen to the dining room, and I got up to raid the refrigerator, dropping Arnold's keys in between the icebox and the wall, as Tommy and Monty came in through the hidden back door off the patio, bumping into each other like a pair of flustered pigeons.

"Upstairs, Viv," Tommy said, pulling off his mud-encrusted boots. "Stat."

"Here," I said, shoving some dish towels at Tommy and Monty. "Wrap up your shoes. You have no idea how hard it is to clean up mud." They did as they were told and padded in stockinged feet after me to the main stairwell.

"How was lunch?" Tommy asked.

"It wasn't polite chat over cucumber sandwiches, I'll tell you that," I said. "Weren't any sandwiches to begin with, and it ended with Hazel in tears and Mrs. Allen becoming my best friend, I think."

"Viv, you gotta tell me how you do it, how you win 'em all over," Monty teased from behind Tommy.

I turned at the top of the stairs to give him the ol' charm, tossing my hair over my shoulder and shooting him a devilish grin. "It's natural."

"I'll say," Monty whistled, and Tommy reached back to cuff him in the back of the head.

"That's my woman, Mont," he said, laughing.

"Well, you two are in good spirits," I said, rounding the mezzanine to the wing that housed our bedrooms.

"We should be. Tommy, I'm gonna go take a long, hot shower," Monty said.

"Good," Tommy responded. "You smell awful."

Tommy followed me into our bedroom and closed the door, shoving the chair under the doorknob as a makeshift lock. Before I could breathe, he was peeling off his clothing.

"We both fell in the damn creek," he said, launching his sodden dungarees in the vicinity of the steaming radiator. "That is one ice-cold wake-up call."

"Don't worry, Tommy—I'll dry these out for you, you don't even have to ask, no siree," I said.

"Thanks, Viv. Sorry, Viv. But," he said, pulling off his shirt, "the bridge is back in business." He was grinning ear to ear and standing in front of me in just his BVDs, hands on his hips like a wartime poster about a man who now knew the power of penicillin.

"And we're not to tell the others?" I said.

"I think we can tell Buster and Paloma and Arnold," Tommy responded. "But no one else. Viv! It felt good to work with my hands again. It's been a while since I got to work up a good sweat. What'd you find out?" He launched himself at the made bed and stretched out on the coverlet in his underwear.

"Well, get your sweaty body off my nice, clean bed, you ogre," I said. "And I'll tell you."

"Fine, fine." Tommy was stripping off his undershirt on his way to the bathroom. "Shout to me while I'm in the shower. I'm ripe. They call that fresh water, but that river is disgusting."

Tommy in his shorts was as close as I'd gotten to spotting him as God made him, in the years we'd known each other, and now he was behind a half-closed shower curtain, tossing his underpants out into the room. "I'm not picking those up," I told him from the doorway.

"So what did you find out?" he shouted at the showerhead, facing away from me. From my vantage point, I could see a bit, but not the specifics, but the general picture wasn't half bad. I shook my head in the steam and looked at myself in the mirror over the sink, staring myself in the eye while I spoke. Daring myself not to take another gander.

Tommy hummed a little tune as he soaped up and listened, peppering me with the occasional clarifying question while drenching the bathroom floor.

"So, Hazel—anything important?"

"No, but I like her." It was true. "And her dress doesn't have pockets, so . . ."

"Liking someone has nothing to do with whether or not they're a murderer," Tommy reminded me.

"Yeah, but she isn't one, I don't think."

"And the Mrs. of the Allen set?"

"There's something off with her," I admitted, watching my hair frizz in the steam. "She's educated. She's got degrees—with an 's,' she said."

"Is she the brains of the operation?"

"Might could be," I said. "She said she was looking into ways of seeing inside someone's body, but without X-rays."

"Well, after Japan, I think we're all squeamish of radiation," Tommy admitted. "Did she go into specifics?"

"No," I said. "And I'm not sure if I would've understood if she had. I'm sorry, I'm a dunce."

"What are you talking about? You did so good, Viv! Toss me the towel, would you? It's freezing in here when you turn off the water."

I strode into the steaming bathroom and handed him a fluffy white towel through the crack, watching a bit as Tommy's shadow rubbed itself dry and wrapped the terrycloth low around his waist. He opened the shower curtain with a giant smile on his face, trails of water still making their way down his chest and stomach.

"We're in the thick of it now, Dollface," he said, and strode up to me, wrapping his arms around my back and pressing his warm body into mine. He lifted me off my feet for just a moment and laughed, placing a kiss squarely on my neck as I tossed my head back. His wet hair dripped all over me, and the heat of the water was making my hair curl. "I can feel it now. Someone's gonna panic."

NIGHT 4

"Will you run down Buster and tell him?" Tommy asked, hitching his towel to remain slightly modest. "I need to clean out my ears."

I sprinted up to the lab to find our client, and the vast space was empty. With the lights on and the window coverings flung open, I could see that it was just a dirty attic with stacks of legal pads and humming boxes everywhere—nothing particularly alluring or even alarming. I thundered back down the stairs and knocked on Buster's bedroom door, turning the knob as I heard a "Who's there?"

The large gentleman was walking back into his bathroom as I walked in. He caught my surprised face in the ornate mirror and turned around to greet me.

"Miss Viviana," he said. "To what do I owe the pleasure?"

"Tommy and Monty are back—the bridge is fully fixed, but we don't want anyone to know, outside of us, Arnold, and Paloma," I said. "We need to keep Stan, Hazel, and the Allens none the wiser."

"Not a problem, I will make sure that Arnold is in cahoots," he said, leaning against the door jamb. "And Paloma, oh, I wish you would tell him yourself." He slipped a hand into his jacket pocket, and in the gap between his elbow and body, my eyes trained on an object sitting on the gleaming porcelain of his bathroom sink. It was clear glass, with a silver cap, a long glass tube sticking out the top.

A syringe. In a bottle. Buster caught me staring and shifted to block my view.

"Of course. Do you know where he is? I was just in the lab."

"He's probably taking a smoke on the back verandah," Buster said, turning back toward the bathroom. "I hate it when he smokes indoors."

"Thanks, Buster," I said, "but it's freezing out there. Can't he smoke inside?"

"Richard has a higher tolerance for cold than you imagine," Buster said, looking wistful. "When we went skiing in Sochi, he even took a dip—"

"Thanks, Buster," I said, cutting him off. I was in no mood to hear about any more fancy-schmancy European skiing parties.

"Not a problem, Miss Viviana," he said again stressing all those airy vowels. "Oh—have you spoken to Hazel recently?"

"Not since lunchtime," I confessed. "What's the matter?"

"She's rather upset," Buster pointed out the obvious. "Though I'm not sure exactly why—a rift between her and Stanley seems to be forming, but then there's also Courtland."

"The death really is weighing on all of us, though obviously for different reasons."

"I don't mean just his passing," Buster said. "She said that he was behaving strangely toward her."

"Strangely? How?"

"I don't like passing along gossip, and if Courtland was on the mend, mum would be the word," Buster assured me with all the facetiousness of a child claiming he didn't steal the last cookie, with chocolate smeared across his face.

"No, Buster, I'm sure you're usually the height of discretion."

"She said that Courtland kept trying to remove her from the company of others," Buster said. "Which is . . . improper. Unless a lady gives all indication that removal is what she wishes."

"When did he do that?" I asked. "Stanley never let her go at all Friday night. It was all hands on Hazel."

"During the day," Buster insisted. "At Mrs. Allen's insistence, she said it was a gorgeous day and that the entire party should go hiking, for a walk in the woods."

"*Our* Mrs. Allen?"

"Evelyn is actually rather outdoorsy," Buster admitted. "She wanted a walk in the woods, so they caravanned to Hook Mountain and went for a climb." Buster winced.

"I'm guessing it was a good thing that you came to see us in the city that day," I said.

"I would say that was rather a stroke of good luck on my part."

"Is that how they all got mucky?" I said. "I remember you saying that on Friday night when I arrived."

"Indeed. None of them, aside from Evelyn and Edward, quite had the right accoutrements, but they gave it the college try. Of course the Allens were the only two who made it to the peak. But while everyone went at their own pace—says Paloma and Hazel, of course—Courtland, it seemed, kept trying to pull Hazel off the trail into a thicket."

"And she gave him the what-for?"

"You've met Hazel," Buster said proudly. "Of course she did. Apparently in front of the entire party. Richard told me he tried to calm the situation, but Mr. Allen was also quite agitated on her behalf."

"Buster, are you suggesting that Hazel is somehow responsible for Courtland's injury and death?"

"Hazel's what-fors can be quite forceful," Buster said. "I've been on the receiving end of some verbal what-fors, but I imagine her physical what-fors pack quite a wallop."

"Thank you for telling me," I said. "I'll circle back with Tommy with this information."

"Of course, Miss Viviana," Buster said. "You should go check on Richard. Those pipes don't last forever, you know."

★   ★   ★

I went to the living room and saw, through a wall of French doors overlooking the sloping yard and frozen river, Richard smoking on the patio, just where Buster said he would be. But in between him and me sat Hazel, curled up on an armchair and clearly trying to disappear into the upholstery. As nonchalantly as I could, I walked into the room and sat next to the fire. Her head perked up when she saw me.

"Viviana," she said, "can I impose on you?"

"Of course," I said. I genuinely liked Hazel, the second heiress I had managed to meet this year. "What's cookin'?"

"If Stanley happens to come in here," she said straightening up a little, with her back to the main entrance to the room, "could you run interference?"

"Of course I can," I said. "My housemates did the same thing for me. A guy I stepped out with for a short period of time decided it was his right to come by unannounced, and the girls managed to scurry me out of the way, no problem."

"Why do they behave like such brutes?" Hazel asked.

"Oh, that's not even the worst of it," I added. "This man tried to set Tommy up for murder."

"No!" Hazel gasped. "What happened?"

Telling the story was a little difficult. I had to pick my way through the details of my summer, trying not to reveal to poor

Miss Olmsted that Tommy and I were detectives and that my boss and I really weren't a couple after all. It was tough doings, but Hazel was enraptured.

"My goodness," she said as I finished up telling how I had managed to save Tommy from the hands of the law. "That's much more exciting than my summer."

"Hamptons? Cape Cod?"

"Oh, that really shows what you think of me," Hazel said, embarrassed. "My mother always taught me not to tell, that ladies with careers just simply cause too much discomfort at social gatherings. Clearly, Mrs. Allen didn't get that lecture."

"I'm not a lady, but I have a career, Hazel," I said. "And I'm proud of it. Tell me all about yours."

"Well, I was so lucky to have the family I have," Hazel started.

"I heard something about a green man?"

"Greensman, yes. The Emerald Necklace and so on," Hazel said, rolling her eyes. I made a mental note to ask Tommy about jewel thieves in Hartford. "But as it turns out, I'm rather adept with figures."

"How do you mean?"

"When I turned eighteen, I took my entire trust—down to the very last penny—and threw caution to the absolute wind," she said, tossing up her hands. "Invested the whole lot. Daring to be the twentieth-century Hetty Green."

"Who's Hetty Green?" I asked.

"The Witch of Wall Street!" Hazel cackled back. "She was the richest woman in the world at some point. Self-made. Invested, guided companies—the whole lot."

"Are you the richest woman in the world?" I asked.

"Not even close," Hazel said. "But I grew my fortune myself." She looked rather pleased with herself, and I couldn't blame her.

"The Witch of Wall Street has a nice ring to it," I said. "My mother would call me *La Strega* when I was a kid, because I could be pretty disagreeable. I don't mind rubbing people the wrong way."

"Neither do I, if I'm being honest," Hazel admitted. "I just wasn't expecting that this witch would stay a spinster her whole life." She glanced down at my stupid diamond ring.

"If I were you," I said. "I'd buy my own damn diamonds and dance in them every night."

"I could, too, you know," Hazel said. "Wouldn't that be a trip."

"How did you learn how to make a fortune?" I asked.

"It's not learning," she admitted, shrugging. "Buy low, sell high is the general gist, and don't overpay for anything. If a figure seems too high to you, it probably is. The hard part is learning who to trust."

"There are a lot of shady characters out there in this big world," I admitted.

"So I really only trust a few people in it," Hazel added. "Above all, I trust my gut. It pays to be very, very conservative when you're handing money to people."

"Did you ever think about investing with Buster?" I asked. "Mr. Allen seems to think that he's the prize-winning pony."

"I did," Hazel said. "I don't hesitate to tell you—Buster is abrasive in his personal life, but his mind is *brilliant.* That's why Stan and Richard hate him so much."

"I thought they were friends?" I asked.

"In their own ways," Hazel admitted. "But alas, Mr. Allen's bid beat out mine. Buster assures me that if Mr. Allen ever pulls his investment, I'm next in line to get a piece of the pie."

"I thought Mr. Courtland was here to represent some investors as well?" I asked.

"Well, yes," Hazel said, blushing. "But I imagine this weekend will have soured Mr. Courtland's clients on that investment.

My instincts tell me to run, and Buster and I have *history*. When word gets out about this weekend, I do worry about his future. That is, should the Allens also pull out."

"You should always trust your own instincts about people," I concurred. "If I hadn't believed Tommy and tossed that man I stepped out with into the trash, imagine what could've happened."

"That *is* a lot more serious than investing half a million dollars," Hazel agreed. "Oh, you know what? I need to check some paperwork my lawyer sent. Thanks, Viv. This meant a lot." Hazel stood up out of her chair and walked back to the stairs. Didn't look over her shoulder once.

As soon as the coast was clear, I popped up out of my chair and checked my hair in the mirror above the fireplace, on my way out to the verandah. The wind off the water struck me like a cab hitting a tourist.

"Jesus Christ!" I yelled.

"You rang?" Paloma did a suave tilt of the head over his shoulder, holding his pipe at a caddishly handsome angle to his face. The collar of his corduroy jacket was pulled up around his ears, and his woolen muffler was almost as high. "Oh, sorry—I thought you were Hazel."

"Oh, so you flirt with all the dames like this, huh?" I said, hopping back and forth to keep from freezing to the flagstones.

"No, she's just been coming around for so long, she's like my sister," Paloma explained. "I would do anything for Hazel. And someone's got her really upset."

"Buster just said Courtland tried something on her."

"Maybe he did. I mean, look at her," Paloma said, eyebrow arching as he craned to look into the now-empty living room. "But he was probably just trying to tell her about Buster, which would upset anyone."

"You don't think Stanley did something?" I asked. "That's the most obvious conclusion to me."

"Stanley? He's not one to sniff around where he's not welcome," Paloma shook his head, and I bit my lip to keep from laughing at this grown man, sticking up for his schmucky college friend. "But he can be coarse at times. Anyway, I *am* sorry about last night—I was rude."

"You were. Tommy is my best friend, and I love him to death," I said. "How would you like it if someone insulted Buster like that to your face?"

"Well, if they were to say I was smarter than Buster, they'd be correct, but it wasn't fair of me to be that rude to your . . . Tommy. Especially when I do know, deep down, we're not in competition." Paloma reached over and tapped the bowl of his pipe out into a planter. "Come inside before you catch your death." He put his hand on my shoulder and led me back inside toward the roaring fire.

"Who says you're still in the competition?" I asked as the heat of the flames warmed me.

"You do," Richard said. "I could've kicked myself last night. I'm sorry, Viviana. I wasn't appropriate. And I really will tell you everything you wish to know."

Few things can get me going quite like a man offering an apology, and Richard Paloma looked rightly shaken. His hair had swooped down over an eye, and I reached up to push it back where it belonged, but something about the gesture no longer felt right. "Listen—is there somewhere we can go to talk?"

"Is suggesting my quarters too forward?" Richard asked. "Anywhere else and we run the risk of being interrupted."

"It's fine, but let's keep the Allens from seeing us, if at all possible. Best to keep up the pretense that Tommy and I are hopeless lovebirds."

Richard led the way up the stairs and to his room, softly shutting the door behind him. He offered me the desk chair and then sat on a bench at the foot of the bed. I got up and sat next to him. Like every other room in the house, it was stately and furnished with dark, carved wood furniture, but in the corner was a record player, a crate of LPs, and a small bar cart. Above hung a nude figure drawing of a woman and a framed advertisement poster for Duke Ellington at the Apollo. Unlike his research partner, who hid in the sticks of Tarrytown, Richard Paloma was a man trapped in seclusion. No wonder he flirted with all the girls.

"I came to find you to tell you that the bridge is back up, earlier than scheduled," I said, still shivering. "But Tommy and I—we don't want anyone to leave. We have to keep it a secret between, Buster, Arnold, and us"

"Do you think I would be able to sneak away to the safe house?" Paloma asked. "I'm afraid they still don't know about Courtland."

"It's a long way to go on foot, and I think the Allens would notice if a car went down the driveway," I said. "It would leave tracks, no matter how thoroughly you shoveled, and we can't have anyone finding an excuse to leave. You said that the laboratory was bugged—can you slip up there alone and say something to the microphones? Hope that someone receives the message, loud and clear?"

"I can try, though I'm not sure if they're back up and running after the power outage, but it's better than nothing." Richard was running his fingers through his hair. "Can I take off my coat? I promise, I'm not disrobing, I'm just awful hot."

I couldn't help but laugh. "It's fine, it's fine. I just practically saw Tommy in his birthday suit. Nothing at this point can surprise me."

"I thought you two weren't an item," Richard said, coiling off his scarf and tossing it onto his desk. He sat back down next to me on the bench.

"We're not, but Tommy and I . . ." I started. "I've seen the man in almost any state of undress and dressed his wounds. It's not that I'm his secretary and he asks me to sit on his lap to take dictation. Without me, he'd be dead—more times than I can count."

"And he asked you to get into this business *with* him?"

"I all but begged!"

"I just can't understand why," Richard said. "It's so *dangerous*." Richard leaned his arm onto the foot of his bed and propped his head in his hand.

"Any more dangerous than microwaves that cause you to go blind?" I asked.

"Ah, so Stan spilled," Richard said.

"Did you know Stan and Hazel are on the outs?"

"No, but I can't say that I'm surprised," Richard said. "He can run through dames, but I'd had hopes Hazel was different."

"Good luck on ever getting Hazel to come back here," I said. "She'll put on a brave face, but she's shook up." Richard's face flickered with disappointment. No matter their relationship, it was ruined thanks to this weekend.

"That would be a terrible pity," Richard said. "Would you like something to drink?"

"Sure, a pre-dinner cocktail sounds great," I said. He got up to carefully select bottles, opening the window swiftly to grab ice cubes from a cotton bag suspended from the windowsill. "Very clever, Mr. Scientist."

"This is clever by necessity. Did you know Buster has a small refrigerator in his room? Must've cost a fortune." He paused to measure, mix, and pour the drink. "Do let me keep my timepiece this time?" Richard asked, handing me a manhattan.

I made a show of closing my eyes and covering them with my hand. "Omega Cosmic, black alligator band."

"Good God," Richard said, rubbing the watch still on his wrist as he sat. "You're deadly."

"And don't you forget it."

"Oh, but it is hard to try to seduce you properly with that ring on your hand."

"You're telling me you've never tried to seduce a married woman?"

"Well, *tried* is an interesting verb, Miss Valentine." He unbuttoned his top two shirt buttons and sighed. "I do hope this case clears up soon."

"Why is that?"

"So I can take you out to dinner, properly."

"A flattering offer, so long as you come to the city," I said. "I am never leaving Manhattan again."

"Oh, don't say that," Richard smiled. "There's Paris and London and Marrakesh to go to, and they're not in New York City at all."

"You have me there."

"I was raised in East Harlem, you should know," Richard said. "After my family moved here when I was six."

"Here?"

"The States. Ricardo Paloma was born in Camagüey, Cuba," he said. "But Richard Paloma has been living here since 1912."

"Then I'm terribly sorry about my own comments the other evening," I apologized. "About you being spoiled."

"Don't be—you're weren't wrong. Meeting the Beacon family opened a lot of doors. And I've been spoiled since I met them." Wind whooshed through Richard's windows, rattling them in their sashes.

"It's so quiet here."

"Usually."

"But quiet men don't have a stack of big band records forty deep in their rooms," I pointed out.

"No, they certainly don't," Richard said, laughing and tasting his drink.

"But quiet men do flirt to try to keep you from asking difficult questions."

"I'm nervous, Viviana—I can't help it," Richard said. "When I said I'd check the backyard, what I really did was run out to the garage and contemplate taking my car. I thought the noise was a gunshot."

"The sound was nothing like a gunshot," I said.

"It was a rather loud bang," he said. "And besides, sound traveling through walls and furniture can distort. All I can say is that, from my position, I thought violence. And I tucked tail and ran."

"Who did you think was on the receiving end?"

"Chester Courtland, of course." Richard was grave. "Someone found out who he was. It was the most logical conclusion for the only person in the house who knew that he wasn't a neighbor."

"Do you happen to know if there's a gun in the house?" I asked.

"I don't have one, and I don't believe Buster does," Richard said. "Arnold? Perhaps. He's rather utilitarian. The guests may— we don't search anyone's luggage. This Monty Bonito fellow might."

"I'm sure Tommy told him not to," I said. "Tommy doesn't work with firearms. Not since the war. And I don't like them much myself."

"Then I'm at a complete loss," Richard admitted.

"Are you being square with me?"

"I swear it. I am." Richard looked ashamed, and the pause lingered. "Do you dance?"

"What? Well, no. Not well," I admitted.

"Then I will teach you." It was not a statement about the future. He put his empty cocktail glass gingerly on his coverlet and stepped quickly to his record player. He plucked out an album with a shocking pick cover and placed it on the table, turning the volume low. A piano and horns began.

"Cugat. I'll take you to see him at the Waldorf," Richard said, pulling me up by my right hand. "Nice and slow, I promise. Follow me."

The tall man's arm slipped behind my lower back, and we started to box step around Richard's room. His hips moved more than mine, but I quickly caught on, and I could feel a smile break across his face.

"Ah, thank you," he murmured into my hair. "It's been ages."

"Hazel doesn't dance?"

"Hazel dances like a fury," Richard said, "but girls from Connecticut don't move their hips."

"Never been to Connecticut in my life," I promised, as he pivoted and swayed me, dipped and moved. We ran out of music but stayed dancing, swaying as the needle skimmed nothing at all.

A music was drifting through the hallway—not music, but noise. The strange sound was leaking through the walls—not loud but certainly playing. Richard dropped my hands, and we rocketed out of the door, meeting Tommy on the landing.

"Listen, and don't move," he instructed. Monty, rounding the corner, stayed behind Tom. We all strained our ears to hear beyond the rattle of radiators and the sound of wind coming through windows and leaky eaves.

It sounded like a woman crying and wailing in sorrow—it reminded me of the time I went to my baby cousin's funeral as a kid, and his mama scared me senseless with her tears. But even though the pitches weren't quite exactly the same, I could sense that it was *almost* a melody, *almost* a pattern, and hummed it back to the menfolk.

"I know that you don't think there's a pattern, Richard, but there *is*," I said. "I swear it. It just sounds like it's a song sung by someone who can't sing."

"But where is the person singing?" Monty whispered, more to himself than any of us.

"Paloma—take Viv up to Swansea's lab and any other part of the attic that might be locked or unused," Tommy ordered. "Monty, we're searching the basement until the dinner gong rings."

"Right," Richard agreed, putting his hand on my back to lead me away.

I heard Monty giggle. Then I heard Tommy hit him. "Shut up, ya lug," Tommy muttered, and Monty laughed again.

The tones continued as we crept through the house.

"The first time I heard them, they didn't go on this long," I said.

"Maybe the ghosts didn't have as much to say the other day," Richard whispered back.

"I've been in Stan's attic," I said as we crept for the stairs. "Take me to the hidden places." Richard pivoted and led me to another door in the hall. At the top of the stairs, he took out two keys and slid them into the two Yale dead bolts that had stopped Monty, the best advance man Tommy knew, in his tracks.

And the bolts were unlocked.

"It shouldn't be like this," Richard said.

"Quiet, and get behind me," I hissed.

Richard was about to put up a fuss about going first, but knew better. Placing his left hand on my hip, he walked behind me into the attic, but the sound grew fainter as we ascended. We weren't yet at the top of the stairs.

"It's not coming from here," Richard said.

"No, but we should try to find out why the door wasn't secure," I said. "Before we get up top—what is it supposed to look like up here?"

"I don't look at the world the same way you do, Viviana," Richard said. "I'm not sure if I'd ever retain the details."

"You're a scientist, Richard. You observe better than probably anyone else who isn't in a life of crime," I assured him. "Whenever it was that you were last up here, what did you see?"

"It's family items, things Buster removed from the main house," Richard said, closing his eyes. "Nothing remarkable—boxes, all jumbled in a heap. It's chaos, from what I remember—he threw things up here without care. He does everything without care."

"Now is not the time, Richard," I said firmly. "Keep it together."

Richard opened his eyes. "Lead the way, Captain," he said. In the dim light, his eyes were steely.

The attic was as he said—an explosion of family history. Dilapidated boxes of documents and photographs, toys spanning the contents of shop windows for at least seventy years, broken furniture, and paintings. The sound of the music was dim.

"I don't see another person, exactly," I said. "But the dust has been disturbed. Is there a light switch?"

"Just a pull cord in the middle, if I remember correctly."

I stuck my hands out in front of me and shuffled into the twilight until I felt the string. Gave it a yank, and the extent of the attic's decay hit me. "This place is a pigsty."

"I've tried to come up here with Arnold on occasion," Richard said. "But who honestly has the time?"

"Has anyone ever come up here with a purpose?"

"Only to drop something off, I believe. Arnold, mostly, and I've never seen anything come back out."

"Was Buster on good terms with his family?"

"You can imagine that he was not the son they dreamed of," Richard said. "He wasn't going to West Point, not going to become an officer, wasn't going to have the fleet of children, isn't going to be written about in any history books."

"I don't know about that," I said over my shoulder. "If your hunches are correct, I want to remind you that we read about Benedict Arnold."

"Excellent point," Richard said.

"Who has keys?" I walked over to a small child's schoolroom desk and took the lid off a box. It was filled with broken picture frames and photographs as old as time. There wasn't a single family memento to tell me about the Beacons in any of the public parts of the house. They were all hidden here.

"The three of us."

"Do you always have your keys on you?"

"I try to, and I know that Arnold certainly does, but who can say for Buster." The hatred in Richard's voice was evident.

"He's really on your shit list right now, isn't he?" I asked.

"It's the suspected selling of state secrets, I imagine," Paloma said, nudging a box with his foot. "I'm not naïve, Viviana. I realize defense contracting is a moral gray area for most people. It's just I do believe in honesty."

"You're lying to your best friend about having him investigated for treason," I pointed out.

From the light of the singular bulb dangling in the center of the attic, I watched Richard's face turn red. "I am *doing* the best I *can*!"

"Okay. Calm down. I need you to look at things without feelings right now. Does anything look strange?"

Richard did a quick pirouette in the dust. "No."

"Stop being an infant. Look at every wall, the ceiling, the floor. Consider it. Don't just throw a hissy fit. And if you continue to act this way, I will tell you to go to your bedroom, lock the door, and stay there until the dinner bell rings."

"Yes, Miss Valentine." His voice was snide, and it was unbecoming of a grown man older than Tommy by a decade. Tommy'd been cross with me in my time, but I didn't know him to pout—just to yell, which I was starting to realize was far preferable. Richard was slowly walking in a circle through the attic, but when he got to his second wall, he stopped and tapped his toe.

"What is it?" I asked.

"There's a crawl space."

"That was always there, wasn't it? It's not like you can add a crawl space without someone noticing."

"No, you can't, but you can hide one by covering it with garbage," Richard said. "I swear to you, I didn't think the attics were connected."

I did my own full-circle turn. "I'm out of sorts—where would that go, if I was to crawl in it?"

Richard looked out a small attic window for orientation. "Toward Arnold's quarters," he said.

"Okay then," I said, dropping to my knees and making my way between the stacks of filthy boxes on all fours. "I'll holler if I need you."

Before Richard could grab my ankle and stop me, I was through the small hole in the wall like a filthy Alice in Wonderland.

A few aspects of the tunnel were unsurprising—it was freezing, dirty, and filled with spider webs. The thoughts of mice and what they'd left behind ran through my head, but I pushed them out and promised myself a hot shower and a load of laundry once I finished my adventure. Some tubes connected with knobs every three or four feet, and my hair caught on the electrical wiring, but thankfully I didn't get fried. Everything met at a small door, maybe forty feet down the shaft from the way I had entered, and the electrical zipped through a hole in the plaster to continue on to wherever it went.

I ran my hand over the painted door, feeling for a handle or knob. The hinges were on my left, near the outside wall, and there was a barrel bolt latch in the center of the right edge. I felt for the toggle but nothing doing. It was rusted closed, and no matter how hard I pried with my fingernails, it wasn't going to budge. I gave the door a bang and waited for any kind of response. But if the wall really did connect with Arnold's quarters, the butler was definitely in the kitchen and wouldn't be able to hear a thing.

It was, like all other leads up until this point, nothing, and I backed out of the crawl space to tell Richard.

My rump hit a hard stack of crates, and I mule-kicked the wood with my foot. "Hey! Richard!" I heard nothing but silence. "Paloma!"

The wind whipped through the space between the lead roof and the gutters. It was colder than a refrigerator in the dark hole, and I thought I felt something skitter across my calves.

"Paloma!" I managed to flip around to sit on my rear end and face the opening to the crawl space. Sure enough, a large something or other was in front of the entrance. I pushed against it with all my strength, but even with ten years of traipsing through Manhattan, my gams weren't strong enough to make it budge.

"Well, that's something," I said to no one but Mickey, Minnie, and Timothy. "I appear to be stuck."

Thankfully, no one answered. But I carried on.

"Yes, you're right, *stuck* is the nicer word for it, Minnie," I whispered. "By the way, did Walt ever explain why he had such a thing for vermin? No offense."

None, apparently, was taken.

"I wonder if there are any Jiminys up here, or his roachy cousins." I pulled the hem of my dress up and tucked it behind my bent knees, to keep any creepy-crawlies that occupied the attic out of my drawers.

A quick trail of my fingertips over my nylons revealed that the rough boards I'd crawled on had killed my favorite pair at the knees. "Rats." I couldn't help but giggle. "Sorry, I didn't mean that."

I angled my watch toward the smallest sliver of light coming between the jamb and the blockade. Nearly time for the dinner bell to ring. And so long as Tommy was in this house and hungry and on time for his third square, he'd see that I was missing and find me at some point. The word for my incarceration was currently *stuck* and not yet *trapped*.

And besides, *trapped* implied intent. One I wasn't willing to apply quite yet.

The wind picked up, and I began to wonder if I could summon some woodland creatures to share their body warmth with me. "I thought heat rises," I said once again to my rodent pals, now more imaginary friends than imminent threats. "You know, if you somehow managed to head on to the basement and get Tommy up here sooner, I'll tell the papers, change your whole reputation." I huddled away from the outside wall and gave the crate another kick for good measure. The sting of the impact shot up my frozen leg.

Sitting in an attic in late November was the pits. I couldn't feel my fingertips, and my nose was running faster than an express train.

"Honestly, though, Mickey, you and Minnie have been an item for over twenty years," I said, trying to distract myself from the fact that I heard something begin to patter on the lead roof above me. "That better be hail and not rain, I have no idea how watertight this hunk of junk actually is. But when are you going to pop the question, Mick? It's been too long, buddy. A girl only has so much patience." I tried to catch the diamond in the weak beam of light next to the crate.

"I know I should be aiming to run down the aisle—you're right," I whispered. "But really, who wants to be in the kitchen when you can be stuck in a drafty attic with so many of your closest friends?'

I slipped the ring off my finger and held it in front of me. "Wouldn't'a minded getting *this* rock for real, though. Gotta thank Tally for lending Tommy quite the humdinger. A broad who goes out with one this big, though, she ain't gonna make it far in Hell's Kitchen without losing it." I slipped it back on, but barely felt it on my ice-cold digits. "Can't lose that. Worth more than I make in three years."

A set of fingers curled around the edge of the crate. "Then Tommy's gotta pay you more, girlie," Monty said as he heaved. "Tom, she's over here."

Eight more fingers curled around the opposite side of the wooden box. "Richard Paloma, if she is anything but dirty and cold, I will—" Tommy started.

"I'm fine, but I can't say the same for my stockings," I said, scooting out of the hole.

"God, Viv, your nose is blue." Tommy grabbed my hand and pulled me to my feet, wrapping his arms around me. I couldn't help but bury my face into his warm, soft shoulder. "Are you wiping your nose on my shirt?" he asked.

"Only accidentally." My arms were curled up in between Tommy's body and my own and for the second time in hours, the heat of his body radiated into me. "Is Paloma okay?"

"I'm fine, just an idiot," I heard the voice say from the far end of the attic. "I thought if there was a crawl space on one wall, then there would be more on others too."

"So you shoved a crate in front of the one with Viv in it?" Monty asked. There was a thrum below the words he was saying, and I knew enough of good ol' boys to know the subtext was *Can I hit him, Tommy? Whaddya say?*

There was a good chance Tommy would say yes.

"You are the biggest bonehead on the face of the planet," Tommy said, turning us both so that he could face Richard and Monty over my head. "Both of you go to dinner. I'm gonna go get Viv warmed up. If someone could tell Arnold, we'd appreciate to eat in our room." And with that, Tommy picked me up and carried me downstairs.

"Okay, now you're just showing off," I said. "I'm cold, not dead."

"You don't see the color of your lips underneath that layer of Stormy Pink," Tommy said. "How long were you trapped?"

"Less than an hour."

"An hour! Jesus Christ, you could've died." Without even putting me down, Tommy opened the door to our room and laid me on the bed. "Your knees are bloody."

"Must've found a nail or two, too." I couldn't quite feel the blood trickling down my leg, which I didn't want to admit was a bad sign.

Tommy went to the bathroom and started the shower, returning with two warm, wet washcloths. He approached my knees and warmed the skin, the blood flow increased and pushed the threads of the nylon out of the open cuts. Leaving a warm cloth on each knee, he took off my shoes, slid his hands up under my skirt to undo my garters, and edged a stocking down each leg, all the while cleaning the blood from my knees. As I regained body heat, my injuries only stung more.

"I'm so sorry, Tommy," I said as my nose ran, a combination of the cold and the pain.

"What are you sorry for? You were doing the job—and damn well too," Tommy said. He placed the bloody cloths on the nightstand—the wood finish be damned—and stood, unhooking the clasp of my dress behind my neck and starting the zip. "There you go. That's a bit easier. Hop in the shower and get all that mouse shit off you. I'll be right back."

"Don't punch Paloma," I said.

"I won't. At least not yet." He left the room and I finished undressing, slipping into the steaming bathroom. The color was returning to my face, leaving me blotchy and as red-nosed as Rudolph. The chill of the tile floor didn't register on my bare toes, and the hot water hurt as it hit every inch of my skin.

There was a knock at the door, and Tommy's voice came through the sound of the splashing water. "My eyes are closed, I promise, I promise," he said. "But you're putting on my flannels. They're clean. Your pjs won't be warm enough."

The door shut again, and I heard the latch click. I was by then starting to feel human, and twenty minutes more under the remaining contents of the water heater completed my transformation back to myself. I dried off and slipped into Tommy's pajamas. Even though they were clean, they still smelled like him, and for that I was deeply thankful. Wrapping my hair in a towel, I found Tommy holding two plates of dinner in his hands, clearly confused about where to eat.

"I guess it's dinner in bed," I said, taking one of the plates from him and swooping a napkin and cutlery off the desk. "I'm getting under the covers."

"You look hale and hearty," Tommy said, sliding off his shoes before climbing on top of the coverlet and sitting with his thigh against mine. "What was in that filthy rathole anyway?"

"Well, rats, from what I gather. Also, wiring, which I think was exclusively electrical for the house. There was a door at the end of it, painted shut, which ought to have connected in some vicinity to Arnold's quarters, so I gather that all the attic spaces are actually connected. Did Paloma give a report?"

"He said about the same, with his tunnel being about fifteen feet long and connecting to Stanley's laboratory."

"Oh, mine was longer than that, so that's interesting. We'll have to check all the garrets."

"Tomorrow. And properly dressed."

"He really hates it here," I told Tommy, shoving forkfuls of chicken cordon bleu into my mouth. "He hates Buster, but that gravy train is too good to pass up."

"I don't even like working for clients I can't stand on a three-week surveillance gig," Tommy said. "Imagine being that smart and supposedly that good at whatever it is you do and not casting a net into richer waters."

"This is pretty damn rich, Tommy," I said. "And Edward Allen seems to think it can get richer. And so did Hazel—she invests her own money, don'tcha know."

"Was she interested in what's happening here?"

"Said she was beat out by the Allens in a bidding war," I admitted. "And that she's still number two on the list, now that Courtland's dead. But she's having second thoughts, which she hasn't expressed to Buster."

"Motive?" Tommy asked. "She says she's not interested, but government contracts . . ."

"For normal people, sure. Hazel might be doing just fine without dealing with Buster's shenanigans—he's not worth the headache he brings—and I would guess she's more likely to kill Mrs. Allen, the way that broad talks down to her."

"Those Allens are pips, huh?" Tommy speared a Brussels sprout and ate it with relish.

"The missus is as sharp as a tack," I pointed out. "I can't quite figure out what the attraction is to Mister."

"Maybe he was just as smart before he was dulled a bit by the drinking. But if he was always this dull before the addiction took hold, I just don't know," Tommy said as he grabbed my empty plate and stood up. "Show me them knees again, Doll-face, I gotta hit 'em with iodine."

"Ouch, absolutely not."

"Well, then, no dessert for you and I was told it's hot apple Brown Betty with vanilla ice cream."

"You skunk, you cheat." I slid my legs over the side of the bed and hiked up my pant legs. Tommy daubed me with iodine and blew on my knees as I winced. "You're not such a bad nurse yourself, ol' Tommy Boy."

"Let's just hope my triage skills never get put to use," he said leaning over and tenderly kissing the top of my knee. "There's gauze on the nightstand. Wrap up and I'll be right back with dessert."

Within an hour, I was stuffed full of spiced apples and asleep next to Tommy, our sticky dishes drawing mice on the floor outside our door.

DAY 5

Tuesday, November 21, 1950

"She's not just any little rich girl," I said from beneath the covers. "I told you—she made plenty of dough all for herself."

"Since when does dough impress you?" Tommy asked, with his red toothbrush sticking out the side of his mouth.

"Normally it doesn't, but Hazel does—I just can't explain it," I said. "She's quite something."

"Don't let this cloud your judgment, Viv," Tommy said gravely. "We're dealing with a murderer here."

"We were dealing with a murderer over the summer too," I reminded him. "When all this is over, I want to introduce Hazel to Tally."

"Cut our girl some slack—she's a kid," Tommy said through his brushing.

"Just Friday you told me not to!"

"That was about coffee," Tommy explained, finally taking his toothbrush out of his mouth. "This is about manners. Hazel is a grown woman. You can't compare the two."

"Fine. And I'm sure Hazel's just as complex as any other Thomasina, Vicki, and Harriet in the world, but involved in murder—even of someone she thought was a business rival?" I shrugged. "Courtland likely wasn't making a pass at her, but how was she to know?"

"I can imagine most of her interactions with men are them making a pass at her," Tommy said. "I mean, Stanley made more than a pass."

"And I've caught Mr. Allen making more than a few mooning glances," I said to Tommy.

"Good lord, he's old enough to be her grandfather," Tommy scoffed. "And he's married."

"I think you might be the only man in this household who doesn't want a piece of Hazel Olmstead," I said to Tommy. "You and Arnold. Or at least you haven't said it."

"Buster?"

"He wants her money," I pointed out. "But no matter what, I don't blame a broad for not running into the woods with a stranger. It was smart moves on her part."

"I tend to agree with you there," Tommy said, wiping foam off his chin and trying not to drool any more down his front. "What about everyone else?"

"The only people really in the clear, I think, are you, me, Monty, and my guts say Hazel."

"Even Buster?"

"Well, Paloma really thinks poorly of him."

"He's Paloma now?"

"When a man traps you in a meat locker because he's too boneheaded to remember you exist, yeah, that douses a flame good and proper. Not that I think that there was even a flame to begin with. In hindsight, nothing feels right."

"If you want me to push him in the river, say the word."

"Perhaps," I said, pulling my watch off my nightstand to check the time. "I really do not care to see the lot of them for breakfast. What should I do instead? Attic search?"

"Monty and I will do that, I think. Do you think you could charm the pants off Mr. Allen instead?"

"Well, I hope he'll keep his pants on, but sure," I said. "It'll be best to get him alone, right?"

"Always is," Tommy said through his foam. "I really gotta go spit."

*　*　*

Tommy paired with Monty in their usual working-man's outfits—dungarees and flannels, and Tommy even managed to find some work gloves in the boathouse for those pesky nails. Supplied with flashlights from the credenza in the hall, they suspected it would take an hour or more to really peel through the layers of maze in the attics, walls, and basement of the house. If anyone asked what they were up to, I was told to lie. With what explanation, I hadn't thought of yet.

Mr. Allen was on a settee by the fireplace after breakfast, and I took a cup of coffee and a fashion magazine to flip through by the light of it. I was barely past the first ad for Chanel No. 5 when Mr. Allen began yapping.

"You and your Thomas, you remind me of myself and my Cordelia," he said, lifting his own coffee cup my way. "So charming together!"

"Thank you, that's very kind," I said. "But I thought your wife's name was Evelyn?"

"Oh, that's wife number two," he said, and I noticed he did not say *she*. "Cordelia was wife number one. Married when we were just babes, I say."

"Tommy and I are a bit more than babes," I said demurely. "Why, he's well into his thirties."

"Then it's about time he settled down!" Edward Allen scolded. "Newborns are quite a bit of work, especially if the father cares at all to take an interest. Not easy as you get older."

"Were you and Cordelia so blessed?"

"We were! Three times over! My children are your age now, I say." He gave me a squint. "The girls are mothers already, naturally."

"Naturally."

"But Evelyn said she was too old for more once we wed," Edward said. "She wasn't—it's harder in your thirties of course, but my mother had her youngest when she was well into her forties. But Evelyn gets what Evelyn wants!"

"Is Cordelia still with us?" I couldn't think of a more tactful way to ask if his first wife was still alive.

"Heavens, no. That was 'til death do us part," Edward said. "But Evelyn was there to pick up my pieces. As soon as it was clear Cordelia was not well, she was there."

"Goodness, how romantic."

"She runs a tight ship! Stepped in, got the children off to school, got ourselves to work—she wouldn't stop working at the laboratory, even after we were married—she did it all."

"Backward and in high heels," I added.

"What now? Backward? That would be risky."

"Never mind. But the children liked her?"

"Well, they resented her somewhat for sending them to Abbot and Exeter, but they're better for it. Top-shelf education, that was."

"Oh! Boarding school! Up until a few years ago, I didn't think those were real."

"Quite! I wouldn't have dreamt of it while Cordelia was alive—and certainly the day schools in Washington were up to snuff—but Evelyn was sure that only proper, New England boarding schools were for her children," Edward beamed. "And she was right, by God."

"Was there an adjustment period?" I asked. "For the children, I mean."

"Oh, goodness, the scraps they got into when they first went away," Edward laughed, wiping a tear from his eye. "My son—goodness. When I got a call to hear that he'd tied his lacrosse teammate to the flagpole naked!"

"Excuse me?"

"Just boys running pranks," Edward explained, waving his hand.

"That's a bit more than a prank," I said. "That's criminal."

"Certainly not, certainly not." Edward was not going to hear—or, clearly, give—any commentary on his kids, so I changed tack.

"I had forgotten that you were centered in Washington. I've never been there."

"Yes, yes. I'm a Navy man," Edward said, puffing out his chest. "I've done my service, believe you me, missy. Not only your man has seen action in this house."

"Oh! You should discuss stories with ol' Tommy . . . I mean Thomas. He was at Midway."

"Splendid battle that was," Edward said. "Splendid."

"Perhaps not the words a man who was wounded there would use," I pointed out. "He watched a lot of shipmates die that day."

"Yes, quite. But the proximity detector we'd worked on was used, and it was something."

"Proximity detector?"

"Radio detection and ranging. If it weren't for the men in my laboratory, your intended might not be here." I knew that Tommy was more likely to claim he was saved by a life preserver and his stubborn decision not to die, but if Mr. Allen wanted to claim he did it himself, I should probably let him.

"Goodness, between that statement and Paloma guaranteeing that radio-controlled fighter planes are not too far off, you might make enemies of the GIs you're working for," I said. "Mr. Bonito and Thomas were both a little ruffled at that."

"We don't work for *them*, Miss Valentine, I assure you. We work for the advancement of science."

"Are you allowed to tell me more about what happened at this laboratory? It sounds fascinating."

Edward went to tap the side of his nose conspiratorially, but missed slightly, landing a forefinger drunkenly on his cheek. "State secrets, my dear. My lips are sealed. The punishment for treason is death, you know."

I felt a giddiness in my stomach. "Oh, Mr. Allen—who am I going to tell?" I asked. "Buster wouldn't allow me to come and visit if he didn't think I could keep a secret."

"Even in a garden, the potatoes have eyes, the corn has ears, and the beans talk, Miss Valentine."

"Oh, that's clever, I'll have to remember that."

"Thank you. My grandchildren love it," Edward said. "Besides, I've given Buster strict instructions not to allow any civilians into the laboratory. Must protect my investment at all costs, of course."

"Oh yes, right," I stumbled. He must have been really out of commission the other night, when all of us traipsed to the attic and he hadn't even noticed.

"If I caught anyone snooping around up there," he said, straightening, "there would be hell to pay, for them and Buster, I assure you, missy."

"Then I will stay dutifully downstairs," I lied.

"Though I confess I did show it off to the little ones when they came to visit years ago," Mr. Allen said. "I'm sure they'll follow in my footsteps one day. Lead investors in life-changing science."

"Were they impressed? I guess they're very intelligent," I said. "Do they also go to boarding school?"

"Of course, of course. Now a family tradition."

"I didn't even graduate high school," I said truthfully. "And Thomas didn't get much further than I did in his education. We don't understand a lick of what Buster is doing in this house, though he's been trying to explain the science to us for years."

That was the ticket in. I saw Edward's cogs line up, and I knew he was ready to spill about his little state secrets.

"Not a lick? Nothing about the radio-magnetic frequencies?" Paloma had said that Edward wouldn't even know how a battery worked, but I think that the old man was sharper than he let on.

"I know that every time I flick on the radio, I hear that blasted 'Goodnight, Irene,' but I don't know much else!" I forced out a giggle.

"Goodness, so it's only with luck that you've found these men, pushing the boundaries," Edward said. Something was hitting him, and I hoped it was the magic of possibility and not a fifth of something strong. It wasn't impossible, of course, but the confessions of someone under the influence of alcohol are hard to submit in court. "I met Balthazar when he toured the laboratory as a student. My staff were men obsessed with the highest of highs and the lowest of lows. And even among them, Buster was quite the beacon, pardon the pun."

"You're excused," I said, wincing internally at the horrible joke.

"But just imagine—aircraft that could go to space and submarines that are virtually silent." I couldn't figure out who was listening to subs underwater, but if Edward thought that silence was golden, then I did too.

"And Evelyn—she worked at this laboratory as well?"

"Of course! That's how Cordelia and I met her. They hit it off so well when I introduced them at the Christmas party." Edward sniffled and picked up his coffee cup, but it was empty. He reached out and rang a small crystal bell on the table for Arnold.

"Mrs. Allen mentioned that she had degrees, but it must have been lonely—there must not have been many women in the lab," I said.

"Well, they were all secretaries, of course. Including Evelyn, as much as it made her bristle." Edward laughed at his current wife's discomfort. "No women in the experimental chambers—too strenuous, too strenuous."

"Certainly her coursework prepared her for the real-life laboratory?"

"Oh, it may have, but imagine letting a woman you care for into the lab!" Edward howled. "I've seen men maimed just setting foot in the wrong place at the wrong time."

"Yes, but Mrs. Allen, by that point, had been on battlefields," I pointed out. "She's extremely careful."

"But even one small slip can be deadly," Mr. Allen reminded me, taking a moment to give the crystal bell another ringy-dingy. "Just remember that poor friend of Buster's who's now in the boathouse. One foot out of place and . . ." He whistled and mimed a slip. "I couldn't let my Evelyn in the laboratory, no matter how much she insisted."

"I'm sorry, I was under the impression that when she started at the lab, she wasn't yet *your* Evelyn."

"Ah, well, yes, . . . uh . . ." Edward looked around and saw that Arnold was not yet peeking at the doors. "If you'll excuse me, it appears as though service is taking a break. I need a refill and, I confess, a small snack. Off to raid the stores. And I really shouldn't keep you from *your* research." Mr. Allen nodded at my fashion magazine as he got up and padded toward the kitchen.

I was left dazed for a moment, wondering how a room filled with boxes with no more dials than a washing machine could be too strenuous for a woman with a degree to use, but I regained composure when I realized Mr. Allen wasn't coming back. I shot up to my room and was on the phone lickety-split. "Miss Svitlana Kovalenko's Girls-Only Boarding House in Chelsea— yes, I know it's long distance," I said in one breath to the opera- tor. There was no response except the sound of the jacks being pulled and plugged, the call going through, and Mrs. K's ring. "Betty!" I shouted when the ring stopped.

"No, I'm sorry, this is Mrs. Kovalenko," I heard my land- lady's voice say on the other line. "Viviana?"

"Oh yes, hi, Mrs. K, how are you?"

"Well, thank you. Are you looking for Tally or Betty?"

I had a brief second of debating whether or not I should update Tallulah Blackstone on the status of her family friends, but practicality won out. "Betty, please."

"One moment." The phone was laid down carefully in its little vestibule, and I waited, spinning the curly wire between my fingers.

"Viv?"

"You up for some more sleuthing?" I asked.

"Of course."

"I need you to call the records department and see if you can get me any information on Cordelia Allen, husband Edward Allen. They must've gotten married sometime between '15 and '25. And the same people should be able to tell you when Edward Allen married an Evelyn Allen—I imagine sometime between '35 and '40—though I don't have any maiden names."

"That's it for now?"

"No," I said. "Something else is sticking in my craw. The main man here, Tally's friend. He's a nut for boats, and he just got a new one. That's strange, right?"

"It's almost winter," Betty agreed. "Wouldn't you get a boat in the springtime so you can use it all summer?"

"That's what I was thinking too," I admitted. "And this one is on par with the party barge Phyllis took us to over the summer."

"Hot damn," Betty said. "How do you end up meeting all the rich and eligible men?"

"Beats me," I admitted. "The boat is named *Captain Ryder*, but no one here has that last name."

"Could be a reference to something," Betty said. "You want me to look it up?"

"Yeah, if you can get the skinny, I'd love it. It's Romeo-Yankee-Delta-Echo-Romeo, Captain like captain."

"I'll get back to you as soon as I can," Betty said. "Just this and the records, right?"

"Yeah, and drop Tommy's name—that should speed things up a bit."

"Can do!" Betty said.

"You're the best."

"Other than that, everything hunky-dory?" Betty asked.

"I almost froze to death yesterday," I said. "But don't tell Mrs. K."

"Almost doesn't count, Viv. I almost froze too, after I got splashed by a cab."

"Oh, golly, I hate that."

"Head to toe—nearly ruined my winter coat. Mrs. K's got the fur trim off and soaking."

"Have you seen Tally at all?"

"She's been in and out of Dottie's room at night but isn't making eye contact with any of us in the halls. Something is on with her."

"Can you leave her a note to tell her what's happening at Buster's?"

"Doesn't mean she'll care."

"From what I understand from stories from her friends here, she's not guaranteed to care about anything but whatever the hell she wants." To tell the truth, as soon as I said something to Betty, my heart felt a little lighter. A good kvetch will do a girl wonders.

"We should all be so lucky," Betty said. "If I don't get another gig soon, I'm going to have to move back home with my ma. You think you and the boss will be by for Thanksgiving?"

"I have no idea, Betts. No idea."

"Okay, well, Mrs. K will have enough food to feed an army, so no worries either way."

"Thanks, honey. You don't call here, okay? I'll ring for you."

"Not a problem—saves on Mrs. K's bills."

"Okay, honey, I'll talk soon." I rang off with Betty, and my mouth started watering for Thanksgiving *holodets*.

The door to the bedroom flung open, and Tommy strode in, covered in dust and debris. Monty followed after, polishing off a sandwich with filthy hands.

"Oh, my noble explorers," I said. "What news have you brought me of the lands afar?"

"Well, we're going to have to check you for plague when all this is over," Tommy said, dusting cobwebs off his sleeves. "That attic is filled with more rat shit than any place I have ever seen."

"It was disgusting," Monty assured me. "You'd have to burn this place to the ground to get rid of all the mice."

"Well, good thing we won't be staying much longer," I said. "Or I hope we won't."

"Nah, we were talking it over," Tommy said. "And frankly, if there wasn't a dead body in the boathouse right now, Monty and I would be inclined to just let all these jamokes make their beds and lay in 'em."

"Honestly, they can all have each other," I agreed. "I've met some entitled schmoes before, but these all take the cake.

According to Mr. Allen, I'm no good to anyone until I start popping out kids like a toaster."

"He seems the type," Tommy agreed. "Evelyn doesn't strike me as Old Mother Hubbard, though."

"She's not. She's the second Mrs. Allen and shipped the kids off to boarding school as soon as she got her cart hitched up to Mister."

"Tried and true method," Monty agreed.

"So, how did the lovebirds meet?" Tommy asked.

"At some laboratory in or near Washington," I said. "Edward is champing at the bit to tell you about how his inventions saved your ass at Midway."

"Well I got a chunk taken out of my ass at Midway, so I won't thank him too much."

"That's what I said, but he was going on about . . . radio something or other? Ranging?"

"Radio detection and ranging, yeah—you know it as RADAR," Tommy said. "It helped, but plenty of us still lie under the ocean, my Bonnie."

"What does RADAR do aside from go beep, beep, beep?" I asked.

"It's a proximity detector," Monty said. "Kind of like how bats see at night."

Tommy and I turned to Monty, our jaws on the floor.

"I like going to the zoo," he said with a shrug.

"Well, go ahead. Explain what you mean," Tommy said with a wide smile.

"You're just gonna make fun of me," Monty said.

"I swear to you, I'm not. I'm impressed," Tommy said.

"Me too!" I agreed. "I'm as lost as a babe in the woods, with electronics *and* bats."

"Well, you ever wonder how those bats find all the skeeters they eat, even in the dark?"

"Honestly, no," I said.

"Well, they couldn't do it if they relied on eyesight, so they rely on hearing instead. What they do, see, is they send out high-pitched screams into the air," Monty said. "The sound bounces off the skeeters and moths and bugs and bounces back to the bat. Then the bat can figure out where the bug is, and he eats 'im."

"So that's how RADAR works? Except you shoot the planes, you don't eat 'em," I said.

"That's the theory." Monty shrugged.

"So, it uses the thingies that Buster and Paloma work on in the lab," I said. "No wonder Mr. Allen was keen to work with them and find different uses for what they do. In the hands of a private company, it could be worth billions."

"You bet," Tommy said. "It's the real American dream—own the patent to something that could be used for the common good. And then hose as many people as possible for access to it."

"It's extortion, I say." Monty frowned.

"Don't say that too loud," I warned. "The FBI has bugs in this house, and I don't want them thinking you're a Communist."

"Do Communists bet on the ponies as much as Monty does?" Tommy asked, throwing an elbow at his friend.

"Doubtful. Anyway, did you find whatever was making the racket?" I asked.

"Nah, but we couldn't get into every hidey hole," Tommy said. Monty waggled his eyebrows at me.

"Oh no."

"Unfortunately, yes." Tommy shrugged. "I got an extra pair of Levi's in my suitcase, and brought up some twine from the kitchen you can use as a belt."

"I just got all the dust outta my 'do, ol' Tommy Boy," I whined.

"Well, Viv, you know I think you're gorgeous no matter how much filth you're covered with," Tommy said. "Get changed. We'll meet you in the lab."

★ ★ ★

I stood in front of Monty and Tommy and held their gazes. I was wearing Tommy's extra pants and a flannel shirt, all of the garments inches too big in every direction. With my saddle shoes, I looked like a child of the Depression, dressed in her older brother's cast-offs. "Cross your hearts and hope to die, you will not let me get stuck in a crawl space again," I said. Both men traced X's over the left side of their chests.

"To be fair, we weren't—" Monty said.

"No more outta you," I said. "Which hole?" Tommy pointed at a two-foot-square hatch that had been hidden behind a stack of electric boxes, about four feet off the ground.

"Where does it go?"

"We're not sure," Tommy said. "East is all we can tell."

"Over to the Allens' suite?" I asked.

"Well, we managed to crawl through one that went over there already," Monty said. "Can't imagine why there'd be two, but in these cockamamie mansions, who knows."

"Hoist me up, Tom, let's get this over with." I put my hands inside the tunnel to position myself, and Tommy's hands wrapped around my waist to help me in. A flashlight slipped between my knees, and I grabbed it to light the way.

"How dirty is it?" I heard Monty ask.

"Honestly, it's not bad," I said. "I wouldn't want to sleep here, but the plaster is smooth and finished. It seems pretty new."

"So people are adding to the house?" I heard Tommy loud and clear down the well-finished corridor.

"Seems like it," I said. "Hold on . . . Ay, if you coulda squeezed past those first five feet, you'd'a been fine, Tom. I'm a little ways down, but I can stand, no problem now."

The square hole containing Tommy's backlit face was smaller, but I stretched out my legs and squatted like a duck to a point where I could nearly stand upright, and I was glad for it. All that crawling and creeping was making my knees bark, and I really didn't want to reopen my scabs.

"Hey, ol' Tommy boy. There are outlets, up and down too, in case you wanted to power something."

"Like an electronic noisemaker, huh?"

"Just what I was getting at," I said. "So, knowing how we can all hear the scream machine, you should keep your voice down. Sound travels."

I had to stoop to make it down the length of the hidden hallway that was now high enough to stand but still narrow enough to brush my hips, breathing slowly and trying to ignore the feeling of the walls closing in. Over time, I could feel that my toes were lower than my ankles, and I knew that the passageway was descending. The flashlight was wobbly, and the beam wasn't terribly focused, but I could see the ledge approaching and the large expanse on the other side of another opening that narrowed to the same dimensions as the hole where I left Tommy, this one about waist high. I jumped up and caught my hips on the ledge, and fell out of the passage headfirst, trying not to crack my neck as I face-planted into what was a small closet filled with luggage. Tumbling over the boxes at my feet, I fell into a wall.

And a false panel opened up into a bedroom suite. By the window was a music stand.

"This is ridiculous." I pivoted on my heel and marched through the house back to the laboratory, sneaking up on Monty and Tommy, who stood with their heads in the hole through which I'd disappeared.

"Back from Wonderland," I said, and Tommy jumped so high he cracked his head on the jamb. "It winds up in a hidden closet in the Allens' room."

"I checked their closet," Tommy said. "All it had was corduroy and tweed."

"Different closet," I said. "This one was behind a panel. Filled with luggage and boxes. They're the only people on earth who come to a mansion with portable desks and a whole traveling church choir." I closed my eyes to try to recall exactly what I had seen, but everything was too dark.

"It was just a regular hallway?" Tommy's eyebrows were all screwed up.

"Let me go through again," I said. "I was so focused on getting to the end, I didn't watch my journey."

"Atta girl." Tommy hoisted me up into the crawl space, and I beat feet to the extended portion where I could stand. As soon as I was vertical, I stuck out my hand and found a switch.

"And the lights come on in the big ball park!" I shouted back up to Tommy. "This is new as all get-out, Tom. Not a crumb of mouse shit to be seen."

"Where's the closest plug to the door?" Tommy asked.

"'Bout another foot down the wall from the switch," I said.

"Any chance there's—"

"Another hidden door?" I said, scurrying back into the laboratory, pushing a heavy leather case in front of me. "Help me with this—it weighs a goddamn ton."

Monty and Tommy lifted the case out of the hidey-hole and plopped it on Buster's desk. They unlatched the lid and started poking.

"No, don't help me down or anything," I said, tumbling out into the lab as I had into the hidden closet. "And you're welcome."

"Do you know what it is?" Tommy found an electrical cord in the case and plugged in both ends—one into the side of the box and the prongs into an outlet. With a heavy click, Monty found the "On" switch, and two lights lit up. Twiddling his fingers above the machine, Tommy fiddled with an antenna, and the box started yelling.

"Good God in heaven!" Monty yelled, flicking off the switch. "Is that what we've been hearing?"

"Sounded like cats being murdered," Tommy said. "Turn it back on."

Monty flicked the switch and plugged his ears. Tommy approached the box again and when he reached into it to adjust a dial, the screaming started up once more.

"Where on God's green earth," said Stanley's voice coming up the stairs, "did you all find a theremin?"

"You know what this is?" Tommy asked.

"I don't know, Stan," I said. "I watched *Spellbound* when it came out in theaters. This doesn't sound like that."

"Of course it doesn't," Stanley said. "This is one of the hardest instruments in the world to play." He took a pause. "Nice outfit, Valentine."

"Thank you," I replied, giving a curtsy.

"Where are the keys? Where do you blow into it?" Monty asked.

"It's an electronic musical instrument," Stanley said. "It synthesizes the sound of an orchestra using . . . well, electricity."

"I'm not a cultured man, Stan," Tommy said, "but this don't sound like an orchestra."

"Not with you playing it. But Clara Rockmore . . ." he looked away wistfully. "She's something else."

"Yeah, but how do you *play* it?" Monty asked.

"So you knew all this time that the sound coming through the walls was whatever this is? A theremin?" I asked.

"Well, up until recently, every time I heard it, I had other things on my mind, so I didn't think too long and hard about it," Stan said. "And Buster never mentioned it or asked about it, so I just assumed it was him, or part of his experiments."

"Do you know a lot about what they do in their lab?" I asked.

"I know the general gist. I'm all ears if they want to share specifics," Stanley said. "Seems to be quite the moneymaker."

"What were you doing just a few minutes ago?"

"Counting the minutes until supper."

"Where were you waiting?" I asked.

"In my lab, just fiddling around with bits."

"And do you know where everyone else is?"

"If I had to hazard a guess, I'd assume Hazel and Paloma are having a chat in his room; they both seem rather rough at the moment. Given *her* location, I imagine Buster is either pawing through Hazel's stuff, trying to glean some stock tips, or if he's already done with that, he's by the bar," Stanley said. "The Allens went for a walk, I believe."

I glared at Tommy. "I don't like the idea of them walking around."

"Me neither," Tommy said.

"You still haven't told me how you play this thing," Monty said.

"With the air, Montague," Stanley said, condescendingly. "You don't blow into it, strike it, or do anything at all. Stand back. Watch."

Monty, Tommy, and I each took a large step away from the box, and Stanley took one toward it. He hit the toggle on the side, and gently lifted his hands toward the upright antenna. Sliding his right hand in flat, he moved his left up, down, in, out, away, and toward his body, and the theremin sang. Off-key and squelchy, but it sang.

"How's it doing that?" Tommy asked.

"It's an electronic field," Stanly explained. "The antennae sense your hands' relative position to them, and each movement controls either the frequency—that's to say, what note it plays—or the volume. Leon invented it as a proximity detector, actually."

"A what now?" I asked.

"Like how we use RADAR." Stanley shrugged. "It works on a small scale, but not quite as well as what we have. I also heard the Soviets wanted something they could use to blow up a bomb as something approached it—a proximity fuse—but this wouldn't work. How it's set up, it's too noisy, obviously. But even if you adjusted the bit that made noise, you have to be real close. Leon, the blessed fool, he was asked to make a weapon, and he made a cello."

"I don't know—listening to you play that is torture," Monty said. "Turn it off."

"When you're right, you're right," Stanley said. "All the best performers can keep perfect pitch."

"Where can we keep this?" I asked. "I don't want it growing legs and walking away."

"Monty's going to watch it," Tommy said. "Sorry, Mont."

"So long as someone brings me dinner, I don't mind."

"Either me or Arnold will do it," I said. "But Tommy, you better help him down the stairs with that or he'll break a leg."

Tommy and Monty packed up the theremin and left with it for Monty's room, leaving Stan and me in the laboratory.

"Why'd you ditch Hazel?" I asked. "You don't want her money?"

"There are easier ways to get money than *that*," Stanley said.

"Than what?"

"The 'death-do-us-part' charade," Stanley shrugged. "My ship always comes in in the end, don't worry."

"You're sounding awfully proud for someone who called himself just a university stiff," I said. "What can they possibly pay you?"

"Enough for what I do for them," Stanley said. "But not enough to live on. I'm going to go check on dinner."

NIGHT 5

More footsteps were coming up the stairs, and Arnold's face appeared in the laboratory. He looked exhausted, and I couldn't blame the man one bit. Taking care of only Buster himself would be a more than punishing full-time job, let alone looking after a household full of silver-spoon charlatans—and at least one person capable of cold-blooded murder—for a goddamn week.

"Miss Valentine," he said. "Miss Blackstone is on the phone for you."

"Thanks, Arnold." I followed him back down the stairs. "Stan—he's up to no good, right?"

"But to what extent, fully, I am not entirely sure," Arnold agreed.

"Capable of murder?" I asked. "He was the first one who brought it up."

"Perhaps that is why Mr. Courtland was dosed in a major muscle group," Arnold said, weighing the possibilities. "With Mr. Swansea's sight failing, it's a very easy target."

"How do you know so much about everything, Arnold?" I asked. "What aren't you telling me?" We were now walking through the mezzanine, and Arnold bottled up.

"May I speak with you and Mr. Fortuna when time permits?" His eyes were dodgy, scoping out every spot where the bedroom wings met the public hallway, while leading me to my own passage. "There may be more information that you need."

"Of course," I said, dipping inside my bedroom. "We'll find you before dinner."

"In the kitchen as always," he said, and shut the door behind me.

I picked up the receiver. "'Evening, Tally."

"What's the big idea, you giving my job to Betty?" a shrill voice came through the wires, and I could picture Tally having a fit on the second-floor landing of Mrs. K's. She'd been insisting on a phone on the third floor since she moved in, and Mrs. K outrightly refused, even when Tally had offered to pay for it.

"Well, someone had to help," I said back coolly. "Nice to hear from you. I called the office yesterday afternoon, but you weren't in. On a Monday. I called home over the weekend. But you weren't in. On a Sunday."

"This is my first real case, Viv, cut a girl some slack," she said with a whine. "How was I supposed to know you needed me?"

"It's fine, it's all fine. How are you? Is everything okay?"

"Everything is not okay. Betty's been going on and on about the case, and she seems to think that everyone over at Buster's house is guilty, throw away the key, kaput."

"Well, it's not looking on the straight and narrow here, Tally," I pointed out. "The FBI is involved." That last part I whispered; only after I said it, I realized it wasn't going to make a difference if anyone was listening in on the line. I had overheard Stanley Swansea making bedroom confessions to a mystery man, and Buster Beacon had revealed himself to be an incorrigible snoop to boot.

"The Feds! You and Tommy shouldn't be investigating when the Feds are involved. *They* can handle it."

"Thanks for the vote of confidence, old chum."

Tally was practically hyperventilating. "*Ma mère* would not have *ever* given money to Buster if he was doing something unscrupulous."

"She was married to your father, who is currently doing time in Fishkill for fraud, blackmail, and racketeering," I pointed out.

"That's low. He wouldn't be in there if it wasn't for you."

"You're the one who set him up for at least one of those charges," I shot back. "Or have all the Champagne breakfasts with Broadway producers rattled that out of your brain?"

"You're a real lousy friend, Viviana Valentine," Tally said, sniffling. "You're given a job and now you're attacking a sick man in his own home."

"I'm doing no such thing," I said. "I was called in to solve a problem, and I'm fixing it. I can't help it if the person who hired me is doing something hinky. Besides, everyone here is hale and hearty except for maybe me. I almost died the other day, you know."

"You did not," Tally scoffed. "No one *dies* at Buster's house. They just get hungover."

"People well and truly do die at Buster's house, Tally. There's a dead man on ice in the boathouse as we speak."

"If you're suggesting Buster had something to do with a man's death, I'll tell Mrs. K on you."

"She knows what I do for a living, Tally! I'm not a child!"

"You're acting like one!" my secretary shrieked. "You're just mad at me for not being at your beck and call."

"I mean, you are my secretary, so you're supposed to be answering the phone. You're supposed to be at the office every day of the week, during normal business hours, even if Tommy and I are out. And I didn't come here with the intent of pinning something on Buster, but he might be breaking laws."

"You said Tommy and you break laws all the time."

"You got me there, kid," I said, laughing through my anger. "Tell me—why should I go easy on Buster? You said he was sick?"

"Yeah. His insides don't work right, and he has to give himself shots all the time."

"Injections? With a needle?"

"Yeah, every day, sometimes many times a day. He hates it. He can't live like he used to."

"I don't know, the house is pretty plush," I said. "How was he living before?"

"The house hasn't changed—well, not a lot since they put in the lab—but it's his life*style*. Less drinking, if you can believe it, less fatty food. He doesn't digest right anymore. But he doesn't like to discuss it." I could feel Tally's eyes narrow at the other end of the line. "It isn't *seemly*."

"Well, Tally, Tommy and I have a higher tolerance for the unseemly than your lot does," I said. "Thanks for telling me." Before my secretary could say a word, I hung up on her.

"Let her tell Mrs. K," I said. "See if I care."

"Let who tell the landlady what?" Tommy was slipping in through the door.

"Ah, Tally's miffed that I roped in Betty to do what she thinks is her job," I said. "And she's acting like a kid about it."

"She *is* a kid," Tommy said, shrugging. "A kid who's been through a lot in the past few months."

"I never acted like that," I said. "And I've been through a lot, too."

"You're right—some of us never got to be kids, not once, Dollface," Tommy said. "But I like to give people opportunities I never got. And you know that if Mrs. K's hit the end of her rope with you—and I couldn't blame her after the summer—I got your back."

"I know, ol' Tommy boy. I know." The phone next to my hand rang again, and I didn't wait for Arnold to pick it up. "What is it, Tally?"

A strange voice at the other end piped up. "Collect call from a Mrs. Cavaquinho's Boarding House. Do you accept the charges?"

"It's Kovalenko, and yes," I said. I covered up the receiver to talk to Tommy. "Maybe she's calling to apologize?"

"She was supposed to let me talk with you before she hung up." Betty was on the other end of the line.

"I hung up on her, so it's my fault, really," I explained. "Oof, everyone's phone bill is going to be off the charts this month."

"Just get *her* to pay for it," Betty assured me, not even saying Tally's name. I guess our local heiress was getting on everyone's nerves.

"I'm sure. So, what'd you find out?"

"Well, you're right on the money for the death and marriage certificates," Betty explained. "The first missus died of some illness in the summer of '36, and the mister wasn't alone for Christmas."

"Good grief."

"I mean, I hope they're good for each other—maybe it is true love," Betty said. "But in my novels, women have to wear black for a *year* before they can find another suitor. Sometimes they have to go through a purple year too."

"Betty, most of your books take place in the 1800s," I pointed out.

"But still! A person needs time to mourn," she said, sniffling. "It's not right for the soul."

"I'm not disagreeing," I said. "The cert—did it really not say anything about cause of death?"

"Not at all." Betty was then suspiciously silent.

"You *didn't*."

"I tried to ask," Betty said, "but no one would spill. Sorry, Viv."

"I'm just impressed you did it," I said. "But what takes out a woman that young in the prime of her life?"

"Usually childbirth," Betty said. "I'm sorry—I don't deal with internal medicine all that much. Most of the time, people in my ER come in for things on the inside suddenly being on the outside. Or things on the outside suddenly gettin' chopped off."

"Ooh, remember the guy who lost his foot under a hansom cab?"

"Remember!" Betty howled. "I saw it every time I closed my eyes for three whole months!"

"Anyway—did you find out who Captain Ryder was?"

"Well, we can thank Dottie for that one," Betty said. "I left my scratch pad on the dining table while I was taking notes and skipped up to the bathroom, and Dottie must've looked 'em over. It's her handwriting that says the name is from a book that was all the rage a few years back."

"I mean, I guess that makes sense," I said. "Buster seems like he's on top of those kinds of things."

"The author's name is . . ." she paused for a moment. "Wow-guh?"

"What a name," I said. "His boss woulda made him change it to Smith or something. Something that sounds better."

"Anyway, I'll spell it for you. Whiskey-Alpha-Uniform-Golf-Hotel."

"Reads like 'Wow-guh' to me too," I said. "Anything else to report, Private?"

"No, sir," Betty said back. "But you know how to reach me if you need me!"

"Bye, Betty!"

I hung up and Tommy set to looking at me.

"It's Waugh," Tommy said back. "That last name is Waugh."

"Well, how about that." I said. "You read the book?"

"Everyone read *Brideshead*, Viv," Tommy said, shaking his head.

"Can you connect Captain Ryder to anyone in the house?"

"Not off the top," Tommy admitted. "Was anyone in the service?"

"No one but you and Monty. Recently, Mr. Allen said something about being a Navy man, but that could just mean who he roots for in a football game," I mused. "He's the right age for . . . the Spanish–American if I recall."

"You can't tease me about knowing authors if you know the chronology of American military campaigns," Tommy said back.

"Deal, I guess."

"But we'll ask around," Tommy said, mentally filing away all his information. "Do the best we can."

"Anyway, I gotta go find Buster—Tally let slip that he's got a medical problem, one that requires frequent injections."

"Nice of anyone to mention," Tommy said. "Meet you in the kitchen after?"

"How'd you know?"

"We have to get to the bottom of Arnold."

"Why are you so interested in Arnold's bottom?" I cackled as I slipped out the door. It closed before I got hit with a throw pillow Tommy had chucked in my direction.

There was no one in the house as I raced my way through the halls to find Buster. Tommy's borrowed dungarees were starting to chafe my thighs, but I couldn't slow down for something as silly as discomfort. I first checked his room, where there was no sound to greet me but the whirring of a small refrigerator, nestled between his own massive, gleaming, dust-free desk and the wall, beneath a window overlooking the entire backyard and its slope to the now-thawing river. Closing his bedroom door behind me and wedging it with a chair, I pulled open drawers and closets, looking for something incriminating, but exactly what, I had no idea. I began with the nightstands and under the mattress, felt under pillows, and then searched robe pockets and suit-jacket linings. The search of all the usual spaces turned up nothing except a startling amount of money in loose bills, stale and used tissues, and an unopened roll of breath mints with packaging that looked like it was from the Hoover administration.

The small icebox itself looked like the usual appliance, only miniature. Inside was a half-empty ice tray, a soda syphon, and a metal laboratory tray filled with small vials of clear liquid, each stoppered with an orange glob of something. The label, in red ink, read "Protamine, Zinc & Iletin. 10 cc."

On top of the refrigerator was a stack of light-blue boxes with "ILETIN SYRINGE NO. 350" scrawled across in big, bold letters. Buster didn't seem to be hiding that he was the one who stuck Chester Courtland in the backside. Next to the refrigerator on the desk was a porcelain enameled box with a gleaming nickel lid, plugged into the wall and humming slightly. Inside were even more needles.

Moving the chair, I left the room armed with at least a little more knowledge and headed into the living room to find Buster sipping on something bubbly next to the fire. I flopped down on the chair across from him, and he looked up.

"Lovely dinner outfit, Miss Viviana," he said, nodding at my dusty clothes.

"Thank you—it's the latest from gay Pah-ree," I said. "Gonna tell me about the needles?"

"Ah yes, that," Buster said. "I was hoping you'd trust me enough to let me keep my medical privacy."

"I don't trust you a fig," I said. "And frankly, if there wasn't a dead man to deal with, we'd just leave you to your little mystery."

"I appreciate your candor," Buster said.

"So, how come you got vials of poison and syringes in your room?" I asked.

"It's hardly poison, Viviana," Buster said, sipping on his cocktail. "It's medicine."

"For what? You look as healthy as a horse."

"Yes, well, I'm not. I have diabetes—diabetes mellitus."

"You've been treating me like an ignoramus since I got here. Now's not the time to act like I know what you're talking about, Buster."

"To put it simply, my body no longer produces a chemical it needs to digest sugar," Buster said. "I must inject that chemical into my bloodstream."

"And what you inject isn't the same thing that was pumped into Chester Courtland?"

"I was under the impression that he died from a leg wound," Buster said.

"Oh, good," I replied. "At least with information, Paloma can be trusted. No, Buster. He didn't die of a broken leg. He was shot full of poison."

"I had no idea the agent was murdered, thank you."

"We're good investigators," I shrugged. "Information is at a need-to-know basis."

"And Paloma needed to know before I did?" Buster arched an eyebrow.

"He did." I left it at that.

"But it *is* possible to kill a healthy man with insulin, if that's what you're asking," Buster said. "Just the amount required would be noticeable."

"And if not enough was injected?"

"The victim would be very, very sleepy," Buster said, "but would eventually survive."

"Courtland was pretty out of it, Buster," I said. "How can you be sure?"

"My medicine is a controlled substance. I only have so much of it in the house at any given time," Buster explained. "I would notice if the amount needed to kill a man was missing, I assure you."

"So, tell me about this diabetes thing," I said. "Tally said you can't eat or drink like you used to."

"She's correct," Buster said. "I could die if I carried on as I did as a young man."

"So, no cake and cookies? Christmas must be a drag," I pointed out.

"My sweet tooth has waned as my years waxed," Buster said. "The hardest part is that I can't drink."

"All the wine at dinner?" I asked.

"Grape juice, if you can believe it."

"The Scotch?"

"An herbal tincture of Arnold's own devising, actually."

"And what's that, if you can't drink?"

"Just carbonated water, a dash or two of bitters for flavor. As much flavor as it gives."

"Be careful with those bitters," I said, getting up.

"They don't have much effect on my blood sugar, Viviana."

"But they will have an effect on your bowels," I said, heading toward the kitchen. "They can really make ya shit."

Buster grimaced, and I was tickled pink to make the man squirm.

★　★　★

Tommy was in the kitchen, eating a bowl of mashed potatoes and chatting with Arnold. "They're extra," he said. "You want some?"

"Thanks, no." I hopped up onto the coffee counter and crossed my legs, less out of modesty than habit. "So, Buster's got a whole pharmacy of needles up in his room."

"He could just be sick," Tommy said, scraping the sides of the bowl with his spoon.

"He says he is. Diabetes."

"Which he does have," Arnold said, pulling a thermometer out of his roast. "And I've been keeping an eye on his needles. None are missing."

"How do you know?"

"There's an autoclave on his desk," Arnold said.

"The little bread box with the plug?" I asked.

"You take apart the syringes, put each element in its correct spot, and turn on the machine," Arnold explained. "It cleans all the parts so you can reuse the syringes with no risk of infection."

"I have to admit, that's pretty neat," I said.

"Any of the other regular houseguests have access to medicine like that?" Tommy asked.

"Mr. Allen gets a touch of the gout," Arnold explained. "Miss Olmsted has been known to pack some smelling salts and aspirins, and Stanley has discovered some rather homeopathic remedies for his anxieties about his eyesight."

Tommy let out a bark, and I gave him a look. "He smokes grass, Viv."

"Ah, okay. Mrs. Allen?"

"Fit as a fiddle, from what I can tell, though she has asked me for some liniment for her arthritic knees on occasion."

"But you haven't seen this extra needle anywhere?" I asked.

"Not in any of the garbage cans in people's bathrooms," Arnold responded. "Not in the kitchen trash. I even went through the bins I bring out to the curb, and couldn't find anything."

"Goodness, you're thorough."

"Thank you. But it would help to search other hiding places," Arnold admitted. "Anyone could have disposed of it anywhere—hidden in the house or thrown in the river."

"Every mousehole we can find, we'll look," Tommy said.

"But after dinner, please," Arnold said, plopping his roast on a serving platter. "I don't want this getting cold." Arnold bumped the door to the dining room and disappeared again in his work.

"Did you get to ask him anything before I showed up?" I inquired of Tommy.

"Just for him to deliver a plate to Monty," Tommy said.

"Every time we get him alone, he finds an excuse to be with people," I said.

"Do you think he murdered the Fed?"

"Not at all," I admitted.

"Then frankly, my dear, I don't give a damn about Arnold," Tommy said.

"Aw, hey! You managed to stay awake to the end!"

"The end of what?" Tommy rinsed his bowl and put it on the drainboard of the sink. "Time for dinner—I'm starving."

"Gimme a minute," I said, pulling at my cuffs. "I gotta go change."

★ ★ ★

Upstairs, the house was quiet. I was going to be late to the table, but at this point, half the house was mad at me for something, so it didn't really matter if I was rude. I slipped out of Tommy's clothes and got a whiff of his cologne still lingering on my skin and girdle. It was comforting and, mixed with the warmth of our room, lulled me into just settling down on the edge of the bed in my lingerie to make the phone call I had been meaning to place since Sunday.

"Madison Avenue Hospital, please," I told the operator. "Personnel Department, if they have their own number."

"They do, hon," she replied. "Please hold."

When the hospital staff picked up, I recited the speech I'd formulated over the past day. "Hello, I'm calling from Sloane," I said calmly, stretching out on the comforter, trying to make myself as relaxed as I needed to sound. "Checking on the employment history of an Elizabeth Wagner, who is applying to work with us. She says she was previously employed at your hospital as an emergency nurse?"

"Let me look up her file," the curt voice responded. There was silence on the end of the line as the body attached to the voice clearly took her time to get the folder with Betty's name on it. "Yes, she was."

"She seems extremely competent," I said. "Is it possible that you may tell me why she was terminated?"

"All I see is that there was a complaint from a Doctor Mitchell," the voice responded.

"Doctor Mitchell—in the Emergency Room?"

"That's correct. His shift starts again tomorrow morning."

"Wonderful, I will give him a ring," I said. "Do you know if Nurse Wagner has had any other complaints against her during her tenure?"

"She hasn't, miss, not according to her file," the woman said. She was speaking slowly and deliberately, clearly scanning a few pages of text as she reported to me. "Over the summer, it went in her record that she served rather admirably during a triage situation, when a man had been gutted with a gaff hook at the fish market."

I knew exactly the incident—it had shaken Betty pretty badly, and she'd told me about it the night we first met Tally Blackstone. "That was only a few months ago."

"Just in June, that's correct. How did you know?"

"She mentioned it in her interview," I sputtered. "And she was still canned?"

"All I know is what's in the file, miss. What hospital did you say you were from?"

"Oh yes, well, thank you for your time." I hung up. "Doctor Mitchell, Doctor Mitchell. I don't like you one bit."

I slipped on my favorite dress, tied my shoes, and went down to dinner, ready to solve a murder.

★ ★ ★

Dinner was a terse and wordless affair, with every adult around the table as taut as a piano wire around a nogoodnik's neck. Just as Arnold was picking up the remnants of the roast, there was a knock at the door.

"Must be a neighbor," Mrs. Allen concluded. "I'll go get the door."

Before we could stop her, Evelyn Allen hustled to the front door and came back fuming.

"It was a delivery man, Buster. From across the bridge."

"Oh, what did he have for us?" Buster's nonchalance was not the answer to Evelyn's anger.

"I was under the impression that the bridge was out," she said. "And that we were unable to leave for our previous holiday engagements."

"Ah, it must be fixed, then," Buster replied. "I tell you, my dear, I had no idea."

"I would have thought the state would disperse a memorandum," Mr. Allen replied. "Wonderful news—we'll be able to see the family for the holiday after all."

"Yes, I think we should leave first thing in the morning," Evelyn agreed, checking her watch. "Let Buster regain some order after these deeply trying times."

"Oh, thank God," Hazel said. "I need to get out of here."

Richard shot her a look. Stanley laughed. "You still have me for Thanksgiving, Buster," Stanley said.

"Viviana, perhaps we should go share the good news with Monty," Tommy said. "And then come downstairs and help Arnold with the preparations for a large, a celebratory breakfast."

"Right-o," I said. My napkin was off my lap in a flash, and we were up the stairs like jackrabbits.

"Monty, they know the bridge is fixed," Tommy said, opening the door.

"Jesus, Tommy, knock, would ya?" Monty was sliding his legs into his slacks.

"Time is of the essence," Tommy said with a grin. "Besides, it's nothing Viv hasn't seen before."

"In the general sense, it isn't," Monty said, tucking in his shirt. "Specifically, I would prefer she didn't. But what gives? What can we do?"

"I don't know how to stop anyone from leaving," Tommy said. "Well, not legally. Got any ideas?"

"Drug 'em, for one," Monty said, holding up a finger.

"Not legal, first of all," Tommy said. "Also, I've had enough of that this week."

"Rapid inebriation?" Monty was focused on chemical warfare.

"Same thing as drugging 'em, but it's an easier option," I pointed out. "Many, if not all, would participate under their own volition."

"If one of us plays bartender with a heavy pour . . ." Monty shrugged.

"It's still morally the same thing as drugging them," I pointed out. "I wouldn't like it if it happened to me, despite our intentions of solving a crime."

"I think we can just ask Hazel to stay," Tommy pointed out.

"But I don't entirely suspect her," I said.

"But letting her leave would tell the others that we *do* suspect them," Tommy said.

"Fair point."

"Who *do* we suspect?" Monty asked.

I paused. "Just about everyone but you, Arnold, and Hazel, actually."

"She does have a motive," Tommy noted. "You said yourself it's always love, politics, or money, if you recall."

"My bet is on one of the two cheap-trick scientists," Monty said.

"The two that live here?"

"No, not the loud one. The one that was getting fresh with Viv and the one that broke that other girl's heart," Monty said.

"I don't think Stan drives," I said. "On account of his being nearly blind. I think he relies on Buster—er, Arnold—to get to and from the train station."

"Okay, so he's stuck too." Tommy was thinking.

"We can always sabotage the cars." It seemed pretty obvious to me, but no one else had said it yet.

"That is . . . significantly less criminal than Monty's suggestions, Viviana. And I don't think anyone is handy enough to fix things themselves," Tommy said. "Viviana, I doubt you've ever had the pleasure of being a grease monkey. Care to join me on a small adventure?"

"Of course, Tommy. I would be honored."

"You two are strange birds," Monty said. "And don't bother coming back to update me. Those pants aren't goin' back on tonight so long as I can help it."

I linked elbows with Tommy, and we went into the body of the house.

"How permanent do you think we should be?" Tommy asked. "'Goes back together with a few screws' or 'Oh, gee golly, we'll have to call a flatbed tow'?"

"Flat bed," I said. "Someone's a murderer, and the ones who aren't . . . well, Buster will pay for it."

"Then, we're away to the kitchen." Tommy was getting playful and it was starting to charm the pants off me too.

"You really love this, don't you?" I asked as we descended the stairs, still arm in arm like royalty.

"Well, I don't like it when people wake up dead at a party, but I do like knowing that I can get the guy who did it."

"Can the next case just be something easy? Theft, maybe? What about a nasty divorce? Find a man is dipping his pen in company ink and get his wife a great, big, fat alimony check."

"Oh, those are nice—I like those." Tommy led me through the living room to the kitchen, picked up the sugar dispenser from the coffee counter, and stopped. "I actually don't know how to get to the garage."

"Exit through that kitchen door, but take a right," Paloma piped up. He was entering from the dining room, looking—and smelling—a little inebriated. "Take the flagstone path as far as it'll go, and it'll lead you to the side door of the carriage house. It's unlocked."

"Thanks," Tommy said. "Numbing some pain?"

"Best medicine for it." Paloma sighed. "Just don't do the Packard, please. You know I didn't do it."

"The person who did could just . . . steal the Packard," I said. "It would negate all of our hard work."

"Fine." He pushed his way through to the living room. And presumably the bar.

"He's looking more and more guilty," I remarked.

"You know what will get your mind off it?"

"Sabotage?"

"Sabotage."

★ ★ ★

The path was still slippery with ice, and icicles from the roof were dripping down the back of my neck as we skated to the carriage house. "If I get knocked dead by one of those things, avenge me," Tommy said.

"Don't they only form when there's something the matter with the roof?" I asked.

"Yup. But you know there's a problem with the attic insulation already, after that lug locked you up in the rathole."

"Ugh, don't remind me," I shuddered. "I have bum taste in men, ol' Tommy boy."

"Oh, I don't know about that," Tommy said. "Just that the odds of getting a good one are pretty slim."

"You said it." We came to the door of the carriage house, and Tommy shoved it open. The garage was barely warmer than the outside, but at least there was no wind. Four gleaming cars sat lined up like sardines in a can. "So, what's the MO?"

"First, we start with the Lincoln," Tommy said. "That's Buster's."

"Which one's the Lincoln, and how do you know?"

"The big one at the far end, and because it looks the most expensive," Tommy said. "Grab that funnel on that wall."

I did as I was told and followed Tommy through the darkness. He pushed down a little flap on the curvy, rear bumper behind the driver's seat. It flipped up to reveal a silver circle. "Gas cap," Tommy said, unscrewing it.

"And?"

"Funnel." I handed it to him. He popped it into the stinking hole of the gas tank and poured in a hefty amount of sugar.

"Oh, that's awful," I said.

"So's killing someone. Next!"

"What is this? I love the color."

"Island-Green Dodge Wayfarer," Tommy said. "They call it a roadster—meant to go fast, nice and sporty."

"Whose do you think it is?"

"Hazel's, I'm sure. Costs an arm and a leg, and she likes to get noticed."

"We can fix the sugar?"

"*We* won't, but someone can. Come on, next is the Packard."

"It's white."

"It's *ivory*. I would've expected black but am pleasantly surprised. Judging by his style, Paloma may not be entirely hopeless—we just have to get him away from Buster. Or someone does. Time to twist, Viv."

"You're having fun, aren't you?"

"Well, this is the first time I haven't had a punch thrown in my mug on a case, so as long as no one gets hurt any further, I consider this a success. Any guesses as to what that last one is?"

"None. Never seen one before in my life."

"1950 Kaiser."

"Still never heard of it."

"Gotta belong to the Allens, though. Our poor, departed Chester Courtland appeared to be a neighbor, so he probably walked or was dropped off."

"That's probably what all the small bills were for," I pointed out. "Cabbed it wherever he needed to go. How did you and Monty get here?"

"I took the train—I know, I promised not to, but I couldn't help it—and then a cab. I didn't ask about Monty because one does not ask too many questions about Monty."

Tommy tipped the sugar bowl into the gas tank, clunking the bottom on the bumper to break up the last few lumps. "Alakazam. No one's goin' anywhere."

"That was quick and efficient. Now let's get inside and get warmed up."

The icicles were dripping, but not dropping, and I beat feet back into the warmth of the kitchen. Arnold was at the phone, and his voice was grave.

"Yes, we need an ambulance immediately," he said. He gave Buster's address and hung up the phone.

"Goddamn it, what now?" Tommy asked.

"Your friend, Montague," Arnold said breathlessly. "He was found at the bottom of the stairs."

"Is he alive?"

My stomach dropped to my ankles.

"Yes."

"Is he wearing his pants?"

"Yes?" Arnold was red at the ears.

"Thank goodness," Tommy said. "Show me the way."

"Tommy how can you joke like that?" I asked. I knew he had gallows humor, but that was too much.

"Honestly, not joking. He hates his war wounds," Tommy said. "He's missing huge, roping bits of his left leg, and half his ass."

"Good Lord."

"If he put his pants on, he was coming to find us. If he was still in his shorts, it would mean someone dragged him out of his room. Let's hope he's awake so he can tell us what he wanted to tell us, before the ambulance gets here."

Hazel, Paloma, and Mr. Allen were crouching next to Monty's head, trying to hold him still. Stanley was sitting on the stairs, his eyes closed. Mrs. Allen was at Monty's side, poking and prodding. Buster was still seated on his favorite sofa, sipping a drink and staring at the flames.

"Oh, how fascinating," Mrs. Allen muttered, pushing fabric against his thigh.

"Mrs. Allen—is he alright? Is he hurt?" I asked

"Extremely," she said.

"What can we do?" Tommy was staring at her with wide eyes, while Monty's were squeezed shut in pain.

"Wait for a doctor."

"What could you tell about the injury, poking his leg?" Tommy's eyes narrowed.

"Nothing," she said. "Something's broken, but I can't tell what or how badly without imaging. What's fascinating is his lack of musculature."

"I . . . don't think . . . my muscles . . . pushed . . . me . . . down . . . the . . . stairs." Monty was seething in both anger and pain, with spit coming through his teeth.

"Tell me—shrapnel? Bomb? I'm just curious." Evelyn's calm in the face of a medical emergency was remarkable but bordering on sociopathic.

"Gangrene."

"Oh, so you were in the Pacific!" She acted like she was discussing a vacation.

Monty's eyes popped open, and he stared at Evelyn Allen without breaking eye contact. "I was in the Philippines, you harpy. Maybe you heard of it. We had a little stroll through the jungle. It was so lovely, it made all the papers," he said, still gritting his teeth. His voice raised. "Whichever of you pushed me, it'll take more than that to kill me." He was hollering, and I couldn't blame him.

"I'm sure no one pushed you, Monty," Stanley said from the stairs.

"I felt two hands on my back and a shove. Someone damn well pushed me, nearly as soon as I was at the top of the stairs."

I hurdled over poor Monty on the floor, then ran up the stairs, two at a time, to Monty's bedroom. The door was flung wide open, and I could see the carnage from the hall. There was debris all over the floor, wooden splinters from the theremin's case embedded in the carpet, and a faint smell of smoke emanating from the torched instrument.

Whoever took out Monty had finally silenced Buster Beacon's ghost.

Every impulse in my body was telling me to frantically search the room for evidence, but I breathed in through my nose and counted to ten before slowly leaking the air back out through my mouth. My heart rate slowed, and I walked into Monty's bathroom. The white and fluffy towels that had previously been stacked on a shelf above the sink were all on the floor; the lid to the toilet tank was in the tub. Monty's entire Dopp kit was spilled in the sink, and the trash bin was overturned on the tiles.

Back into the main bedroom and my eyes finally turned away from the busted musical instrument in the middle of the floor. The desk in Monty's room had all six drawers askew, along with the drawer in each nightstand. I moved to the phone and picked up the receiver, circling the dial to get the operator.

"How may I help you?" asked the young voice on the other end.

"Yes, hello. Would you be able to tell me the last call that was made from this line?" I asked.

"If it was long distance," she affirmed.

"Great, just let me know what you can find. Maybe the last five?"

"Who, may I ask, is inquiring?"

"Uh . . . Mrs. Balthazar Beacon."

"Hold on."

There was silence on the end of the line for some time before the same young voice came back on. "One to an office in Hell's Kitchen, two to a boarding house in Chelsea, one to Hartford, and the last one was to the Weather Bureau," she said.

"Interesting."

"Someone wanted to know the weather, 'tis all." The operator was sounding impatient.

"But why not just listen to the radio?"

"Got me. Is there anything else I can help you with?"

"No, thank you. I've taken too much of your time." The grunt on the end of the line implied she agreed, and then I got a dial tone.

Leaving Monty's, I slipped into Tommy's and my room and found nothing disturbed—even the ring box for my bauble was sitting in the exact place I'd left it on my nightstand. It looked like someone was suspicious of another person in the house, but they'd managed to finger the gangster and not the private eyes.

At the top of the stairs, I caught a glimpse of Monty's gurney being rolled out the front door by two technicians all in white. I stopped four stairs from the bottom and cleared my throat.

"I think we should all go to bed," I said quietly. "It's been a terrible evening, and we should all just get some rest." I turned on my heel and ascended the stairs, Tommy following behind me with his hand at the small of my back.

"You're sure all the cars are disabled?" I whispered.

"I think I'll nip out once everyone's in bed and slash some tires, to be on the safe side."

"Good thinking."

"I guess I could take Monty's bed tonight," Tommy said as we made it to our hallway.

"Don't you dare," I responded, taking his hand. "Not with a damn murderer in the house."

As I got ready for bed, Tommy listened for a silent moment before stepping soundlessly into the hall. He was back in no time with a schmutz-smeared screwdriver he wiped off on a kitchen rag.

There would be more filth to clean up in the morning.

DAY 6

Tommy was out of the shower, and the hum of his shaver eventually woke me up. At least now that I knew what the noise was, my subconscious didn't have me hopping out of bed like a frog on a hotplate anymore.

"Rise and shine," he shouted as he left the bathroom. "The game is afoot."

"You're too excited about this," I said, rubbing sleep from my eyes. "Monty could've been killed."

"But he wasn't, so that's a point on our side," Tommy said. "He may not be walking, but he's definitely talking. Besides, I already called the hospital, and they said he'll be fine in a few months, and Buster said he'd write him a nice check for his troubles."

"That's kind of him."

"Kind or *too* kind, you think?" Tommy was musing as he pawed through a pile of clean and pressed shirts that had appeared overnight through the magic of Arnold. I didn't like the fact that he repeatedly slipped into my room unnoticed while I was sleeping, but Tommy didn't seem to have the same train of thought while he rummaged through the perfectly creased shirts. Even after my house had been broken into by a murderous gangster over the summer, I didn't lock my door at Mrs. K's boarding house. But one butler had me questioning my habits—and Arnold's role in the goings-on at Buster's house.

"Just nice," I said, tossing the idea around in my head. "I think the only way he's ever made friends is by buying them. Paloma was telling me that as soon as they met in college, Buster was flying him all around the world. Skiing in Europe and the USSR . . . maybe it was still Russia then, I don't know the ins and outs of that. I think Paloma feels somewhat indebted to him for all the presents."

"Glad that never happened to me, I guess," Tommy agreed. "I hate having debts. But that leaves me to make friends the hard way, with my good looks and personality."

"Oh God, you must be so lonely," I snorted, and Tommy flipped me the bird. "Did you get to ask Monty why he was leaving his room?"

"No, not yet—we'll have to try back," Tommy said. "They had to take him to surgery to fix his bones."

"Bones *plural*?"

"He's got no meat to protect 'em," Tommy explained. "Monty's in bad shape, but he's alive."

"Good grief." The thought of Monty being that injured for one of our cases weighed on me, even if it didn't seem to be weighing on Tommy. "What do you think he wanted to tell us?"

"It was something about all the electric doodads we've been dealing with, I'm sure," Tommy said.

"I wonder what he figured out that we haven't yet," I said. "So, when it comes to suspects, we're down to who?"

"Stanley Swansea, Richard Paloma, the double-Allens, and still Buster Beacon," Tommy said. "Buying people's affection might be his SOP, but it's still suspicious."

"Can we ascertain where everyone was last night at the time that Monty was pushed?"

"We can try, but courts can get a little iffy on spousal testimony," Tommy reminded me. "And if Stanley and Hazel are each other's alibis, then that's not going to hold up to scrutiny either."

"Even if they're on the outs?"

"Ins or outs, we can't trust them entirely," Tommy said. "Intimate relations complicate things."

"Then I hope Paloma doesn't have to come under any scrutiny," I said. "I had a drink in his room."

"While masquerading as another man's fiancée, no less," Tommy said. "No, we have to get this buttoned up tightly."

"Sorry if I jeopardized the case," I said, examining my cuticles. "I mostly just wanted information."

"You didn't hurt the case one bit," Tommy assured me. "Courts that expect all women to be nuns is the hurdle—not your behavior. Your behavior was fine."

"Speaking of behavior," I said, "I got a sneaking suspicion that I know why Betty was fired. Can I get your help once you're done doing what you have to do?"

Tommy came out of the bathroom, once again slapping on some Charter House. He looked handsome as all get-out, his eyes sparkling now that he was ready for action. "I thought you'd never ask."

"I'm gonna call up Madison Avenue Hospital and ask for a . . ." I consulted my notes by the phone. "A Doctor Mitchell. Seems he had something to do with Betty getting canned. You're going to pretend you're from Sloane and find out why. Capisce?"

"Consider it peeshed," Tommy said, sitting next to me on the bed. "What should my name be?"

"How about Doctor Fortuna?"

"Have some imagination, Dollface," Tommy scolded. "What about *Attraente*?"

"And if he speaks Italian, how is he going to like speaking to Doctor Handsome?" I asked.

"A man with the last name Mitchell doesn't speak Italian," Tommy huffed.

"Okay, well, it's your gamble." I dialed the operator and had her connect us to the Emergency Room at the hospital.

"Hello, this is Doctor Attraente," Tommy said into the receiver. "I'm doing interviews for candidates for an opening here at Sloane and I wanted to ask about a Miss . . ."

He put his hand over the receiver. "What the hell is her name, again?"

"Elizabeth Wagner."

"A Miss Elizabeth Wagner, who recently left your emergency room," Tommy said. "Her employment history is glowing, and we should be lucky to have her. I need to ask—why was she dismissed?"

Tommy listened to Doctor Mitchell drone on and on for a moment, and every so often his side of the conversation was peppered with a manly chuckle or a "don't I know it," which clued me in good and proper to the reason for Betty's dismissal. By the time he hung up the phone, I was fit to be tied.

"Tell me that wasn't what I think it was," I said.

"Well, if you figure that he put the moves on Betty, she declined—rather forcefully, I should say, as he needed stitches—and she got canned well, I can't help you, Dollface."

"Remind me to buy Betty a drink when we get home," I said. "How is that allowed? She's amazing at her job!"

"That's what this schmuck said," Tommy agreed. "But he was afraid she wasn't going to listen to him anymore so . . . away she had to go."

I sat with Doctor Mitchell's decision in silence, fiddling with the ring on my finger. "Of all the rotten things a fella could do to a girl . . ." I said, finally.

"This is bad, but it coulda been worse," Tommy said. "Plenty of men like Mitchell just take what they want anyhow."

"Any way we can avenge Betty?" I asked.

"Someone very smart once said, 'Living well is the best revenge,'" Tommy said. "I think that's the best avenue for Betty."

"That's the pits," I said.

"We can also anonymously mail him a dog turd," Tommy offered.

"Now you're talking!" I checked my watch. "Drats. I need a few minutes to gussy up, and then we have to go down to breakfast," I said. "Then we'll divide and conquer and finish up with these miserable people."

We started out in our usual pattern—helping Arnold in the kitchen while everyone else was behind the swinging door and away from the dirty work, waiting to be served.

"Good morning," the butler greeted us from his usual space at the stove, his face sallow and eyes rimmed by dark circles.

"Please tell me you get a vacation after this," I said, filling up the coffee urn.

"We shall see."

"Arnold, are you selling American scientific research to a foreign government?" Tommy picked up a piece of crisp bacon and snapped it in front of the help before munching on each of the halves.

"No." Arnold's face was calm and ready for interrogation, but he was stirring a pot of porridge and not looking up.

"I'll find out if you are." I've heard Tommy threaten a man at least once a day for a decade, and this wasn't that, which made me feel overwhelmingly relieved. Arnold was crooked and hiding something, but I couldn't help it—I liked him. I wanted him to be innocent. Or at least innocent of the murder of Chester Courtland and the international espionage happening under this very roof. I just hoped his crimes were something fun and a bit glamorous, like fixing pony races or contriving some complex money-laundering scheme. Something tough to prove in court.

"I assure you I am not."

"Look at me, man." Tommy wasn't fooling. Arnold looked up from the stove and held Tommy's gaze, still stirring the oatmeal as if he really was the greatest butler on God's green earth, and not whatever else he was being paid to be on the side. "I do not care what else you are doing, but if you are responsible for that man's death or Monty's maiming, I will report you to the proper authorities."

"I assure you, Mr. Fortuna, that is not my crime." Arnold banged the cooking spoon against the side of the pot, and wet, spattering bits of oatmeal hit with a sickening *thwack*.

"Then carry on, Mr. Arnold, the butler who may not be only a butler. Squeeze every penny from this bastard that you can, if that's your racket."

The servant acknowledged Tommy's absolution with a wry smile and carried his large silver serving dish into the dining room.

"What do you think he *is* doing?" I asked Tommy.

"Some government that's not ours put him here," Tommy said. "That's all I can figure."

"And we're gonna let him stay?"

"We don't have much say in the matter." Tommy shrugged. "Let's go get the good grub before everyone comes and sits down."

I grabbed my coffee service and moved into the dining room, where Buster Beacon and Hazel Olmsted were sitting next to one another, the tenseness between them utterly unspoken but utterly obvious. It would have been rude for Hazel to sit far away from her host, but no one could blame the girl for pinning the disastrous weekend on Buster's cavalier shoulders. Hazel's jaw was set so firmly, I was afraid her perfect pearly whites were going to crack. Stanley Swansea was at the opposite end of the table, ignoring his past lover and his host, all the while digging into his plate like the happiest, fattest pig at the trough. I wondered if he knew what usually happened to the fattest pig.

"Top of the morning!" I said cheerily, placing the coffee-pot next to Buster's elbow. He immediately snatched it up and poured only himself a cup before slamming the coffeepot back down. Hazel gaped. "Just to let everyone know, our dear friend Monty Bonito will be just fine." I was so bubbly someone was going to get the burps.

"That's wonderful news," Stanley said, getting up and bringing his own coffee cup and saucer to the pot. He filled his own and then, chivalrously, Hazel's, who ignored his entire existence before he moved back to his seat, slowly, his hip brushing against the back of everyone's chair for orientation. "Now, if anyone would like to tell me who Monty Bonito actually *is* and why he's at this house, I would be much obliged. He isn't one of Buster's crackpots. Buster's usuals might be strange, but at least they have manners."

"So how do you fit in?" I said with a grin. "Because you're one of the biggest assholes I've ever met."

I ought to have timed my barb a bit better; Hazel was finally sipping her hot coffee as I bantered with poor Stanley Swansea. She dribbled over the side of her porcelain cup, and the brew went spilling onto her plate.

"Sorry, honey—I'll just make you up another one," I said, sashaying behind Hazel and picking up her half-finished breakfast. "Same as usual?"

"Yes, please," Hazel responded, turning to look up at me. I gave her the slightest nod and knew immediately she was on my side.

"Your wish is my command." Arnold had already zipped in to take the plate from me, and I went to the buffet to pluck another dish from the gleaming stack and portion Hazel up some new eggs and toast.

"I'm not at liberty to tell you who Monty Bonito is," Tommy assured Stanley, cagily, "but he's here at my request."

"Keep your secrets," Stanley said to Tommy. "But before I forget, here's what I owe you for the camera." Stanley threw some greenbacks onto the floor, where Tommy didn't even glance at them. Hazel gasped.

"We have more news once the Allens get downstairs," I said to the room.

"And Richard?" It was Buster's voice that rang through the room. "He's late for breakfast."

"I suspect he went for a long walk," Tommy responded. "I checked his bedroom at six this morning, and no one was there."

"Surely he's got to be somewhere," Stanley responded. "Did you check the lab?"

"And the cellars and the attic and the boathouse," Tommy said. "His car is still in the garage, where it will stay with everyone else's."

"How's that?" Mr. Allen was now seated across from Hazel at the other hand of Buster Beacon. "Oh, is Miss Valentine finally dishing for everyone? I'll take a heaping pile of it all."

I hadn't planned on serving more than just poor, jilted Hazel, but it wasn't much to me if Mr. Allen expected eggs to appear in front of him. I dished out almost everything I could onto three plates—one for me, which I placed at the empty seat next to Mr. Allen; one for Tommy; and one for the only other innocent person in the house, who had spilled coffee in her bacon—and delivered them to the table before circling back for Mr. Allen's portions. All that was left was a crumb of egg and some hideously gluey oatmeal, which his plate and his wife's received, split down the middle. He looked crestfallen but stopped short of demanding someone fix him some fresh bacon. Mr. Allen eyed the crystal bell next to Buster's elbow, but Buster didn't ring for Arnold to whip up a new batch of breakfast for his investor.

"So where is Richard?" Hazel asked Buster.

"I assume he's taken to his heels and walked to the FBI safe house in Nyack," I said, weighing his options. "Or at the very least, walked to the bridge where a cab could meet him and take him to the FBI safe house in Nyack."

"I'm sorry, the what?" Mr. Allen seemed awake for the first time all week.

"The Federal Bureau of Investigations," Tommy explained very slowly. "It was created in the 1930s and is helmed by J. Edgar Hoover? I'm surprised you haven't heard of it, given your Washington connections."

"I have heard of the FBI, Mr. Fortuna." Mr. Allen was hot under the collar. "I just want to know why a man in my employ is in communication with them."

"Oh, I'm not aware of the specifics," I said quietly, reaching out to pat his hand. "But the general gist is that the mansion is bugged, and they've been listening in to the whole household for quite some time."

"And how would you know this, missy?" Mr. Allen wrenched his hand away from me, as if I was a rottweiler starting a snarl.

"My dearest Tommy, would you care to explain?" I batted my eyelashes at my boss.

"My name really is Tommy Fortuna and this really is Viviana Valentine, my partner. Together, we're New York City's premiere private investigators." Tommy flipped open his wallet to show his license, and the result was so smooth and so upsetting to Mr. Allen that I regretted that mine was in my wallet, which was in my handbag, upstairs, so I couldn't do the same. "Chester Courtland was an agent of the FBI, brought in by Richard Paloma, to pretend to be one of Buster Beacon's neighbors and spy on the entire household. Until he was poisoned some nights ago and left to die a horrific, painful death surrounded by strangers. He did not die of an accidental embolism. Chester Courtland was murdered by someone in this house."

The reaction, I would say, was mixed.

Hazel yelped, and her hand immediately covered her mouth, her eyes searching for mine for confirmation. I gave it when our eyes met, and she said nothing else. A woman of her breeding knew people with connections in the government, undoubtedly, and would know the seriousness of having an undercover investigator embedded in a household. Buster's face was ashen and grim, but he continued to calmly slice his sausages and eat breakfast. Stanley stood up and punched the table.

"Prove it," he snarled.

"Which part?" I asked sweetly. "I can go get my license too, if you'd like."

"The bit about Courtland, you *ridiculous* broad," he said. "Why should we believe a thing you say?"

"Oh, you shouldn't," I said, hopping up and giving Tommy's shoulder a squeeze. "I've been lying to you for nearly a whole week. I'm not a friend of Buster's, and you couldn't pay me to actually be one, but he is paying me to fake it. But I have plenty of proof of Chester Courtland's employment. I'll be right back."

As I maneuvered out of the dining room, I heard Stanley ask, "So she's not really your fiancée?"

"Oh no," Tommy responded. "But she really is something else, isn't she?"

Heading back into my bedroom, I found Chester Courtland's identification wedged between the toilet tank and the wall, exactly where Tommy—and the snoop that tore through poor Monty's belongings—had left it. I flipped the cracked, black leather back and forth on the way back to the dining room, the golden badge glinting in the weak, winter morning sun. For extra protection, just in case, I slipped my own ID into my brassiere. I hoped someone would ask to see it, just to see the look on Mrs. Allen's face when I slipped it out.

"Head's up!" I tossed Stanley the wallet over the dining room table, and Mrs. Allen, who was now seated nowhere near her husband and was tucking into her plate of cold gruel, flinched at my lack of decorum. Stanley couldn't see the billfold until it hit him in the chest and landed with a splash in his plate. "Sorry, my friend, I forgot about your eyes. Truly, my apologies."

"His eyes?" Hazel asked.

"Cooked through, thanks to his experiments," I explained. "Mrs. Allen told me about it. Horrible shame to be hurt by your own work that much. Cruel."

"Well, that's something," Hazel said. "At least now I know everything wasn't about my looks, just about my money after all."

"When did he start badgering you?" I asked her. "For cash, that is."

"Saturday," Hazel confirmed. "It was gentle at first, but it ramped up over the course of a day. His plans were changed once we all learned the bridge was out—I don't think he usually has to spend so much time with the girls he's bilking."

"Did you know about this?" I pointedly asked Buster. "That your friend was wooing and screwing the female houseguests?"

"I assumed they were providing money for Stanley out of their own free will," Buster explained. "It's hardly a crime to give gifts to a lover."

"That's a very loosey-goosey interpretation of that law," Tommy said. "Hazel, I'd be more than happy to walk you through the process of pressing charges against Stanley Swansea once we get back to our office in New York City. Free of charge."

"Oh, it was simply attempted extortion, Mr. Fortuna," Hazel said, glowing. "I didn't give him one red cent."

"Small miracles!" I said. "Good for you."

Arnold came swooping through the dining room with a fresh pot of coffee, and I turned to look at him. "Oh, Arnold, I don't suppose you have a running list of female houseguests who have been successfully swindled by Mr. Swansea here, would you?"

"Of course, madam, I can have it for you shortly, complete with telephone numbers and mailing addresses." He bowed a bit before exiting to the kitchen.

"Your butler is spying on me too?" Stanley demanded of Buster.

"What on earth makes you think he's a butler?" Buster asked.

"Is everyone here some kind of double agent?" Mr. Allen scoffed.

"Someone is a spy too." I shrugged. "But I'm not sure which one yet."

Arnold returned with a small sheet of paper and handed it to Tommy. "A short but meaningful list, Mr. Fortuna."

"Thank you, dear Arnold," Tommy said, folding the sheet and slipping it into his pants pocket.

"Oh! Stanley. This explains the little camera stunt!" I said.

"What does?" he asked. He blanched a little and looked down at the cascade of bills still sitting on the floor.

"Why Tommy's Polaroid went in the drink," I said. "If we ever got wind of your little dealings . . ."

"Or if Hazel soured on you . . ." Tommy added

"No one could go around to that little list o' girls there and make a positive identification," I said. "Or find out that he was steppin' out with another broad."

"The river of green is gonna dry up pretty soon, buddy boy," Tommy admitted. "It was an instant camera. I have a whole set of photos in our room upstairs."

Stanley let out an audible curse.

"Do you know it? It was invented in Boston," I said.

"Cambridge," Stanley corrected. "It was invented in *Cambridge.*"

"The only people who get touchy about that are the most high-falutin', eggheaded—"

"That's enough, Tommy," I said. "He's shaking in his boots—we don't have to gild the lily."

"Fine. Back to business. Arnold, if you'll be so kind, will you please guard the doors and keep every single person who is in this room, in this room?" Tommy asked.

"Miss Olmsted, if you could help him, we'd be much obliged," I agreed.

"Me?" she squeaked.

"Aside from me and Tommy," I explained, "you're the only other person here we're reasonably sure didn't kill off the local G-man. I don't think."

"I have no reason to kill anyone," she said.

"You said you were second in line to invest in Buster's research, however," I pointed out. "And if Courtland's clients—fake clients, I should add, because obviously, he wasn't here representing anyone—won the business instead, you'd be out a pretty penny."

"I have many avenues of investment open to me," Hazel demurred. "I don't put all my eggs in one basket, unlike Mr. Allen."

"Buster tried to serve you up on a platter, though," I mentioned. "He said Courtland was badgering you in the woods, and you took offense, and he heavy-handedly suggested violent offense, at that."

"If a dame took violent offense every time a man badgered her," Hazel said, "there would be no men left. Except maybe Tommy." She flashed ol' Tommy boy a smile, and he winked.

"Should we be so lucky," I said.

"Agreed," Hazel said. "But I believe all parties in this room would concur that I did not step away alone with any man other than Stanley. But if Stanley approached me at this point in time, I confess I would wring his little neck."

"Don't blame ya."

"And Arnold?" Stanley Swansea asked. "What makes you so sure he didn't murder this Courtland fella?"

"That's more of a hunch thing," Tommy explained.

"But he's the *butler*," Swansea yelled. "He could've slipped into the man's room and offed him at any time!"

"You're right," Tommy allowed, "but I tend to trust my hunches."

"You're insane," Stanley muttered. "Absolutely insane."

"So, Arnold—would you like anything to keep these jamokes in line? I don't have a pistol," I said.

Arnold cracked his knuckles. "That shouldn't be necessary."

"Hazel?"

"Oh, my, now that you mention it," she said with a purr, "I think Richard has a Louisville Slugger in his room—would you mind grabbing that?"

"Not at all," I said, and curtsied. I doubled up the stairs to Richard's room and noticed the wooden handle tucked into the corner behind his nightstand. Grabbing it, I took a moment to peep into his closet. Sure enough, his galoshes were gone, along with an overcoat. The man had fled in the night.

I delivered the stick to Hazel, whose hands smoothed the wood like an old pro's, and she caught me eyeing her. "Miss Porter's," she said. "Varsity. Center field."

"I like you more every day," Tommy declared, and turned to address Stanley, Edward, Evelyn, and Buster. "So, here's what's going to happen. You four are going to stay here, at the insistence of Arnold and Miss Olmsted. Viviana and I need some time."

"To do what?" Mrs. Allen asked.

"To look through all of your belongings." Tommy shrugged, and we edged out of the dining room as Hazel Olmsted whacked the end of her baseball bat into the palm of her hand.

"Oh, I really do like her," I said.

"Let's do her room first, then."

* ★ *

Tommy and I wound our way to the suite of rooms in the northeast corner of the house. Two gleaming wooden doors stood side by side, one leading to Hazel's room and the other to Stanley Swansea's. Peeking into the one on the left, it was clearly Hazel's, with the window curtains open and delicate pink luggage on stands next to the desk. The luggage was all empty, and she had unpacked fully into the chest of drawers and expansive closet. Her unmentionables were pure silk of varying soft shades; her pajamas were thick, utilitarian flannel. Though she had only initially been scheduled to stay at the house for three days, the closet held at least ten dresses, of varying levels of formality and slinkiness. Hazel was an adventurer, and a pair of muddy boots was lined up next to several pairs of pumps. In the bathroom, a small vase of flowers stood next to the toothbrush.

"Is someone sweet on Hazel?" I asked. "Not just jonesing for her money?"

"My guess is Paloma," Tommy said, "no matter how much he doth protest."

"Or it could be Arnold," I admitted. "He might be a crown prince back in Hungary, for all we know."

"Could be. So we should check every inch of this place for glaring evidence he may have missed in his daily, butlerish snoopings."

It took close to an hour to turn over every object in the room that wasn't nailed down, but no, Hazel Olmsted would leave this house with her reputation intact. Nothing in the room pointed to her being the one who did in Chester Courtland. But bank statements revealed that Stanley Swansea may have wanted to hang on for the long haul.

"Onward to Swansea," I muttered.

"I hope it's him too," Tommy admitted. "Imagine using your friend's friends as piggy banks. That's pretty low."

Stanley's room was pitch-black, so we pulled open the curtains for light. The layout of his quarters was a mirror of Hazel's, but every single item in his room was a shade of gray, black, or blue. None of his drawers were silk, I noted, but they were clean. Stanley had been planning on staying a week or more, and the contents of his trunks backed up the claims he'd made. Unfortunately, nothing in his room was more incriminating than his breakfast behavior.

"Rats," I said, kicking my toe into the corner of his traveling trunk. "But Dottie told me over the summer that even clearing someone of suspicion is forward momentum in a mystery."

"Does Dottie want a job?" Tommy asked. "That's very good advice. Should we check out Stan's lab?"

"Yeah, but it's just nuts and bolts."

"How would you know?" Tommy asked. "You haven't been in a science lab since freshman year biology."

"How would you know I was wrong?" I swung right back. "You haven't either."

"Good point, Dollface." We went to the unmarked door between Stanley and Hazel's bedroom suites and walked upstairs.

"Want to see a great party trick?" I asked, picking up the kalimba. Tommy was rooting through a metal box of small thingamajigs and doohickeys and didn't answer, so I plucked the tines. The TV across the room turned on to blaring static.

"Jesus, Mary, and Joseph," Tommy said, jumping out of his skin. I plucked the tines in the opposite direction, and the TV turned off.

"Stanley said you could hook this kind of thing up to almost anything," I said.

"What kind of thing?"

"The wires that cause the TV to listen and react to what it hears," I explained. "You just have to make them know what to do when they hear the right noises."

"What kind of noises?" Tommy asked, and I saw the glint in his eyes.

"Any kind of noises, now that you mention it. Even spooky, scary noises." A broad smile ran across my face. "You stay here and guard the lab. I'm going to run downstairs and grab Buster's and Arnold's keys. Then we're going to lock the doors, Buster's aversion to locks be damned."

I was there and back before Tommy could even say *boo.* "Did you find anything else while I was gone?" I asked.

"Just an absolutely *felonious* amount of marijuana," Tommy said, holding up a brick wrapped in plastic. "There's no way Arnold missed it, but I guess he's not here for trafficking. I think we can let it slide."

"Good grief. I wonder how much of his ill-gotten fortune was spent on grass?"

"More than his paramours would like to know, I'm sure. He sold them a bill that was probably all about sacrifice and king and country . . ." Tommy petered off.

"What?"

"I wonder if he had intent to sell? That sits different with the coppers. Anyway, I didn't find anything that looked related to the death of Chester Courtland," Tommy said. "Let's lock up and move on."

We moved methodically through the common spaces of the upstairs, into the Allens' guest rooms, where I showed Tommy the extra cupboard for luggage behind their expansive closet. It was fishy and unusual, but clean of evidence, so we moved on, circling back to check Stan and Hazel's rooms for the same feature and found it in both rooms, dusty and unused. Only the Allens seemed to know about the extra space built into the mansion's guest rooms.

"Buster did say that Edward funded much of the house's renovations," I said. "I wonder if the extra storage space was part of his plan, but it just slipped his mind to mention it to the other guests."

"Probably. Edward has a very slippery mind."

Our search took us to the public rooms of the house, through the library, the central living room, the solarium, the occupied dining room filled with sour-faced prisoners, and into the kitchen.

"While you're in there," Buster mused as Tommy pushed the swinging door open, "would you mind bringing us some lunch?"

The door swung shut behind me. "There's some bread in the pantry. I suppose ham sandwiches are enough?"

"Better be." Tommy was already in the fridge, pulling out condiments and giving everything a scrutinizing eye.

After a tense and quiet lunch—without poor Monty, there was no one to break the ice, though I'm sure the violently imposed house arrest also put a damper on the excitement—Tommy and I circled back to the kitchen.

"I hope we find *something* in here," I said. "I don't want to search the cellars. I've spent enough time in the dusty bowels of this house."

"Get the pantry, and I'll get the cabinets," Tommy instructed. "If you see anything tasty and expensive, eat it."

"You know, I might actually do it," I said. "I feel like I've walked six miles today just inside this goddamn house."

Thanks to Arnold being the most excellent plant-turned-butler-turned-heavy I had personally ever met, the pantry itself was orderly and clean. I started at the top and worked my way down—dried chanterelles, dried beans, jars of soup stock ready for winter, preserved peaches. Sacks of sugar and flour were waiting for eggs and baking soda, and beneath it all, a large basket of potatoes. I slid the basket away from the wall and heard a small, glassine *tink*.

"I need a flashlight!" I hollered at the top of my lungs. I immediately heard Tommy's thumping run out of the kitchen, and he was back and panting, with a torch from the upstairs credenza and a hand broom.

"What'd you find?"

"Something in a dark hole, and if it's a syringe laced with poison, I'm not just sticking my hand in there to find it," I explained. "Scoot back—I need more space to look."

I lay flat on the floor of the pantry and pressed my cheek into the tiles, grabbing the flashlight and swishing it to try to find what had made the tiny, barely perceptible noise. There wasn't a dust bunny in sight, and the light caught the metallic tip of the needle in no time flat.

"Don't worry—I'm being careful," I said, and I reached the sweeper under the shelving, all the way to the baseboard, squinting to focus on swatting the glass tube of the needle instead of the deadly end. It skittered out and Tommy handed me an empty jar, its previous contents of beans now scattered in a pile on a shelf. I urged the glass tube into the jar with the handle of the broom and sealed the lid.

"Nice way to avoid prints, Dollface."

"I suppose you could be neater about this, ol' Tommy boy," I said, eyeing the beans.

"The FBI will clean it up," Tommy said. "Who could've dumped this back here?"

"In actuality? Anyone. In reality, I have one good idea." I led him back into the main part of the kitchen.

"So, if you try to convince me that Hazel is actually an Italian spy or something, I'm going to think you're crazy," Tommy said.

"She isn't. I don't think Il Duce there sent girls to Miss Porter's in the mid-thirties," I said. "That's what Switzerland was for. No, Hazel is still in the clear. But you're on the right track."

The kitchen phone was jangling, and Tommy moved toward it. "Tell me after I get this," he said. "Beacon residence, how may I help you?" he spoke into the receiver.

For a man who'd had a secretary for about a decade, Tommy had decent phone manners.

"Hold on—let me get Viv on too," Tommy said, and bent the receiver away from his ear. "It's Paloma. Things are on the move."

NIGHT 6

"Hi, Richard, how's it going across the way?" I asked, curling the cord of the phone around my little finger.

"I'm no longer in Nyack," he replied cagily. "But I need you two to stay where you are. The FBI is coming to arrest Buster as soon as they get some paperwork squared away."

"It's not Buster, you fool," I said with slightly more certainty than I felt. "At the least, the syringe used to kill Courtland isn't his brand. He uses Lilly's, and this one is an . . ." I squinted at the label through the jar. "Injecta? That's what that says, right?"

Tommy nodded. "The smart thing woulda been to use one of his," he said.

"Maybe they came prepared?" I asked. Tommy's short nod was an agreement—this was likely premeditated. The thought sent a shiver down my spine.

"Okay, I'll tell the Feds about the needle, but that's not going to make a lick of difference," Richard shouted into the phone, growing angrier and angrier as he spoke. "It's Buster. It's always *been* Buster."

"What's their ETA, Richard?" Tommy barked. "How long do we have?"

"A few hours at least, Fortuna." Richard sounded furious. "They have to make sure all their *I*'s are dotted, I suppose. If he disappears before then, you'll be charged with something, I'm sure of it."

"Don't worry—he'll be here. But whether or not he's still your man, that's to be seen." Tommy slammed down the receiver and looked at me. "What now?"

"We need to check on the . . ." I stumbled. "Both 'hostages' and 'prisoners' sound terrible."

"Just call 'em suspects, Viv," Tommy said. "Takes some of the edge off."

"Then, the suspects it is. They probably have to go to the bathroom, anyway, and Arnold could use some extra muscle."

Edward Allen, Evelyn Allen, Stanley Swansea, and Buster Beacon had not moved from their spots at the table since the morning's breakfast. Hazel stood sentry at the door next to the kitchen, her Louisville Slugger still at hand but laid now on top of the cold and smelly chafing dishes that contained the remnants of breakfast.

Mr. Allen's eyes stormed with rage, for the first time unclouded by drink in the week that I'd known him. They were a beautiful shade of cornflower blue, and it broke my heart to see him fully lucid and at his strongest, even if he did look like he wanted to punch Tommy's lights out.

"Let me out of this fetid, stinking room!" He ran at Tommy like an outraged ram, but stopped before striking ol' Tommy boy, who was fit as a fiddle and close to forty years Edward's junior.

Tommy was, as they say, *nonplussed*. "If you think this is fetid and stinking, I would like to remind you that Montague Bonito, an innocent man who was recently maimed by someone in this *very* room, a person who had the intentions of ending his young life, spent six days marching through the jungles of the Philippines, losing half of his lower extremities to gangrene and infections that took eight months to fight off, nearly dying himself and watching countless of his fellow soldiers perish, for all of your freedom.

"And Chester Courtland, in service to the Federal Bureau of Investigation, himself a war hero who survived the bombing of Pearl Harbor almost exactly nine years ago to this very day, currently lies dead and forgotten in a rich man's boathouse, untended to and uncared for by nearly every single person in this room save the butler and the two private investigators who were hired to be here, and was murdered by the very Soviet spy he was sent here to uncover." Color was rising in Tommy's cheeks, and the color was draining out of Mr. Allen's. "The only person we have any desire to detain and try is the soulless, craven individual or individuals involved in the death and near-death of two of America's greatest heroes."

I took the time to study the wood grain of the dining room floor. I had the appearance of being reverent, but mostly I was trying not to laugh at Tommy's theatrics.

"And what we need from you now," Tommy said, his voice coming deep from within his chest for the full effect of the song-and-dance he was putting on, "is your full cooperation. If you are innocent, Viviana and I need your help. For our nation, for our future, for *justice*."

"That's a little much, isn't it?" Buster said through a laugh. He looked exhausted.

"It works on more people than you'd think," Tommy said with a shrug. "If they're less cynical."

"Making up a service history for a dead spook is rather cynical itself," Buster said. "Chester Courtland wasn't at Pearl Harbor, for crying out loud. He was never in the war. He's a lawyer—*was* a lawyer. Wouldn't know a battleship from a catamaran."

"And you only do because you collect boats, you high-falutin' bag of wind," I said. "But the worst part is, I need your help. Tommy, you stay here and make sure no one makes a scamper, but maybe let them take a piss. I need Buster for something."

"You gonna be okay, Dollface?"

"He can't hurt me," I said. "Not in any meaningful way."

"Holler if you need," Tommy said. "I'll send hard-hittin' Hazel to your rescue."

"Thank you much."

Buster got up from his chair at the head of the table, with a moan. "Do you mind if I check my blood sugar, first?" he asked. "We'll have to go to my quarters."

"Will you die if I say no?"

"I may not be very useful to you in a coma," he responded.

"I'm sorry, I should have made sure you were more comfortable."

"It's alright," Buster said. "You were invited here for something much less deadly. I realize you're playing from behind the totemic eight ball."

We marched up the plushily carpeted stairs slowly, and Buster meandered toward his bedroom. "If you'll excuse me," Buster said, stepping toward his washroom.

"Not out of my sight. You're still a suspect, Buster."

"Miss Viviana," he said, once again turning on that darned accent and stressing the vowels in my name, "I regret to be so uncouth, but I test my blood sugar via my urine. Surely . . ."

"Hon, if you think I haven't heard a man take a leak before . . ."

"I'll leave the door open."

"Thank you."

Buster went about his business, flushed, and sat quietly on the edge of the tub as he waited for his test to run its course. "It looks as though I need a small dose," he said. "Do you have a macabre interest in watching me take my medication?"

"Honestly, I do," I admitted, "if you don't mind."

"Not at all. I'll consider it part of public outreach on behalf of all diabetics."

Buster went to his refrigerator and pulled out the clear glass vials of liquid. "This is manufactured insulin," he said, shaking the bottle a bit. "Insulin is a chemical made by an organ in everyone's body called the pancreas, and it's essential in the breakdown and absorption of various sugars in food that are required by the bloodstream."

"And your guts don't make it anymore, correct?"

"Oversimplified, but correct." Buster pulled a syringe from the autoclave on his desk, plunged the needle into the top of the vial, flipped the whole apparatus over, and drew out a precise amount of liquid. He flipped the whole thing back over, drew out the needle, and plinked it a few times with his fingernail.

"Air bubbles. Deadly."

"Noted."

"I must admit, Viviana, I have been hesitant to inject myself with any of my medicine since you told me Courtland died of poison," he said, pulling the hem of his shirt up to reveal his midsection. He sank the metal tip of the needle into the fatty section on his hip with a wince. "Will someone have tainted my medication? Will this be my last day on earth?"

"Honestly, I hope not, Buster," I said as he drew out the needle and disassembled it, putting it back into the device that would clean it for his next use. "I think you're smart, and I think you have real honest-to-goodness friends who would miss you. And I also think that whoever has been stealing your work would still like to have you around."

"You make me sound so loved, Miss Viviana," Buster said, tucking in his shirt. "Now what do you need me for?"

"We're looking for something very specific somewhere in the house, but only you'll know it when you see it."

"I do love to be needed," Buster said. "Lead the way."

First stop was Stanley's laboratory.

"Look at everything," I instructed, "and assume it was being used for nefarious deeds."

Buster immediately sat down at Stanley's desk, and paged through the man's notes. "Some of this is just what he was working on at Princeton," Buster explained. "The microwaves that are robbing his eyesight."

"Those microwaves," I said, "they sound awful."

"They can be," Buster equivocated. "But we shall see."

"What else was he up to?" I asked, plinking at the kalimba. The TV turned on.

"Oh!" Buster seemed genuinely surprised. "That's rather delightful."

"Did you not know he was doing something with sound too?"

"I suppose once his eyesight began deteriorating, his brain went skipping over to sound. It's only natural."

"He called it 'ultrasound,'" I explained. "Aside from turning on and off the television, what else can it be used for?"

"Oh, the possibilities are endless," Buster said. "Certainly detection and ranging is practical, but even down to building and construction. Since different materials react differently to sound waves, you can perhaps tell whether there's an air crack in a building foundation. Certainly, that's how Evelyn's imaging experiments were working."

"Whose what now?" I asked.

"Evelyn. Brilliant woman," Buster explained. "Ever since she saw people blown to bits in the war and saw so many people get sick from X-ray radiation."

"But she knows what ultrasound is? Is that why she asked if Stanley was doing research in it, when she used the word 'too'?" I asked. "She meant in addition to *herself*."

"I'm sure she meant in addition to his microwaves," Buster said. "She doesn't like to let on how adept she is in the lab."

"It appears as if even her husband doesn't know," I pointed out.

"Edward has his own issues," Buster said. "Mustn't hold it against a man."

"I don't hold it against him exactly," I said. "But he isn't very nice to her."

"Yes, well," Buster said. "He loved his first wife deeply."

"What does she have to do with the way he treats Evelyn?"

"Now I tell this to you in the greatest, utmost secrecy," Buster started. "But Edward—in the throes of drink, I assure you, when he has no control over his mind or speech—has suggested on more than one occasion that Evelyn perhaps sped up Cordelia's condition."

"You mean he thinks his second wife offed his first wife."

"Again, if you wish to be so uncouth."

"Could she have?"

"Of course." Buster didn't mince his words. "She's a trained medical professional and brilliant beyond that."

"You sound like you respect her?"

"I do, very much," Buster agreed. "She is an impressive woman, a brilliant scientist, and a gentle soul underneath it all."

"Evelyn told me that she was interested in how to look at people's insides without X-rays," I said. "Can you do that with ultrasound?"

"There are people around the globe trying, of course." Buster was clearly pleased that only he was privy to Mrs. Allen's apparent genius. "I don't believe anyone's unlocked the secret yet, but it is theoretically possible."

"Are there people around the globe who would also pay handsomely for the ticket to the technology?"

"After the war, my dear, people will pay handsomely for anything."

"You're proof enough of that," I said to my host. "Let's go look at the Allens' stuff."

We traipsed to the Allens' suite of rooms, and I flung open the latch to their secret compartment of luggage.

"Oh, when they requested this, I couldn't fathom why," Buster said. "But it does keep their room so much neater and easier to walk around. Especially as Edward is here so frequently."

"I'm sure it makes it easier on Arnold too," I said. "It's hard to vacuum around piles of junk, I'll tell you. Here—lay all the trunks and stuff out on the bed. And the desk. Wherever it fits." I began a bucket brigade of boxes and suitcases to Buster, who placed them about the room.

"Now what?"

"We open them."

"This feels like an invasion of privacy," Buster said, scrunching his nose at the various toggles now staring at him expectantly.

"But your searching through my train case wasn't?"

He had no response to that.

"Someone in this house is a murderer," I said. "I don't care about any dirty laundry but that."

Buster went to the tall standing trunk in the corner. "They don't make them like this anymore, really," he said, rubbing a hand over the smooth leather at the edges. "Vuitton, from at least twenty years ago, you know."

"We're not assessing their choice of luggage—it's what's inside that counts." I flung open the top of another bag and found the main compartment empty. Feeling about the lining, there was nothing concealed, but I did want to take a knife and separate the canvas from the leather. However, I'd save the finality of destruction for if I came up empty-handed.

"Do you have any inkling of what we might be looking for?" Buster asked.

"It'll be electronic—that's all I know," I said. "Keep searching. Tommy and I took a gander at all of this stuff, but nothing jumped out at us. That's why I need you. You'll be able to see a few things I couldn't."

I went through four hat boxes, two train cases, and Mr. Allen's Dopp kit before Buster had finished with his first standing trunk, and I came up with nothing.

"There's one left in the closet," Buster said. "But by the weight of it, I believe someone packed a pallet of bricks. Give me a hand."

Together, it took us quite a bit of huffing and puffing to get Mr. Allen's travel desk out of the hidey-hole.

"Should a desk be this heavy?" I asked. "Does he correspond in clay tablets?"

"It shouldn't," Buster conceded. "But it's mightily locked."

"Even more suspicious," I pronounced. "Do you have a screwdriver in your lab?"

"Of course," Buster said. "I assure you, I'll be here when you get back. My absconding years are far behind me."

"If you're *not* here when I return, I will hunt you down!" I said cheerily, and I slipped up to Buster and Richard's lab, unlocked the dead bolts with his keys, fetched two screwdrivers and some wire, relocked the door, and was back to find Buster sitting exactly where I'd left him.

"I want this done as quickly as you do, I assure you."

"Thank you for that. Now, skootch aside. I think I can pick it rather than destroy it."

It took a bit of fiddling with the wire, but I managed to snap the locks open. Inside the pristine leather case was a box covered with lights and switches.

"Is this going to explode?"

"Not at all," Buster said, fishing out a power cord and popping the plug into a nearby socket. "It's a standard-issue radio with some extra baubles." He grimaced as the wires and lights stayed dead.

"Hold on a second." I stood up and exited to the main bedroom, returning to the closet with the Allens' pitch pipe. "How many different note combinations can there be with a three-tone pitch pipe?"

"Well, endless, it depends on how long the melody is," Buster said.

"Start with three notes."

"Then there are 27 different note combinations if you limit the melody to three notes," Buster said smugly. "It's basic multiplication."

"Let's start trying."

I put the tiny instrument to my mouth and began huffing, filling the room with the music of a half-hearted, low-talent subway busker. My cheeks were getting tired by the time I played the magic combo. The radio flicked on, and Buster's face lit up almost as bright as the lights.

"*Dobryy vecher, Vorobushek. Nemedlenno dolozhi, Vorobushek. Zakhodi, Zakhodi.*"

"Well, that isn't English," I said to Buster.

"No, Miss Valentine, it is not."

I reached past Buster Beacon and yanked the plug out of the wall, to a bright spark and a whiff of ozone.

"How far could that little boxy thing get a radio signal by its lonesome?" I asked.

"Well, it depends on weather conditions and geology and . . ." Buster began, but then caught me glaring at him. "Not very far, Miss Viviana, without an antenna."

"Is it using one of *your* antennae?" I asked. "If you have antennae in the lab?"

"No, all of our laboratory is switched off at the moment," Buster said. "I believe, for any sort of significant distance, it would be using an external relay antenna."

"And that is?"

"A thingie outside the house to make the signal bounce farther."

"Thank you." I popped the lid back on the radio and locked it up tight. "Help me lug this to Stan's lab. We'll keep the evidence against her there. There's a bit more space up there than in your pigsty."

If Buster was doing his fair share of the heavy lifting, I couldn't tell, and it took literally all my strength not to shout for Tommy to lend his biceps to help me get the overladen writing desk out the door, down the hall, around the bend, and up the stairs to Stanley Swansea's laboratory. I shoved Buster out of the room and locked the two Yale dead bolts behind me. With Buster's keys.

"Miss Valentine," he scolded. "How on God's green earth . . .?"

"You really shouldn't try to hide anything from a pickpocket," I said, staring at Buster down the length of my nose. "I heard them jangle when you gave yourself your shot."

"I do not like locked doors," Buster reminded me.

"Your own lab was locked up tight," I reminded him. "And I should tell you, I don't like filthy rats and liars."

"You seem to appreciate Monty Bonito," Buster said. "And your boss."

"Monty never once lied to me." I urged Buster down the stairs. "And Tommy's my partner, not my boss. Now let's go check on the dining room. Our spy has to know we're onto her by now."

I pushed on the swinging door, only to be greeted by Tommy, cursing and bleeding from the nose. "That didn't go as planned," he said. Stanley sat at the table, bewildered. Arnold and Hazel were nowhere to be found. Buster entered the room behind me, collapsed into his chair at the head of the table, and began to sob.

"Where are the guards?"

"Arnold is bringing Hazel back around in the kitchen and checking her for a concussion."

"What happened?"

"Well, Mr. Allen was fit to be tied and took a swing at me," Tommy said, sniffling. "We got into it a little, and during all the confusion, Mrs. Allen declared she had to use the facilities."

"That couldn't wait?"

"She claimed it couldn't, so I told Hazel to accompany her."

"And Hazel took the bat? To the bathroom?" I asked

"I would've," Tommy admitted. "Every person here is a suspect."

"I guess Arnold warned us that Mrs. Allen was hale and hearty, only with bad knees," I mused. "She wrestled the bat from Hazel?"

"She did," Tommy said. "She chose the moment of confusion with her husband rushing me to catch everyone off guard. Spirits were high."

"And defenses were low," I said, putting it all together.

"I do think poor Miss Olmstead let her guard down a bit too much around Mrs. Allen."

"Clearly," I said. "And the mister provided an excellent distraction. *Ouch.* Is she going to be okay?"

"Arnold called the hospital, and they're sending yet *another* ambulance," Tommy assured me. "Now the bigger question is: Where are the Allens?"

"They have to be here somewhere," I said. "I'm going to go get Arnold, so long as Hazel isn't on her last legs."

In the kitchen, I found Hazel drinking tea and holding an ice bag to the back of her head. "That bitch clocked me," she said, drooling a little.

"Is anything broken?"

"I don't think so," Hazel admitted. "In my defense, I *was* in the process of ducking and tackling her when she connected."

"You're some woman, Hazel Olmsted," I said. "But where's Arnold?"

"He went to the garage." Hazel hooked a thumb at the back door.

"Thanks." I beat feet out the utility door after the not-butler, and found him on his way back.

"Someone intelligently sabotaged all the vehicles," Arnold said as we made our way down the path and back toward the kitchen.

"Golly, who could that have been?" I asked, shrugging. "But where would they go after they saw the getaway cars were down and out?"

Buster was pushing past me now, hollering as he ran down the lawn. "Evelyn! Evelyn, my love. Don't!"

It was the unmistakable hum of an outboard motor on the wind. "Tommy!" I hollered at the top of my lungs, as if he'd be able to do anything we couldn't. "Tommy, come quick!"

Arnold and I were racing down the back lawn toward the river, and Tommy came thumping up behind us in no time flat. We were just in time to see a speedboat burst through the doors of the boathouse, cutting through the skim of ice on the frozen river. Two figures, silhouetted in the dark and standing together so closely, I couldn't tell who was at the helm, but in my gut, I knew who was in charge.

"Stop! You're going to freeze to death!" Buster shouted at the back of the retreating figure.

"Evelyn doesn't give a hoot, Buster," I said. "We need to call the police. And tell them to set up a cordon on the river."

"There may be no need," Tommy said, motioning toward the bridge to the north, over the river, coming East from Nyack. "The Feds will be here in a second. We'll let them know their spy is heading south on the Hudson, as fast as her engine will carry her toward the city."

"Someone called the weather bureau," I told the three men around me. "Wanted to make sure the skies were going to be clear for the trip."

"Well, if they're going south, we can call the Coast Guard," Buster said, tears still streaming down his face. "I have the number. I've had to call them once before."

DAY 7

Thursday, November 23, 1950

"Happy Thanksgiving," Tommy muttered as the anonymous Fed slipped some steel bracelets onto his wrists. A nearby cathedral bonged one AM. "Don't get 'em too tight. I don't want the mother-in-law seein' bruises at dinner tonight."

We had at least managed to make it back into the warm kitchen from the backyard before the entire Westchester Division of the Federal Bureau of Investigation was banging at the door. Arnold, still acting as butler for the time being, rushed to open the front door, and the cavalry ran in, not quite guns a-blazin' but at least ready to blaze. The feeling had just started pinging back into my fingers and toes when the Feds declared us under arrest and said we were going to be dragged back outside.

"You may not be seein' the mother-in-law for quite some time, pal," the Fed smirked.

"Don't get between this man and her mashed potatoes, sir," I said, as my own skin felt the sharp sting of cold metal. This wouldn't be the first time in my life some authority figures wished to ask me some questions, but it was my first time in handcuffs. I had to admit, I did not like the sensation.

Arnold was not quite as quick tongued—maybe his instructions were to keep silent until silence was no longer prudent—and accepted the cuffs without remark. Hazel was on a gurney, but attached to it now, her grin wicked as she flirted with the man in charge of her. She, unlike Arnold, had no compunction about blathering away.

"And then that bitch *hit me* with a *bat,*" she explained. "The woman you're looking for will have four fingernail scratches down the side of her face, though—I got her pretty good. You don't spend thirteen years at boarding school without learning how to scrap a little. Tommy and Viv were amazing. *They'll* tell you *everything.*"

"Feel better, Hazel," I said as I was walked past her bed. "I'll catch up with you as soon as we're clear of this whole mess."

"That's okay, Viv," Hazel said. "You're sweet, but I'd like to forget this entire weekend ever happened. Which I might, thanks to Mrs. Allen and her bat."

"Makes sense. Anyways," I said, craning to keep my head in the kitchen, "it was nice to meet you."

We were led through the dining room en route back to the front door, and the other men—Stanley Swansea and Buster Beacon—had already been removed from the premises.

"Can Viv at least get a goddamn coat?" Tommy asked. "It's midnight in November. She's going to freeze to death."

"The car is plenty warm," a voice from the crowd explained. And then we were shuffled through the remainder of the Beacon mansion and into a waiting sedan. It was far from the most pleasant car ride I've ever taken, but I'll give the Feds this—the car was so warm, I managed to conk out on Tommy's shoulder for at least half the ride.

★   ★   ★

We were shuffled into a two-story office building surrounded by a small parking lot, lit with sodium lamps. The only thing that made it look different from your basic suburban gas company headquarters was the fact that I could hear the hum of an electrified fence through the quiet night. The entrance was a heavy steel door, and the lobby was a room of worn cement floors and the scent of industrial cleaner. I guess the men in suits thought we weren't much of a threat, because we were left alone to sit on some cold metal chairs for what felt like hours, but in a windowless room with no clocks, and unable to see my wristwatch with my hands cuffed behind my back, it could've been only twenty minutes. No matter what, though, it was uncomfortable, and not even Tommy's mindless chatter could calm me down.

"Well, Viv, how much of this do we parlay to Mrs. K when we get you home?"

"As little as possible, please," I said. "Tally let on that she's fit to be tied about my employment, and I don't want to be kicked out of the house, right?"

"Don't worry about that," Tommy said. "Remember, I've always got your back."

Our treatment remained cold and standoffish until we managed to produce our licenses—Tommy's was found quite quickly in the wallet that the G-men collected upon our processing, but I needed my hands, and it took a fair amount of pleading and insinuation before the gents unlocked me and I could slip the piece of paper out from my undergarments. Tommy about fell over laughing as the older gent at the desk turned beet red and sputtered at taking the small slip of paper, holding it between his fingers like he was going to catch something from the surface.

"Well, perhaps dames could get a dress with pockets," I said, matter-of-factly. "Until then, we make do. If you want more paperwork than that, you'll have to find my purse at Mr. Beacon's house."

It took only a few minutes for the swarms of men in suits to check their databases and confirm that ol' Tommy boy and I were in fact licensed private investigators, and a few more minutes before we were settled in different—I wouldn't say more comfortable—chairs, with a hot cup of coffee each. Arnold was shuffled past us by a group of bleary-eyed, older men in noticeably more expensive suits.

"Like we said, we're fairly sure the butler did not do it," I said. "Where are they going with Arnold?"

"He's with The Org," the fresh-faced man said. "West Germany. Can you believe it?"

"Absolutely," I said back. "With my whole entire soul."

"I guess we weren't the only folk who wanted to take a gander at what was going on in that house," the desk Fed whispered. "We'll get you in a room soon. Clearly not with the top brass—they're with the butler—but someone."

"I'm fine with medium brass," Tommy said. "As long as I can get another cup of coffee."

★ ★ ★

The sun was coming up through the trees by the time we were presented to a group of nameless men sitting at the far end of a dusty wooden conference table.

"Names?"

"Viviana Viola Valentine."

"Tomasso Antonino Fortuna," Tommy said. "And you all are?"

"What's your business?"

"Private investigators." I hadn't slipped my license back into its hideaway since its last reveal, so Tommy and I just slid the paperwork across the table, where it was glanced at with raised brows.

"The girl too?"

"The girl too," I insisted. "Or do you not trust paperwork from the state of New York?"

"Story?"

"Viv, you start," Tommy said, taking another swig of coffee. "I'll fill in details if you forget any."

"Thanks, Tommy," I said. "To start, we were brought in last Friday evening by Balthazar Beacon, nicknamed Buster, to investigate what he called 'strange noises' at the estate. I feel like you probably already know this."

"Buster owns the joint," Tommy interjected.

"Actually, he doesn't," I said. "His family did once, but his research partner, Ricardo Paloma—who goes by Richard, now, although I'm not sure what his documents say—informed me that he, at some point, sold the estate back to the government and was allowed to set up shop there."

"So my taxes have been paying for that whole schtick?" Tommy goggled.

"Yeah, I thought it best not to tell you," I said, patting his hand. "Clearly, I was correct."

"I got a thirteen-year-old kid at the end of my block who lives in a box with his mom under an overpass, but the government pays for *that*." Tommy was livid.

"Not now, Tommy," I said. "I just wanted to inform the investigators, here, that I knew about Buster's arrangement with the government."

"Understood, Viv."

"No problem," I said, continuing. "He's friends with our secretary and thought we were just the folks to help him out with a problem."

"How would he know your secretary?" The only word for the Fed's look was *dubious*.

"Our secretary is worth at least twenty million dollars, I think," I said.

"Probably closer to fifty," Tommy added. "You forgot about her maternal trust fund."

A Fed sputtered on his coffee.

"Anyhow," I continued, "the first evening, I was introduced to fellow houseguests, including Miss Hazel Olmsted—who I hope is feeling better?"

A man at the end of the table nodded. "She'll be fine. The hospital reports a small concussion, but no fractures."

"Thank you," I said, then ticked the other houseguests off on my fingers: "Stanley Swansea, who is another scientist; Chester Courtland—God rest him; Edward Allen; and Evelyn Allen, who was introduced to me as his wife, and I gather actually is."

"They are legally wed, yes." Every man at the end of the table looked like he'd been directly copied from the man on his left and right. It was a whole lot of pale skin, high-and-tight haircuts, and starched collars digging into neck fat. They were all starting a collective sweat, to boot, as the sun finally started to trickle through the east-facing windows and heated up the room. The effect was not pleasant, especially on little sleep and less coffee.

"Also at the home was Ricardo Paloma, as mentioned, and myself and Tommy here."

"As well as an associate of mine, Montague Bonito," Tommy added. I hadn't mentioned Monty, but if Tommy thought him fit to mention, I guess Monty's beef would be with him.

"What would you need Bonito for?" another suit asked. I guess Monty, and his particular set of skills, was known to them.

"Monty has a way of getting into places where no one wants him," Tommy said. "It seemed like a good idea at the time to get him there before Viv and I could show up."

"I think he'd disagree with you on that point," another suit said. This one at least wore his wedding band. "He called here incredibly upset."

"Oh? What'd he say?" I asked.

"More four-letter words than I feel comfortable saying in front of a lady," one of the brass said in my direction, "but in between the shouting and the slurring—I think he's still on pain meds—I heard 'mountain' and 'signal.' And something about bats."

"Oh, he's a smart one," I said to Tommy. "I'll get to what he's talking about in a bit."

"I have no doubt," Tommy said, grinning. He turned to the Feds. "She's great, isn't she? I wish I'd thought to have her join me on cases ten years ago."

"The first night, there were cocktails in the main living room," I said. "And spirits were high. And expensive, by the way. You might want to audit Mr. Beacon. From what I gather, he spends a lot of taxpayer money on non-research items. I spoke with every guest, and all seemed fine, if not a little tight. During the night, we heard a loud noise and found Chester Courtland in his room, sick and injured. Within a day, a doctor, from some hospital in the city . . . I'm sure Arnold—is his name Arnold?"

"I can neither confirm nor deny his name," a Fed replied.

"Then the man I know as Arnold, rather, can give you the doctor's real name and information—if the doctor isn't also in cahoots with another country's government, I guess? I hadn't really considered that." I lost my train of thought. "The doctor told us Courtland had been poisoned, and tests revealed that it was a poison called curare. Which Richard Paloma informed me was well-known to be used by the Soviets."

"That's correct," someone confirmed.

"But he shouldn't have told you that," another man said.

"Well, it set us down the right path of investigation," Tommy said. "You can't do your job without all the details."

"The fact of the matter was, as you know, there was a spy in the house, someone working on behalf of the USSR," I said. "Paloma thought it to be Buster, but Tommy and I had our doubts. There are smart people coming and going out of that house, and it could've been any one of them."

"Well, now we know exactly which one it is," someone said.

"You're awfully confident," I declared.

"They always are, Viv," Tommy said. "I bet they think it's Mr. Allen."

The suits clammed up.

"Oh, boy." I laughed. "You can't be serious."

I was met with grim faces.

"Virtually everyone in that house had better means, motive, and opportunity than Mr. Allen," I said. "Good grief."

"Why don't you enlighten us, missy," some younger fella in the back spat out. "If you're so smart."

Tommy giggled, and I took a deep breath.

"Before I start," I said, "have one of your errand boys call all the DC hospitals and get the medical records for Mrs. Cordelia Allen."

"Why should we?"

"If you want to arrest the right person for treason, you will."

The oldest gentleman in the room snapped his fingers, and someone left out the door.

"Thank you. Now, obviously, I first had to take a glance at the butler," I rationalized. "For some reason that I couldn't figure out until we got here, Buster had a tendency to tease Arnold in German. The butler had an uncanny knack for slipping in and out of all of our rooms unnoticed—and could've easily gone into Chester Courtland's room to administer the shot of curare long before Courtland fell out of bed and made the racket that woke us all up."

"That's very classist of you to suggest the butler first," someone said from the back.

"Thanks, Mr. Marx," I said, rolling my eyes. "Arnold's a great butler, but I've never known service workers not to trash-talk their boss or spread rumors about the people they served to other peons like me. Arnold was way too tight-lipped with gossip and avoided pointed questions about certain people in the house. He was great at being a butler, but he was a *lousy* butler."

"I'll pass along the notes," one older man said, laughing, "just in case he gets another assignment like this."

"Oh, give the man a break and let him take a vacation first," I said. "He looks exhausted."

"He's been in far more compromising appointments than this, miss."

"I think you've certainly removed Miss Olmstead from your suspects list," I said, "given her head injury. But you should know—she had better motives than even Mr. Allen. Did you know she's . . . well, she's not a self-made millionaire—she started out with plenty of millions—but were you aware that she's a keen investor?"

"Of course we know that," someone scoffed from the back of the room. "We're the FBI. Anyone who makes that much off the markets gets a file."

"Ah, the promise of capitalism," I said. "Be a broad and do it well enough, and the state thinks you're cheating."

"I assure you, it's not just the women."

"That's hardly comforting," I said. "But Hazel was chatting with Mr. Courtland the night I got there, the night he was jabbed, and all the following day she was more concerned than anyone else for his well-being. Later, it was revealed to me that he'd tried to interview her in the woods while the guests went on a nature walk, and she took it to mean he was trying some funny business. Trying to get her alone for some hanky-panky."

"She thinks highly of herself, for a woman almost forty."

"Do shut up," Tommy said. "Whoever that was."

"She told me as Tommy was attending Courtland that she knew the whole house, up and down, and I'll tell you why that's meaningful in a bit," I said. "And I should also say that Courtland's cover was that he was representing potential investors in Buster's private work, and apparently Hazel had been promised—verbally, I think, not in writing—that if Mr. Allen ever pulled his funding, she would be next in line."

"She would've seen Courtland as competition?"

"Stiff competition at that," I said. "Apparently, he made quite the story about his investors. But I took a peek at her bank statements and had a little chat with her about her money strategies. I think she was already souring on Buster and his trustworthiness and didn't have the heart to tell her friend that she was rescinding her offer, even if he had no opportunity to take it."

"And speaking of friends," Tommy added, "Buster knew how to collect some of the worst ones. Who are we going to talk about first—Stan or Richard?"

"Ugh, *Stan*." I recoiled. "I feel bad about his eyes, but what a schmuck."

"His eyes?"

"Ruined them with his experiments," I said. "Be careful of microwaves, if you ever have to be around them or if eggheads like Stan ever find a practical use for them. They cooked his eyeballs! He's nearly blind."

"We thought for a moment maybe that's why poor Courtland was jabbed in the ass," Tommy said. "It's a pretty big target, easy to hit, even for someone with failing eyesight."

"Stan is very canny," I said. "He managed to see through Tommy at some point and knocked Tommy's camera into the drink during a boat ride. He's got a criminal's mind, but most of his crimes appeared to be crimes of love rather than passion."

"We'll keep names out of it for right now," Tommy said, "but as greedy as Swansea is, and as jealous as he was of Buster's outside funding, he seemed to find a way to his own river of dough. He was seducing some of Buster's finer houseguests and requesting monetary gifts from his lovers."

"Though to be fair, I think he had his sights ultimately set on Buster's income," I said. "Paloma said that if anything happened to Buster, both he and Swansea would be in line to take over the governmental work, and presumably, the Allens wouldn't change horses midstream on their privately funded research."

"That certainly is a motive," someone muttered while fountain pens scratched against notebooks.

"Sure, but both Swansea and Paloma are not men of action," I said. "But my god, did Paloma like to ski! Do you know how many times he mentioned skiing? Insufferable."

"What does that have to do with this?"

"At least three of the ski resorts he mentioned were in the USSR," I said. "And I don't mean to be uncouth, but he was born in Cuba, and from what I've read in the news, some people down there are really cheesed off at Batista."

"That's a polite way to say it," the man in charge said with a smile.

"I don't want to raise suspicions just based on where a man was born and where he vacations, sirs," I said, "but I do have to admit, he was acting very fishy. He said that when we all heard the noise that woke us up—that ended up being Mr. Courtland falling and getting hurt because he was poisoned—he thought it was a gunshot and went to scram."

"It didn't sound like a gunshot," Tommy said. "But I suppose if you're waiting to hear a man get knocked off, any noise will make you jump."

"And speaking of noises," I said, "we have to get around to Buster, who called us in."

"What, exactly, did he say to you to get you to show up?"

"The dollar amount or . . .?" Tommy asked.

"He said there were 'woo-woo creaks and ghastly sounds,'" I said. "And that we had to get there as soon as possible. To be honest with you, he must not have correlated the theremin to the espionage."

"The what?"

"It's an electronic instrument," I said. "Named after the man who invented it."

"It's louder than the dickens, and if it's not played by someone with perfect pitch, then it sounds like two cats drowning," Tommy added.

"And I'll tell you what—it was the source of all of Mr. Beacon's ghastly sounds," I said. "I guarantee it. Too bad it's now in pieces on the floor of the room Monty Bonito was staying in at Buster's, or I'd show you how to play it."

"Don't you just press keys or blow into it?"

"Not even slightly," I said. "It has an electronic field you move your hands in and out of, and the position of your hands tells it what squawk to squeak."

"You're joking."

"It looks like magic, but I gather it's mostly just electronic science," I said. "Too bad Buster didn't figure out why the theremin was there or why anyone was playing it."

"Enlighten us, Miss Valentine."

"Happily," I said, straightening up. "The process of spying was multifaceted and used all the latest technologies, as you would expect. How much do you all know about ultrasound remote control?"

The men stared at me like they were dead fish.

"Mr. Stanley Swansea can explain all the technical mumbo-jumbo, but it's not like you'd understand any of it . . ." I said. "But long story short, people have figured out how to wire electronic devices to, I guess, hear certain noises and behave in certain ways. Stan showed me how to turn on a television just using a little kalim—um, a thumb pianny."

"Interesting."

"I tell you, it was very interesting," I said. "He said you have to use something that makes a consistent tone—the same sound, over and over again—or else the circuits won't know what they're listening to."

"So, Swansea was involved in this?"

"Not at all," I said. "When I told Mrs. Allen about Stan's electronics, she asked if he was working in ultrasound 'too.' I took that to mean that he was working in ultrasound in addition to his microwaves, but I think she meant that she was *also* working in ultrasound, or knew what it was and how it worked."

"Perhaps her husband spoke of it?"

"If you want to be pigheaded, sure," I said. "But I'm telling you—Mr. Allen really wrote off Mr. Swansea, but perhaps that's because Swansea was having a lark with Miss Olmstead, and Mr. Allen harbored a bit of a crush on her."

"He's old enough to be her grandfather!" someone scoffed.

"When has that ever stopped an old dog before?" Tommy pointed out.

"I think the first purpose of the theremin at Buster's was to serve as the sonic control for a spy radio," I said. "The inventor of the instrument was himself a Soviet and was returned to the country in the 1930s. I'll bet they have him working on all sorts of fun gadgets for the KGB."

"You mentioned this theremin was difficult to play?"

"It is," I agreed. "I tried it myself when we found it. But there was a pitch pipe in the Allens' guest suite. I think that Mrs. Allen had a pretty good ear and was very good at correcting her pitch. She had very steady hands, nurse's hands, and probably took to the instrument well."

"And this radio she was controlling," a man laughed. "Tell me about *that*."

"Can do!" I normally needed at least three more cups of coffee in my bloodstream to get going, but proving these men wrong was starting to be quite the picker-upper. "That's hidden in a portable writing desk that I found in a hidden closet in the Allens' suite. I locked it in Stan's lab to be safe, but you should find it there."

"That's an awfully small radio," someone said.

"None of you fellas saw an SCR-300 in the war?" Tommy asked, to some murmuring. "That thing would fit in a backpack."

"But I'll tell you it's awfully heavy," I said. "I practically lugged it up the stairs myself. Someone with enough motivation could bring it anywhere in the house—including all the secret passageways in and around the lab."

"You're joking," a young 'un in the back said. "Secret passageways?"

"I explored at least two of them myself," I said.

"And Monty and I went through the rest of 'em," Tommy added. "That house is like Swiss cheese. With a radio in the right place—especially one you can control from anywhere in the house—you could spy on anyone and everyone. And all the scientific goings-on."

"Mr. Allen was adamant, time and time again, that he'd put in a huge amount of money on renovations to the house," I said. "But it was drafty, filled with mice, and the basement hadn't seen a living soul for ages. So where did the money go?"

"To back alleys and all sorts of hideaways his wife asked for," Tommy chimed in.

"Exactly," I said. "That laboratory was a basic room—nothing flashy. She probably had all sorts of sneaky secrets in that house, to hide her spy technology."

"Didn't Arnold say something about liniment?" Tommy asked.

"You're right!" I snapped my fingers. "After I crawled through the passageway in the Allens' closet where I found the theremin, my knees were barking. Arnold said that Evelyn was hale and hearty—except she sometimes asked for something for her arthritic knees."

"Spy technology that was in a writing desk," a suit scoffed back, with no inflection in his voice. "We're supposed to believe that?"

"Who is going to investigate a travel writing desk?" I asked. "It blends in everywhere, especially when you have frequent guests with professional jobs."

"So who do you think our spy was broadcasting to?" someone asked. "*We* know, but who do you think?"

"Well, when I flicked it on . . ."

"You did *what?*"

"I turned it on!" I said. "How else was I to know what it did? And I've played enough poker with my Ukrainian landlady and her son to know when I hear a language that ain't English."

"Did you speak with the person on the other end of that radio, Miss Valentine?" a man asked while leaning forward.

"Absolutely not," I admitted. "I pulled the plug on it ASAP. But I should tell you—the reason Monty Bonito called from his hospital bed. If you send another young fella up to the top of Hook Mountain, you'll find a relay antenna."

"Did Monty Bonito plant a relay antenna at the top of Hook Mountain?"

"No, Jesus—aren't you listening?" I said. "Monty knows it's up there because he knows about bats."

"Pardon me?"

"He says they find skeeters to eat by sound," I said. "And that has something to do with radar and bouncing sound. I don't know—I didn't think I liked bats until Monty started talkin' about them. But *Mrs. Allen* put the antenna there. When she arrived at Buster's on Friday, she insisted on going for a hike, and only she and her husband made it to the top. It's the tallest peak around for miles, and unless you've got a secret Soviet cell in Poughkeepsie you don't know about, she needed an antenna all the way up there to get her signal out to where it needs to be."

"So far, Miss Valentine, you haven't given us a single reason as to why the spy is Evelyn and not Edward Allen," someone spoke up.

"Would it matter that she was having a relationship with Buster Beacon?" I asked.

"I find that very unlikely," someone scoffed.

"Well, when she got away on his speedboat, he did shout after her, 'Evelyn, my love,'" Tommy said.

"In addition to that, she was giving him expensive presents," I said. "The sailboat—named after the lovelorn main character from a book by Evelyn Waugh."

"Wait, so you've read *Brideshead*?" Tommy asked.

"Of course," I admitted. "I had only just ever read the author's name, never heard it said out loud before. And forgive me for not connecting the dots right away on *Captain Ryder*. It happens."

"Well, I'm sorry I teased you then," Tommy said.

"No problem," I said. "But I think you'll find when you go snooping that Mrs. Allen was neck deep in you-know-what. She was keeping international correspondence that she told me had nothing to do with her husband—while she was snitching all of Buster's airmail stamps."

"Don't forget," Tommy chimed in, "she was adamant that Courtland likely died of an embolism, and nothing else. Do you know how many people die of bone marrow dislodging every year?"

"No, how many?" I asked.

"No idea," Tommy admitted. "But it can't be a lot. That seems pretty far-fetched to me. But she was so insistent, it got all my hackles up."

Tommy talking about his hackles must've made me jumpy, because I was on edge when I saw that the young buck who had been sent to ask around about Cordelia Allen had slipped back into the room.

"What'd you find?" the senior agent barked.

The younger man whispered into the room.

"Speak up, speak up!" the older man shouted. "Everyone in the room can hear whatever it is you have to say."

"The notes made me think of something specific," the boy started. "Nerve twitching, hair loss, and extreme pain in her feet."

"They thought that was cancer?" I asked. "Cancer of what—the soles of her feet?"

"You're right, Miss Valentine," the boy returned. "I called up the lab at headquarters and they suggested—

"Thallium," the man in charge said before staring me right in the eyes. "They call it the poisoner's poison."

"I just wonder when she stuck him," Tommy mused.

"Probably when she spilled her drink on him," I said, Courtland's small yelp now ringing in my head. "Buster did something ostentatious, and the next thing I saw, Courtland was doused. I'll bet she distracted him with the ice-cold drink and jabbed him at the same time. Old nurse's trick, distracting people from pain."

"And what? She just pocketed the syringe?" Tommy asked. "Risky."

"She dropped the murder weapon in the pantry as soon as she could," I said. "When I got her and Hazel in there to discuss Thanksgiving. She was probably trying to frame Arnold. He may have been made."

The suggestion hung heavy in the air for several minutes as the men all stared at their hands.

"Not to harp on this," I said, piping up, "but I also think that Mrs. Allen was using the theremin to communicate in some kind of code—she had blank pages for sheet music all over her desk in her room, and I bet if you set your best code breakers on it, you'd find out she wasn't composing hymns on the side. She was writing code, but with music."

"That's pretty advanced stuff right there, Miss Valentine," someone informed me.

"I'm sure that all the technology is related to whatever Buster and Richard were doing in that laboratory," I said. "Why don't you figure it out by listening to your bugs? The microphones you have hidden in Buster's lab?"

The room fell dead silent. "What bugs?"

Two Days Later . . .

Saturday, November 24, 1950

The poor taxi cab driver at the curb looked like he was going to burst into tears as he lifted the last hat box off the snowy sidewalk—the only square inches of his cab left free of baggage were the few square inches where his fare, and his own keister, were going to sit.

Tally stuck her head out of the front door and shouted. "Just leave it on the curb! I'll hold it in my lap—it's okay!"

The cabbie put the box down gingerly and waved his cap to salute that he understood. He shut the back-seat door and retreated to the warmth of his ride, undoubtedly with the meter running. He didn't know it yet, but not only was the fare to the airport worth all his trouble in the cold and snow, but his passenger was the heaviest tipper south of 81st Street.

"That's the *second* fella in one of your cases," Tally said quickly. "The *second* one that tried to get one over on you."

"And Tommy too, don't forget," I said. "They found Paloma fast—he didn't have a vehicle. They found him at a Greyhound station outside of Oneonta."

"Was he also having an affair with Mrs. Allen?"

"No! If you can believe it," I said. "Mr. Allen was paying him off under the table."

"You're kidding!" Tally gasped.

"You're right, I am," I admitted. "He and Mrs. Allen maybe weren't an item, but she was having him steal work from the laboratory for her. Every single file, every single note. He was passing straight on to her. Maybe he thought it was business. He'll have to say that under oath."

"Was it *Mrs. Allen* who told him there were bugs in the lab?"

"She did, indirectly," I said. "She was the one sending him transcripts of what was said up there. He only talked about business, business, business, but she was manipulating Paloma by telling him what Buster said behind his back. He was losing his marbles."

"Poor guy," Tally said. "Buster really put him in a sore spot."

"Buster selling the government's cast-offs to the Allens is what started this whole mess," I admitted. "Whatever chum Buster threw in the waters to get investors . . . it attracted the worst sharks. He had the government contract, but that wasn't good enough, and instead he got in bed with a spy and her loaded husband."

"He's not going to fare too well at trial," Tally said. "He has no idea how to act in situations where he isn't in charge."

"Let's just hope his lawyers can help him."

"Did Buster and Richard know she worked for the Reds?" Tally asked.

"They say they don't," I assured her. "Buster himself was a pretty big snoop—maybe he was being willfully blind. Oh!"

"What?"

"Come to think of it, Buster called Mr. Courtland an agent before I told him that Courtland worked for the government."

"That doesn't mean that Buster killed him," Tally said with a sniffle.

"No, it doesn't," I admitted. "I am still fairly certain it was Mrs. Allen who tossed the needle in the spuds—they'll run fingerprints to be sure. But it does tell me he knew an awful lot about everyone in his house. He knew the butler worked for the West Germans too."

"Did you tell the FBI all this?" Tally asked.

"Not yet," I admitted. "*If* Buster and Paloma can prove that they had no idea about Mrs. Allen—and they may be able to because Tommy and I *will* say on the stand that they didn't know about the theremin or the radio, because the noises were why Buster called us up there in the first place—then maybe the jury will go easy on them."

"Awful. Just awful."

"I've seen Tommy get messed up in some pretty heartbreaking situations over the years," I said. "But never before have I seen two men be threatened with the firing squad for selling out the country."

"Is there any way to save their lives?" Tally asked.

"Maybe they can spy too," I said. "They certainly know more about science than any people I've ever met."

"Welcome to 1950," Tally said. "It's a great, big, strange world."

"And you're about to see a lot more of it, honey. I want you to know I'm proud of you," I said, giving Tally a squeeze. She lingered at the front door.

"I was afraid you were going to be furious with me," she said. "You just got me this job two months ago."

"Yeah, but you're much better suited for another line of work," I pointed out. "You're going to be a producer?"

"Or a writer or something—not sure if it's been defined quite yet. After I met with *ma mère*'s friends," Tally explained, "they thought I had a good head on my shoulders and might just be the right person to tell them what kids today want in motion pictures."

"That's a lot of responsibility."

"You're telling me. I was so worried—every night I was in Dottie's room, fretting, making myself sick. But she was so supportive, told me you'd understand."

"She's right. Did she also tell you it's going to be a lot of work?"

"Yes, and she also said that it's going to be very expensive, but if I learned anything from *mon père*, it's that if you're paying the bill, they can't tell you 'no.'" Tally was fairly used to being able to pay her way into what she wanted, and that kind of treatment was much more comfortable territory than brewing coffee and opening the mail for a couple of working stiffs in a mouse-riddled office in the heart of Hell's Kitchen.

"Got any ideas in mind? What kind of pictures you want to see made?"

"Oh, all sorts," Tally said, her eyes growing wide. "What if we moved away from flashy song-and-dance shows and pirate movies? Imagine if they treated kids my age like people with real problems."

"Considering what you've been through in the last six months, I hope they start treating people your age with some respect," I told her. Tally had singlehandedly contributed to a gray hair I spotted at my temple that morning, but that didn't mean she didn't have grief of her own.

"Yeah, this decade is going to begin the era of the teenager— I can feel it." Tally started toying with the clasp on her bag. "But first on my to-do list is to talk to kids who had a more normal life than mine."

"Tally, what on earth are you saying?" I asked, laughing. "The granddaughter of two millionaires who never went to high school—let alone a *public* high school—doesn't know what regular kids like?"

"We're all the same, Viv," Tally said with a smile. "We hate our parents and would rather spend time kissing than learning about the Revolutionary War."

"Oh, I almost forgot." I fished a box out of my cardigan pocket and tossed it to her. "I should give this back to you." It felt strange seeing the diamond I'd worn for a week heading back to its rightful owner. "Sell it, if it's real, I guess. You could use as much capital as you can get out there in the City of Angels."

Tally flicked open the box with her thumb. "This isn't mine," she said, snapping the ring box shut and handing it back.

"It's the dummy I wore at Buster's," I explained. "Mrs. Allen wouldn't give the other girl the time of day, but me? The diamond opened her right up. For a traitorous spy, she sure was old-fashioned."

"Well, I'm glad to hear it helped, but I would recognize a two-carat Tiffany setting," Tally said. "I'm telling you, Viv—this isn't one of mine."

"Tommy brought it up with him on Friday night," I explained, trying to jog her memory. "It was only like a week ago."

"Then maybe you should ask Tommy about it, Viv." Tally blushed before resuming to dig in her purse. "I almost forgot." It was her turn to toss something through Mrs. K's foyer. A set of silver keys flew at my head. I snatched them out of the air before they collided with my nose.

"To the office?"

"The office, here, and the Caddy," she said. "I'll get that Porsche I always wanted once I'm in Los Angeles."

"That's too much," I said. "I can't take a four-thousand-dollar car."

"Sure you can." She shrugged. "The signed paperwork is on my desk at Tommy's. Along with the receipt from Mrs. K."

"What receipt?"

"Your room and my room through the end of 1951, you silly. You can stay in the room—or, I guess, rooms—upstairs for the next year, on me. Keep a window."

"You're too much, Tally." I hugged the keys close to my chest as a memento of one of the best friends I'd ever had, even if she was a rich goofball who'd flown in and out of my life in less than six months.

"And don't forget it." The heiress stooped to leave a peck on my cheek. "I'm just a phone call away, Dollface."

"Since when did you ever pick up the phone?"

Tally let out a cackle and closed the door behind her. Through the streaky and foggy glass of Mrs. K's front door, I watched my friend and secretary skip down the stoop, pluck up her hatbox, and slide into the back seat of her waiting cab. The bright yellow sedan slid away from the curb, turned left, and was on its way to Idlewild.

"Our Girl Friday off to greener pastures?" Tommy emerged from the dining room, eating a plate of Thanksgiving leftovers Mrs. K had heated up for him at her own insistence. Tommy looked happier than a pig in mud, cozy warm in his gray flannel slacks and a maroon sweater with leather patches on the elbows.

"She is indeed. And look." I jangled my keys. "She left me her car."

"Have you ever driven before in your life?"

"Nope, never once. Actually, the first time I was in the Caddy I almost upchucked everywhere."

"*Vaffanculo,*" Tommy groaned. "Even when she's gone she's going to be the death of me."

"You don't have to teach me to drive in the city," I said. "We could drive out to the country. Teach me on a dirt road where I can't hit anything. I've never been to Connecticut, and I hear it's just lovely."

"There's plenty to hit in Connecticut. It's nothing but trees," Tommy said, sitting on Mrs. K's stairs and putting his empty plate aside. "And besides, I thought you hated the country."

"Maybe I just hated being in the country with *that* lot." I scooted over to Tommy and sat in his lap, leaning my head on his shoulder and leaning up to kiss the underside of his jaw. "It's all in the company you keep, I think. But, ol' Tommy boy, I see we find ourselves without a secretary again."

"Oh, I don't know about that," Tommy said. "Betty sounds like she needs a job."

"She didn't do half bad," I agreed. "Should we ask?"

"Sure, why not?"

I leaned back on Tommy's lap and hollered up the stairs. "Hey, Betty! Get your butt down here!"

My housemate popped her head out of her room and skipped down the stairs. "Hey, Viv. Hey, Mr. Fortuna."

"Call me Tommy," he said. "It's been years, for Christ's sake."

"Okay, Tommy."

"Betty, why didn't you tell us you got canned because you stood up for yourself to some piece-of-garbage doctor?" I asked, and Betty blanched.

"Viv! You went snooping on me?"

"Old habits, etcetera, etcetera," I said. "Sorry, honey, but I just couldn't let that slide."

"Oh no. What did you two *do*?" she asked.

"Literally nothing, Betty," Tommy assured her, wrapping his arms around my waist. Betty's eyes goggled a bit, but then she settled against the banister with a smug smile on her face. "But I suggested a special delivery of a fecal sample to Viv, and she thought it might be appropriate."

"No, no, *please* don't," Betty said, somewhat humiliated. "It's okay, the Emergency was getting to be a little overwhelming anyhow. A girl can only be ankle deep in blood so many times before losing her grip. And besides, he'll have a nice scar on his eyebrow to remember me by."

"If you need a way to pass the time, how would you like to be our secretary for a bit?" I asked. "At least until you find another sawbones to work for."

"Really?" Betty's eyes lit up.

"Yeah, you really helped me out of a jam," I told her. "And besides, I bet Tommy would like to be fixed up by someone with actual medical training for once."

"Viv's been doing your sutures?" Betty's mouth fell open.

"Rather admirably," Tommy said. "But that's not her job anymore."

"What will I have to do?" Betty asked.

"Pick up the phone, greet people, keep notes, make coffee."

"Can you make coffee?" Tommy asked. "Our last one couldn't, and I have very high standards after nearly a decade of Viv."

"I make a *mean* pot of coffee," Betty assured. "When can I start?"

"How's Monday?" Tommy said.

"That's perfect!" Betty squealed and grabbed my hands, pulling me off Tommy's lap. "Told you," she whispered, and hugged me a bit tighter before letting go.

"Oh, shush," I whispered.

"Oh, I gotta call my mama," she said. "Thanks, Mr. Fortuna!"

"Thank Viv," Tommy corrected.

"I do, I swear!" Betty ran to the phone on the landing and got the operator, stretching the cord of the handset as far as she could into her room for privacy.

"Well, that's settled." I laughed, settling back down on Tommy's lap. "Oh—and Tally said I should give this back to you, ol' Tommy boy."

The cream-colored box was out of my pocket again and Tommy was quiet.

"Had it since the day I turned twenty-one, huh?"

"I don't fib about things like that, Viv," Tommy said, wrapping his arms around my waist, one more time. I leaned against his chest and breathed him in. He smelled like cigars and a hint of old whiskey, just like usual. It was perfect.

"So, what about all those dames you used to run around with," I said, teasing him.

"Just killin' time," Tommy said back, kissing the top of my head. "You were just a kid when you got here. I wasn't takin' glances at you like that."

"Nah, you're no creep, Tommy Fortuna," I admitted. "But some of us ain't never been kids in our life."

"Well, then I was just a kid," Tommy said. "Runnin' around with girls and gettin' in fights, being a PI—seemed a lot more glamorous than settling down with anyone. But over the years, there was no one I could ever rely on more than you. You're the one and only, Dollface."

"You're the one and only too."

"So, yes. I admit it, under extreme duress—I admit that on the day you turned twenty-one, after five years of knowin' ya, I bought the ring," Tommy said. "You never noticed I stopped wearing the Rolex?"

"Of course I noticed," I said, teasing him. "I just thought it got snitched one time you got your lights knocked out."

"No chance," Tommy said. "The Rolex brought you in. I just hope this ring keeps you forever."

"Well, I don't think we can live here at Mrs. K's," I said. My stomach was giddy, and I couldn't wait for the question, but I had some details to iron out and things to consider, just like I told Mrs. Allen I would.

"What do you mean?"

"Well, after we get hitched. This is a girls-only boarding house. And I'm not living in that building of yours either. Some of your neighbors are real pieces of work."

"Well, I was jawing with Mrs. K just before, when you were saying your goodbyes to Tally," Tommy explained. "We might have a solution."

"Good grief," I laughed. "You two were conspiring?

"Lana and I have been conspiring since summer," Tommy said. "She's a great cook, but a man doesn't spend his Friday nights with a boarding house o' dames unless he's sweet on one of 'em. She knows that. You can't sneak anything past her."

"Okay, then. What'd you two figure out?"

"Well, I'd never make you live at my place—that's no place for you," Tommy admitted. "Mrs. K's brother—you remember Mr. Doroshenko, yeah?—he said he'd be willing to finish off the top floor, make our own little apartment. Betty and Dottie can stay on the second floor."

"With a kitchen and everything upstairs?" I asked.

"Well, kitchenette, so I can make some things if we want," Tommy assured me. "But Mrs. K will still cook breakfast and dinner for us if we pay board too."

"Tally said she paid for the rooms through the end of next year," I told him. "Is that enough?"

"Seems enough," Tommy agreed.

"Well, then, we have some planning to do."

"I didn't ask you yet, Viv."

"Well, what are you waiting for?"

"To tell you the truth? I have no idea anymore." With that, Tommy pulled the two-carat diamond out of its little box and slipped it on my finger—for real this time. He lifted me up off his chest and kissed me—good and proper—so good and proper I thought I was going to faint.

"I love the hell outta you, Dollface."

"I love the hell outta you too, ol' Tommy boy."

ACKNOWLEDGMENTS

First and foremost, I must thank my husband, who has given me the room to explore my creativity, grow as a writer, and calm down.

A huge thanks to my brother, Peter, engineer extraordinaire, who answered a thousand and one questions about mid-century technology and electronics when he could've been doing something much more interesting and productive.

Thanks to my editor, Faith Black Ross, for taking a chance on these cockamamie ideas; you continue to shape my thought spaghetti and plot threads into a real story.

Endless gratitude for my incomparable agent, Anne Tibbets, who paved the way for Viv to shine, and Donald Maass.

My thanks to the entire team at Crooked Lane Books: Madeline Rathle, Rebecca Nelson, Dulce Botello, and Melissa Rechter. I promise to keep the emails to the absolute minimum I can.

A special thank-you to cover designer Rui Ricardo, who continues to encapsulate Viv in all her "mid-century broad" glory.

And to my friends who have nudged me along the way: Andrew Rostan, Michelle Athy, Taverlee Laskauskas, Will

Wallace; and Lauren and Dani and Val and Emmett and Lilah and Philip and Derik and Rob and everyone I've met through FBOL who has turned into a true friend and cheerleader—thank you. You are an amazing community, and I owe you.